FORTUNE & FAME

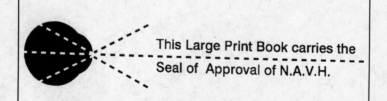

This Large Print Book carries the
Seal of Approval of N.A.V.H.

FORTUNE & FAME

VICTORIA CHRISTOPHER MURRAY & RESHONDA TATE BILLINGSLEY

THORNDIKE PRESS
A part of Gale, Cengage Learning

GALE
CENGAGE Learning·

Farmington Hills, Mich • San Francisco • New York • Waterville, Maine
Meriden, Conn • Mason, Ohio • Chicago

GALE
CENGAGE Learning®

Thorndike Press, a part of Gale, Cengage Learning.

Thorndike Press® Large Print African-American.
The text of this Large Print edition is unabridged.
Other aspects of the book may vary from the original edition.
Set in 16 pt. Plantin.

LIBRARY OF CONGRESS CATALOGING-IN-PUBLICATION DATA

Murray, Victoria Christopher.
    Fortune & fame / by Victoria Christopher Murray & ReShonda Tate Billingsley. — Large print edition.
        pages ; cm. — (Thorndike Press large print African-American)
    ISBN 978-1-4104-7197-0 (hardcover) — ISBN 1-4104-7197-7 (hardcover)
    1. Bush, Jasmine Larson (Fictitious character)—Fiction. 2. African American women—Fiction. 3. Spouses of clergy—Fiction. 4. Reality television programs—Fiction. 5. Large type books. I. Billingsley, ReShonda Tate. II. Title. III. Title: Fortune and fame.
PS3563.U795F674 2014
813'.54—dc23   2014016891

Published in 2014 by arrangement with Touchstone, a division of Simon & Schuster, Inc.

Printed in Mexico
1 2 3 4 5 6 7 18 17 16 15 14

A NOTE FROM VICTORIA

I love writing novels, but these acknowledgments right here are always so difficult. I never want to leave out anyone because feelings get hurt, and folks stop speaking to you, and then you have to buy them dinner to get them to forgive you. It's just too much! So because of that, I've limited my acknowledgments to the professional side of my life. Well, the professional side and the spiritual side because nothing I say, do, or write would be possible without God, who just keeps pouring His blessings down on me. He just doesn't stop and I truly hope that I'm pleasing Him with my life and my writings. I thank God every single day for the life He has given to me.

I have written twenty-something novels, most of them with Simon & Schuster. The team at Touchstone is always so amazing and I look forward to writing twenty-something more! Thank you, Lauren Spie-

5

gel (I'm really looking forward to working with you), Shida Carr (we've been doing this for ten years and you are still the best, by far, publicist in the business; ask any author I've ever talked to, they'll tell you!) and the rest of the Touchstone team, which makes me feel like I truly have a publishing home.

It wasn't enough that I was blessed with a great publishing house; God blessed me with my agent, Liza Dawson. Thank you, Liza, for your never-ending support and belief in me and my talent. Every book I've written you've helped me to make better, and I have such hope in this publishing journey because of you and the team at Liza Dawson and Associates.

I have been writing for over fifteen years (ouch!) and I love it. But there is nothing, I repeat, nothing like writing and working with ReShonda Tate Billingsley. With Re-Shonda, not only do I have a blast, but I learn about the important things in life, like where are all the designer discount shops on Interstate 95, and what happened on *Love and Hip Hop* last night. If I could write every book from now on with you, I would. Thanks for bringing the fun back.

I have to give a special shout-out to one of my best friends, Candy Jackson, who reads all of my novels first and is an honest enough friend to tell me when I need to get back to work. You rock, Candy! And Victor McGlothin, who came up with the catch-phrase, or catch line, or whatever it's called, for Jasmine Cox Larson Bush. Victor, who knew?

Finally I want to thank the readers, especially all the readers whom I have the pleasure of interacting with just about daily on Facebook. I truly wish I could list every single one of you, but the list might be longer than this novel, and I wouldn't want to leave anyone out. The way you encourage me, support me, inspire me, and are willing to take off your earrings and Vaseline up (you know who I'm talking about!) . . . it all means so much to me. Thank you so, so much, and as long as you keep reading, I will keep writing.

Now, onto my next story. . . .

A NOTE FROM RESHONDA

With every book, my editor has to dang near threaten to go to print, sans my acknowledgments. That's because the book I write with no problem. The acknowledgments, or note from the author, as I like to call it, well, that one isn't so easy. Particularly because I wouldn't be where I am today if it weren't for some really fantastic people. And since I'm not trying to create Encyclopedia Billingsley, I simply can't name them all. But we're at the ninth hour, about to head to print, and my wonderfully patient editor is like, "It's now or never." So the time is now.

Time now to say my usual thanks — to God, for blessing me with the talent to craft stories people want to read; my husband, for all his support; my three wonderful children, who are so patient in letting Mommy do what she does. Thanks also to my agent, Sara Camilli; the awesome folks at Touchstone who worked on this book —

Lauren, Miya, Shida, and everyone else. Thanks also to the wonderful team at my home for the past twelve years, Gallery Books.

And of course, a huge chunk of gratitude to my yang, Victoria Christopher Murray.

It's not often that you meet someone who could be so completely different (I'm a little bit country, she's a whole lot of citified; I'm a Southern girl, she's a true northerner; I'm the saint, she's the sinner) . . . it's not often you can meet someone so different, yet you're alike in so many ways. When it comes to what we create with our fingers (I won't say "pen" because neither of us write longhand anymore), it's like we are one. It's amazing that this is our third book in the Rachel/Jasmine series and we haven't changed one single word that the other person wrote. Not one. That shows you how in sync we are with each other when it comes to writing, and we hope the readers feel that. She gets me. I get her. Sounds like a sappy Hallmark card, but as seriously as I take writing, it's refreshing to work with someone who feels the same. Not only is she an awesome writing partner, she's an even better friend. So, VCM, thank you for teaching me, for challenging me, and being an all-around great friend and, yes, even my voice of reason when I turn into Psycho Mom.

I don't want to get into naming a whole lot of other names, but I'd be remiss if I didn't give a big hearty thanks to Pat Tucker, who always has my back and listens to my countless ideas, providing feedback and helping me work through story ideas.

To Yolanda Gore and Gina Johnson, I don't know where I'd be without you two. To my Motherhood Diaries sisterhood, you ladies are phenomenal. And to my Facebook family, yes, social media, I couldn't ask for better friends and supporters.

To Regina King, Reina King, Shelby Stone, Queen Latifah, Shakim Compere and Flava Unit, Roger Bobb and your crew, everyone at BET and the amazing cast and crew of *Let the Church Say Amen,* including Naturi Naughton, who played the heck out of Rachel — thank you for bringing my words to the screen. I can't wait for the world to see it!

Like I said, I could go on and on, but since my editor is waiting, I will end with my biggest thanks — to you, the reader, for your continued support! You are why I continue to write!

Until next time, enjoy!

CHAPTER ONE:
JASMINE COX LARSON BUSH

Jasmine sat with her eyes opened wide and her mouth clasped shut. But even though not a word passed through her lips, the living room was filled with the joyful sound of laughter.

Slowly, Jasmine rose from the sofa, leaving Mae Frances sitting alone. There was no way her friend would be able to stand right now; Mae Frances was buckled over, laughing so hard that Jasmine was sure she was going to bust a vein.

But Jasmine didn't turn her head to the left or the right. Her eyes remained focused only on the plasma TV centered on the wall.

"I cannot believe this," Jasmine said, finally speaking.

She took two steps toward the television as if that would help her hear Shaun Robinson, the anchor for *Access Hollywood,* a little better.

"This has to be quite an exciting time for

you," Shaun said. "Especially since you're going to be on the OWN network."

Rachel Jackson Adams stood next to Shaun, cheesing like she was in a Colgate commercial. Her hand was on her hip as if she was posing for the camera, though she came off looking more like a posing seal.

"Well, you know, I was supposed to be on Oprah's show last year," Rachel said to Shaun, though her eyes were on the camera and not on the anchor. "But due to circumstances where somebody else acted like a fool, my appearance was canceled."

"Fool?" Mae Frances cackled as she pointed at the television. "I think she's talking about you. She just called you a fool on national TV."

Mae Frances cracked up, and Jasmine's eyes narrowed as she watched the unfolding interview. For a moment, she wondered if the steam coming out of her ears would set off the smoke alarm in Mae Frances's apartment.

On the screen, Rachel spoke, her eyes still on the camera. "But even though that didn't work out, Oprah and I kinda became friends and after we hung out a couple of times, Oprah said that I would be the perfect First Lady to be on television because there are so many misconceptions about pastor wives."

"Liar!" Jasmine growled at the screen.

Still chuckling, Mae Frances said, "Why're you calling her a liar? There *are* a lot of misconceptions about First Ladies."

Jasmine shook her head. "I'm not talking about that part. This whole story about how she and Oprah are friends, you know that's a lie. Oprah's not her friend. Nobody's Rachel's friend. Anyone who knows Rachel for more than five minutes would never be a friend of hers."

"Hmph . . . I thought you two were friends."

"No," Jasmine said, sinking back down onto the couch. "We're more like frenemies. I would never call someone that I couldn't trust a friend."

"Y'all were sure acting mighty friendly last year when you were in Chicago. By the time we got down to the Caribbean, I thought you two would be BFFs forever."

"Yeah, well," Jasmine said, thinking about everything that she had done for that juvenile-delinquent-on-the-loose. If it hadn't been for her, Rachel would be sitting in a ten-by-ten concrete cell facing the death penalty for the murder of Pastor Earl Griffith. Of course, it might not have played

15

out that way once the world discovered the truth that Earl Griffith wasn't dead. But in her mind, right now, Jasmine had wonderful images of Rachel being dragged down a long corridor toward the death chamber.

"So, the reality show is set to begin soon, right?" Shaun asked Rachel.

Rachel nodded, though she still didn't face Shaun. Her eyes were steady on the camera. "We're going to begin taping in a few weeks, and Oprah told me she expects this show to be one of the fall hits."

Yes, Jasmine should have definitely left Rachel rotting in that Chicago jail. If she had, then she'd be the one with a reality show. Not that being on one of those shows had ever been her heart's desire. Reality TV was just not her thing. Jasmine found the women on those shows uncouth and classless. She had too much intelligence to sit in front of a television and watch women share the misery of their lives.

But the fact that Rachel was about to have a reality show made Jasmine reconsider. Maybe a reality show about First Ladies was just what America needed. A show with class and substance — the kind of show that had nothing to do with Rachel Jackson Adams.

"How in the world did this happen?" Jasmine wondered.

Though she hadn't directed the question to Mae Frances, her friend answered, "That Rebecca girl must have more than those two brain cells you're always talking about. Somehow she figured this out."

"Her name is Rachel, Mae Frances!" Then she groaned out loud. "I can't figure out how she kept this from me. I've talked to her at least a dozen times over the last year and she didn't say a word."

"We're still in preproduction right now," Rachel said with her eyes still on the camera. "We're trying to figure out everything about the show. Of course, I'm the star, but the producers are still trying to determine who will be in the supporting roles." Rachel grinned and her eyes peered into the camera as if she was trying to see into everyone's living rooms.

Silly woman! She didn't even know that she was supposed to be looking at Shaun, not at the camera.

Shaun shifted, taking two steps to her right as if she was trying to get Rachel's attention. But Rachel wouldn't turn her head. "Well, we're excited," Shaun finally said, speaking to the side of Rachel's head. "We'll be watching. By the way, Oprah hasn't released the name of the show yet."

"Oh, it's a secret," Rachel said, then batted her false eyelashes.

Jasmine hoped that a couple of those lashes would fall right into her eye! Blind her right there on TV.

"But we will announce it soon," Rachel added.

"Just make sure you come back here and tell us first."

"Definitely," Rachel said.

"Thank you for sharing this with us."

"Thank you for having me."

Jasmine shook her head. That was what . . . a two- to three-minute interview? And that swamp pony had never once faced Shaun. How was she supposed to carry a show? There was no way that Oprah had ever spent any time with Rachel or else there wouldn't be a show. How had Rachel pulled this off?

To the camera, Shaun said, "Who's the latest Hollywood couple to adopt a baby in Africa? We'll be right back with that story after this break."

Jasmine grabbed the remote, pointed it at the television as if it were a weapon, and clicked it off. The moment the screen faded to black, Jasmine opened her mouth and released a scream that shook the bricks of the Upper East Side building where Mae

Frances lived. And as Jasmine shrieked, Mae Frances howled with laughter.

"Ugh," Jasmine growled as she paced in front of her friend. "I just cannot believe this. Rachel is going to have her own television show." She spoke as if she was trying to convince herself that this was a fact. "This cannot be happening to me."

"Well, this is gonna happen, unless you're thinking about shutting it down."

Jasmine slowed her steps. "Yes! That's what I need to do. I need to shut it all down before Rachel becomes a star. Because can you imagine what she'd be like if that was to happen?" Jasmine shuddered. "There would be no talking to her. No." She shook her head. "She cannot have that show." But then Jasmine paused and tapped her forefinger against her chin. "Wait a minute. Maybe I shouldn't shut it down. Maybe what I need to do is get on that show."

"You want to be on the show with Raquan?"

"Yeah," Jasmine said, this time, ignoring the way Mae Frances had made up yet another new name for Rachel. She couldn't focus on that while this idea was still forming in her mind. "First, I have to find out what's really going on because Rachel is such a liar, she could have made this whole

19

thing up."

"Well, you've told a few lies in your lifetime, Jasmine Larson," Mae Frances said, calling her by the name she'd been using from the first day they'd met. "So, maybe you shouldn't be so quick to call that buffoon a liar."

"My past sins have nothing to do with this. This is all about Rachel. I have to get some information. But how?" She took a few more steps, then stopped. Her eyes settled on her friend.

Mae Frances.

The two had been friends for more than eight years, since weeks after Jasmine had moved to New York. And if there was one thing that Jasmine had figured out during that time, it was that Mae Frances knew everybody in America, and beyond this county's shores. That meant that Mae Frances surely knew Oprah.

Jasmine sat down next to her friend on the sofa. "You can help me."

"How?" Mae Frances looked at her sideways.

"You need to call Oprah. You're friends with her, right?"

Mae Frances crinkled her nose like she smelled something bad. "Did I ever tell you I was friends with Oprah?"

Jasmine's shoulders slumped. This was unbelievable. There was someone that Mae Frances didn't know? "I thought you knew everybody."

"I do. But Oprah ain't everybody. In fact, she's nobody to me."

"Well, Oprah's the person I need for you to know right now because I have to get on that show with Rachel," Jasmine whined like she was about to throw a tantrum. She surely would if she couldn't find a way to contact Oprah.

"Well, if that's all you need to do, we don't need to be talking about Oprah." Mae Frances pushed herself off the sofa. " 'Cause I can make a call right now and get in touch with the person who's in charge of everything that has to do with Oprah."

Jasmine blinked like she was trying to clear her thoughts. "If you're not friends with Oprah, who are you gonna call? Gayle?"

"Gayle King? Please. She might run one or two things here and there, but I'm talking about the real Negro in charge of Oprah and her business. I'm calling Stedman."

Now, Jasmine's eyes were wide. "Stedman Graham?"

"You know another Stedman?"

"Oh, my God, you know him?"

21

"Yeah," Mae Frances said in a tone that sounded like it was no big deal. "Stedman's the reason why Oprah and I aren't friends."

"Because of Stedman?"

"Yeah," Mae Frances said with a little chuckle. "He's one —" She glanced over at Jasmine, who was staring at her with wide eyes, and Mae Frances cleared her throat. "Let me just make this call. Stedman will get you on that show."

Mae Frances turned toward her bedroom, and Jasmine followed. Suddenly, Mae Frances stopped, making Jasmine bump right into her. She faced Jasmine. "Where are you going?"

"With you. I wanna hear what Stedman's going to say."

"Excuse you . . . but this is a private call. You don't need to know what Stedman says to me as long as he says yes." Mae Frances walked into her bedroom. "I'll be out when I'm finished." She closed the door, and Jasmine's mouth opened in shock when she heard her friend click the lock.

Jasmine folded her arms and stood in the middle of the living room, stunned. She should have been insulted, but how could she be? Mae Frances was about to hook her up!

"Oh, yeah," Jasmine said as she plopped

22

back down on the couch. It wouldn't take Mae Frances more than ten minutes to work it all out. Jasmine Cox Larson Bush was about to crash Rachel's party.

She laughed as she thought about the look on Rachel's face once she heard the news that she wasn't going to be the only First Lady of reality TV.

There was a new First Lady in town. And this one had class.

CHAPTER TWO:
RACHEL JACKSON ADAMS

"Get it. Got it? Good."

Rachel Jackson Adams frowned, knitting her eyebrows together as she studied her reflection in the floor-length mirror. "No," she mumbled, then said, "Google me, hun."

She shook her head, trying to keep her frustration from overpowering her. "No. That doesn't work either."

Rachel took a deep breath, wagged a finger at her reflection, and said, "I'm about to situate the situation."

"What in the world are you doing?"

Rachel spun around to see her husband, Lester, standing in the doorway of their massive bedroom. He was sweating profusely. Why her husband continued to go running in this brutal Houston heat was beyond her.

"I'm trying to come up with my catch-phrase," Rachel replied.

Lester walked in and began removing his

T-shirt. "Your what?" he asked.

Rachel sighed. She was really not in the mood to explain Reality TV 101 to her husband, but she knew he wouldn't get it any other way. "My catchphrase," Rachel said, walking over to her husband. She leaned in to peck him on his lips, but backed up when she noticed just how sweaty he really was. "Every reality star has a catchphrase. Like Sheree says, 'Who gon' check me, boo?' Tamar says, 'Bomb.com.' Mama Dee says, 'In that order.' "

"Who are these people?" Lester asked, looking confused.

"From the popular reality shows."

Lester released a small chuckle as he walked into the bathroom, stepped out of his shorts, grabbed a towel, and began wiping his face. "See, I can't with you today. I will never for the life of me understand why you watch that foolishness."

Rachel jabbed a warning finger in his direction. "Don't judge me, Lester. Me 'watching that foolishness' is why I landed my own show."

He wiped himself some more, then wrapped the towel around his waist.

"Well, I still don't support that," Lester said, heading to his closet. "I am head of the American Baptist Coalition. The last

thing I need is to have my wife on TV looking crazy," he called out from the walk-in
closet.

Rachel rolled her eyes. She liked her timid
husband better, the one who let her run all
over him. But Lester was feeling himself
now that he'd gotten a little power as
president of the ABC. Beating the esteemed
Hosea Bush had given him some "oomph"
and made him a little cocky. Add to the fact
all the flak he'd caught because of her
behavior this past year, and now he was trying to get all caveman on her. Well, he'd
better recognize. She may have evolved from
the slash-your-tires preacher's daughter. But
she was still a forge-her-own-path preacher's
wife.

Lester walked out of the closet holding a
dress shirt and tie. Rachel couldn't help but
notice it was his Valentino tie. Hmph, when
she first met him, he didn't even know how
to spell "Valentino"!

"Number one, I'm not going to be on TV
looking crazy. I'm too classy for the trashy."
She smiled. That had just come to her. She
would definitely have to use that phrase.

Lester didn't bother trying to hide his
exasperation as he laid his shirt and tie on
the bed. "Is there even such a thing as classy
reality TV?"

"If there wasn't, there is now," she replied.

"I'm going to take a shower," he said. "I worked out and ran two miles, so I know I'm real tart right about now."

Working out. Something else the new and improved Lester had started doing. Rachel followed him into the bathroom.

"So, you're not behind me on this?" she asked, her arms folded across her chest.

Lester inhaled and turned to face her. "Rachel, you know I try to support you. But I just don't understand the need to do this show."

She released a long sigh. She'd already had this conversation with her father, Simon, who was completely against her "airing all her business." Now here Lester was giving her a hard time. This had been a dream come true that had fallen into her lap. No, Rachel and Oprah weren't exactly the best of friends. But Rachel's friend Melinda, a former reporter in Los Angeles, did just get hired as OWN's vice president of programming, so when she shared the good news with Rachel, Rachel had suggested her reality show. Melinda had set up a meeting and Oprah loved the idea (which was a shock in itself because of the disaster Rachel and Jasmine had at the *Oprah* show last year). But the reality show — *The First*

Lady — had been fast tracked and here they were. It was divine intervention.

"Lester, it's not like I went out looking for this. It fell into my lap and I would be a fool not to take advantage of this opportunity," Rachel protested. He didn't need to know that she *had* actively pursued her own show.

He leaned in and turned the shower on. "As long as this doesn't make us look bad. No fighting, hair pulling, and all that other stuff."

Rachel had to convince Lester to get behind her on this. She didn't want to go to Atlanta, where they were filming, if her husband wasn't completely on board. She *would* go, but she didn't want to.

"Of course not," Rachel said. "It's not like I'd get caught up in some mess like that anyway."

He smiled. "Don't act like it's beneath you."

"See, why'd you have to go there? That's the old me. I don't fight. Anymore. I'm above that. You're always talking about spiritual growth, but you don't want to believe that I've grown spiritually."

He leaned in and gave her a big kiss. She ignored his pungent smell and let him kiss her. "I believe you have, honey," Lester said.

28

"I'm just concerned."

"I'm serious, Lester. This is a great opportunity and I plan to take full advantage of it." Rachel had put her foot down when Lester first said he'd been called to preach. But ultimately he'd called her bluff and did it anyway. She'd caved that time, but there would be no caving this time. Not where Oprah was concerned.

"I just can't believe Oprah gave you another shot," Lester said.

"She knows all of that drama wasn't my fault. That was straight Jasmine."

"Why are you putting all the blame on Jasmine? I thought you two were girls."

"We are. Kinda sorta," Rachel replied. "I mean, since I lost my mother, it's great to have a mother figure like Jasmine in my life."

Lester laughed. "Mother? Really, Rachel?"

Rachel frowned. "You're right. Grand-mother."

Lester laughed as he stepped into the shower. "Some things will never change," he said over the running water. "I thought you all were over taking digs at each other."

"We are. But you know, with Jasmine, you just never know. You have to keep one eye open. Like Ephesians 24:7 says, 'Keep your friends close and your enemies closer.' "

Lester paused and frowned like he was

thinking. He leaned his head out the shower. "Rachel, that's not in the Bible. And Ephesians only has six chapters."

"I know, baby. I was just testing you. You know I was raised in the church. I know all the bible verses."

Lester laughed as he leaned back under the water. She could tell that even though he wasn't feeling this reality show idea, he wasn't going to fight her on it, which was a good thing because that was one battle he would not win.

Rachel made her way downstairs just as the front doorbell rang. She peeked out the window and saw her best friend Twyla's car. There went her peaceful evening. Rachel's brother, David, had taken Rachel's sons — Jordan and Lewis — to a baseball game and Twyla had taken the girls to a ballet performance at The Ensemble Theater. Now Rachel was going to have to listen to Brooklyn's exciting recap for the next hour.

Rachel swung the door open. "Hey, my —"

"Shhh," Twyla said, motioning toward Brooklyn, who was sound asleep in her arms. "She's knocked out."

Thank goodness, Rachel wanted to say.

"Where's Nia?" Rachel asked as Twyla walked in.

"I hope you don't mind. My niece is at my house and Nia had a fit to stay, so I let her stay. I'll bring her back in the morning." She laid Brooklyn down on the sofa in the living room. "But this one, she's a handful."

Rachel laughed. "That she is."

"Well, she's all yours now," Twyla said, setting her little backpack down. "I need a bottled water."

Rachel motioned for Twyla to follow her into the kitchen.

"Oh, yeah, I caught your interview on *Access Hollywood* earlier. Girl, you rocked it," Twyla said as Rachel handed her a bottle of Oasis spring water. "But umm, why were you looking straight at the camera? Weren't you supposed to be looking at the reporter?"

"*Supposed* to, but when has Rachel Jackson Adams ever done anything she was *supposed* to do?" Rachel replied. "You know I wanted to be a reporter so I know how the game is played."

"Then, educate me because it looked crazy."

"Are you talking about it?" Rachel asked matter-of-factly.

"Well, yes . . ."

"I rest my case. I know how an interview is supposed to go, but the reality stars who are successful are the ones who are over the

31

top. That's going to be my thing. I'm going to be *Gone-With-the-Wind* fabulous. I have to be dramatic. That's what the whole purpose of looking at the camera was. Get people buzzing."

Twyla released a small chuckle as she sipped her water. "I should've known you had something up your sleeve. What did your new BFF say when you told her about the show?"

Rachel waved her comment off. "First of all, Jasmine is not and never will be my BFF. That's reserved for you. Second, I didn't tell her."

Twyla's mouth fell open. She'd never personally met Jasmine, but she knew all about her and she definitely didn't care for her. "So, she doesn't know?"

"She probably knows now if she was watching TV. My agent told me to keep it under wraps until we went public with the announcement."

"So, you got an agent now?" Twyla raised an eyebrow like she was really impressed.

"I told you, I'm big time, girl. Anyone who doesn't recognize needs to exit to the rear!" Rachel pointed over her shoulder.

"Huh?" Twyla frowned.

"I'm trying a few catchphrases."

Twyla laughed. "You are silly. But I still

think your girl is gonna blow a gasket."

"Jasmine and I are cool now but you know, with her backstabbing history, I have to keep one eye open. Even if she tries to do right, Harriet Tubman might start planting some ideas in her head."

"Who?"

"Mae Frances. You know I told you about Jasmine's decrepit old friend/nanny/maid/lover, I don't quite know what that old woman does. But she knows everybody and I don't need her or Jasmine trying to pull any strings and get my show canceled."

"Why would they try to get your show canceled?"

"I don't know, but I'm not taking any chances."

Twyla shook her head. "Honey, just let me have a front-row seat when she finds out because something tells me she's not going to take too kindly to this news."

"I'm not worried about Jasmine," Rachel responded. "All I have to do is keep being friendly with her. She helped me out in Chicago so she thinks we're all buddy-buddy now. I just need to keep making her think that and we'll be fine."

"Okay. I guess you know what you're doing."

"I do. I'm not trying to trip on Jasmine

now. We seriously are in a much better place. As long as she stays cool, I'm cool."

"Why do I have the feeling that she is so *not* going to stay cool?"

"Whatever. I'm the head diva in charge. I think she's finally realized that." Although Jasmine and Rachel talked only occasionally, Rachel thought Jasmine really had gotten over her jealousy at Lester's winning the presidency of The American Baptist Coalition, which made Rachel the top First Lady. So, they were in a good space. And since no one was buying Jasmine's claim of how she threw the election and let Lester win, Jasmine had finally let that ridiculous notion go and the two of them were getting along just fine.

"From your lips to God's ears," Twyla said, heading toward the door. "Because neither you or the ABC can stand anymore drama."

Rachel followed her best friend out. "Oh, I'm done with the drama. This will be smooth sailing. After all, it's my world. My rules." She snapped her fingers. That was it. That was her catchphrase!

"I like that," Twyla said.

"Me, too." They hugged and said their goodbyes.

My world. My rules. That's what her signature phrase would be, Rachel thought as she made her way back inside.

Now that that was out of the way, Rachel was ready to get this show started and show the world the real First Lady of reality TV!

Chapter Three:
Natasia Redding

Divine intervention!

There was no other way to explain it. All it could be was God and His hands all up in this.

"So, I take it that's a yes!" Melinda said.

"It's a definite yes." Natasia laughed. But then, she coughed.

"Are you all right?" Melinda asked.

"Yes, yes. Something caught in my throat." She coughed again this time putting her hand over the phone, and when she found her voice, she said, "And yes to the job, too. I thought about it," she continued, then added, "and, I prayed about it. I'm on board for *First Ladies.* Again, I have to thank you for thinking of me."

"You're welcome. There are so few of us in this business; we have to stick together. And I've been a fan of yours since we met at the Emmys."

"Well, I'm a fan of yours, too," Natasia

said, and once again raked through her memories to find one of this woman. From the moment Melinda had called her last week about being the executive producer on her new reality show, to this minute, Natasia couldn't ever remember meeting her. Even when she'd Googled her, Melinda's face wasn't familiar. But as Natasia had researched the new VP of OWN, she'd found Melinda's accomplishments impressive, though not nearly as impressive as her own.

But with the way Melinda kept raving about her, Natasia wasn't about to tell her new boss that she wouldn't even be able to pick her out of a police lineup. She may not have remembered the woman before, but from this point on, she'd always remember and think of Melinda as her angel. Natasia was riding Melinda's angel wings right back to Hosea Bush.

"So, we have a contract ready for you," Melinda said. "I can email it to you and after you review, you can print out four copies, sign, and get it back to us."

"That's fine. I'll want a couple of days to go over it with my attorney."

"Of course. But if you can expedite this, I'd really appreciate it. Like I told you, we're ready to begin filming within the next few weeks. So, we'll relocate you down here to Atlanta as soon as it's a go on both ends."

Natasia frowned. "Atlanta? Aren't we filming in New York?"

"No, I'm sorry, I thought I told you Atlanta. That's not going to be a problem, is it?"

"Uh . . . no," Natasia stuttered, as all kinds of questions galloped through her mind. "I just thought . . . you said Jasmine Larson Bush was the First Lady on the show, correct?"

"Yes, but she's not the only one. I just mentioned her because I knew you'd worked on her husband's show years ago." Melinda paused for such a long moment that Natasia wondered if there was something more behind Melinda's wanting her on the show. When Melinda first called, she'd mentioned Jasmine's name as if she was just an ordinary First Lady in America. But now, Natasia wondered if Melinda knew any of the dirty details that were part of Natasia and Jasmine's history.

Melinda continued, "The show centers on Jasmine and another First Lady, Rachel Jackson Adams out of Houston."

"Oh, I didn't know that."

"Yes. And we're looking for a third person, but we want someone out of Atlanta so that we won't have the expense of relocating her. You'll be involved in helping us choose the third one."

"So, that's what you're going to do? Relocate Jasmine and her family?"

"Well, I'm not sure if she's bringing her whole family. We have to sit down with Jasmine and Rachel to discuss that. Sometimes husbands, especially ones who are as prominent as Hosea Bush and Lester Adams, don't want to have anything to do with these shows. But whatever, both Jasmine and Rachel will be relocated to Atlanta for the six weeks of taping. We figured that would be neutral territory."

Natasia leaned forward, resting her elbows on her cherrywood desk. The lines in her forehead deepened. If they weren't going to tape in New York, what would this mean? Would Hosea actually leave his church for six weeks to film a reality show? Natasia couldn't imagine that happening. So, if he wasn't going to be in Atlanta, how would she make contact? He was the reason she was getting involved in what she anticipated to be nothing but a hot mess. A reality show? Really? Total madness!

Maybe she could convince Melinda to tape the show in New York. She said, "I don't get it, Melinda. Viewers surely know that Jasmine is married to Hosea Bush. And if they know that, then they know that he's the pastor of one of the largest churches in New York. So, what's he doing in Atlanta? How are you going to explain this to the viewers?" Even though Melinda couldn't see her, Natasia shook her head. "That won't work. The viewers will never believe it."

Melinda laughed like she'd just heard a good joke. "Obviously, you're not a reality TV fan. The viewers don't care where these people live or where they lived before. They don't care if their husbands are there or not. These viewers just want the drama. And the more ratchet, the better."

Natasia groaned inside. See? Definitely madness! There was no way that she would ever lend her name to such a show — except, she had to do this. This was the doorway she needed.

"Well, you're right about that. I don't watch reality TV." Natasia paused. She hoped she hadn't said that too emphatically, or said too much. She really wanted and needed this job.

"And that's exactly why I want you as the EP," Melinda said. "I want a fresh eye from someone who can bring something to the table besides drama."

It didn't sound like Melinda knew any-thing of her history with Jasmine, which was a good thing. Because those months that Natasia had worked on Hosea's TV show had been nothing but drama.

"Well, if that's what you want, that's what you'll get. Because I'm not into drama," Na-tasia said.

"No problem. I'll handle the drama part. Your job is going to be to make sure that drama is not all that we're about. We need some positivity because I definitely don't want to portray the First Ladies in a *completely* bad light, even though we know there is often more drama in the pews than in the streets. But at the same time, we do want viewers to walk away, at least some nights, feeling uplifted. That alone will make our show different . . . and a success."

"Then, that's what we'll do!"

"Perfect. I'm telling you, Natasia, we can ride this reality wave. Especially with Jas-mine and Rachel, I can see this going on for three, six, or nine seasons."

Natasia closed her eyes. No matter which way all of this played out for her, she wouldn't need more than one season. She just had to figure out how she was going to use this to get to Hosea. How was she go-ing to get to New York, or get Hosea down to Atlanta?

"So, what I was thinking," Melinda said, breaking into her thoughts, "is that I'd like to fly you into New York within the next few weeks before we start filming."

New York!

Melinda continued, "I'll be there . . . taking care of some things, and this will give us a chance to sit down and talk this show out face-to-face. Will that work?"

You have no idea, was what Natasia said inside. Aloud, she said, "Yes, the sooner, the better."

"Okay, well, I'll get back to you on the exact date." She paused for a moment. "There are some arrangements I have to make."

After a few more thank-yous and then the final goodbye, Natasia hung up the phone, still amazed at how God had stepped in. When Melinda had first called her, Natasia had been sure that this was all about God giving her the desires of her heart. But now with New York added in, Natasia was sure that not only was God going to give her what she wanted, but He was setting it up so that it would be easy. And to think, she'd only been back to going to church on the regular for three months.

She leaned back into the soft leather of

her executive chair and reflected on these past months. She thought about all that she'd been learning, the faith that she'd been building, and the prayers that she'd been sending up. God seemed to be coming through for her in every single way. And this call was the best way possible — she was going to New York; she'd get to see Hosea.

Hosea Bush. The man she hadn't seen for more than a minute. She hadn't seen him since he'd had her thrown off as the producer on his TV show *Bring It On,* almost seven years ago.

Natasia had had such high hopes at that time. Her desire had been to be reunited with the man whom she'd loved like no other. Of course, when she'd finagled that position, she knew Hosea had a wife. But surely Hosea couldn't have loved Jasmine the way he'd loved her.

In the end, though, Jasmine was still there and Natasia was the one who'd been kicked to the left.

Natasia slowly pushed herself away from the desk. Those memories, especially of the last time she'd been with Hosea, were not the ones she wanted to remember. She preferred to think about the days when she and Hosea Bush had been planning *their* wedding and *their* long life together.

That would be what she would focus on from now on. Those memories and the new images she had in her thoughts during the day and in her dreams at night. It was always the same — Hosea was always glad to see her once again. He was always thrilled to have her back in his life.

The irony of all of this wasn't lost on her: Her dreams were about to become a reality because of reality TV.

Natasia chuckled at that thought as she took slow steps toward her bedroom. All she had to do was figure out the right way to make her presence known. And once she did, she'd see Hosea Bush again.

This was truly an answer to her three months' worth of prayers.

CHAPTER FOUR:
MARY RICHARDSON

Air had never smelled so fresh.

Mary Richardson recalled an article that said Huntsville, Texas, had horrible pollution, ranking at the bottom of the list in air quality. But to Mary, the brisk wind sweeping across her face was Febreze fresh.

Fresh air. Something she'd known nothing about for the past four years.

Mary looked to her left, then her right. She wanted to cry when the realization set in that she could go in whichever direction she wanted. There was no CO telling her which way to turn. There was no warden dictating what she should do next. Every step she made from now on would be on her own terms.

Mary closed her eyes and inhaled deeply. She only opened them when she heard someone say, "There she is! My baby!"

"Babyyyyy," she said, running into his arms.

Nathan Frazier picked her up and swung her around, smothering her in kisses. He wasn't the most handsome man she'd ever dated, but he looked magnificent to her right now. Even though her friends used to tease her in high school, Mary had never been able to shake her preference for black men. Men like Nathan were the reason why — tall, dark, and good looking without even trying.

Mary didn't know how long they'd been lost in their embrace when Nathan finally pulled away and said, "Okay, babe, we have many more nights of holding each other. We need to get to the airport. Our plane leaves in three hours."

She smiled and hugged him tightly one last time. He took her hand and said, "And the first thing we're going to do when we get back to Atlanta is go and get this band replaced." He fingered the small metal band on her ring finger.

The old Mary, the con artist always looking for a come up, the one that was out to get money by any means necessary, would've been all set and ready to go. But the new and improved Mary, the one who had found herself in prison, who had renewed her relationship with God, and who had vowed to become a law-abiding citizen, was happy with the ring that was on her finger. Nathan had given her that ring in a small, quaint ceremony in the prison chapel. It was more than enough.

"Honey, I told you. We don't have to get another ring. This one means the world to me," she told him.

Nathan took her hand and led her to the rental car. "And you can keep it in a box somewhere as a memento." He turned to her. "But baby, I told you, things have been really good this past year. This church business is *the* business. Everyone is excited and ready to meet you."

She'd been real nervous about that. "How are they going to feel about having a First Lady who's been in prison?"

"Half the congregation has been in prison. That's how we've been able to build Pleasant City up so. This is a no-judgment zone and the folks are eating it up!"

She hated when Nathan talked like he was in the ministry for the money. When she'd first met him as part of the prison ministry for a Houston church, he'd seemed genuine in his desire to spread the gospel. Their relationship had quickly flourished and she'd fallen madly in love with him. He'd proposed in the prison chapel, promising her that he would do everything in his power to get her out. Then, just a month after they'd gotten married, he'd received an offer to lead a church in Atlanta. He'd taken it and each time he'd returned to visit, he was hungrier and hungrier for money and power.

"I told you, we've been doing big things," Nathan said. "I hired a top-notch marketing team. We got a grant. And you know the actor, Laurence Hill?"

She smiled, enjoying his enthusiasm. "Yeah, he went to prison for tax evasion. Right?"

"Yeah, but he's out and he's bankrolling a whole new facility at Pleasant City. Once word started spreading about his support, everyone else started getting on board. I told you, moving to Atlanta was the smartest thing I'd ever done!"

She loved seeing her husband so excited. She snuggled closer to him as he pulled out of the parking lot and away from Huntsville Correctional facility for the last time.

Her husband.

Mary still couldn't believe that she'd met and married her soul mate while in prison. She had a flash as she recalled the man she'd *thought* was her soul mate — Lester Adams. She'd gone to great lengths to get Lester, especially because his wife, Rachel, treated him like dirt. Seducing Lester had started out as just a job, something set up by Rachel's enemy. Mary had pretended to be in need of counseling, and the more time she spent with the good pastor, the more she wanted him. For real. He'd been attentive, loving, caring. All things she'd never had from a man. Not even her absentee father.

She had seduced Lester, they had a brief affair, and Rachel and Mary both ended up pregnant at the same time. Confident that she was meant to be Mrs. Lester Adams, Mary had shown up at Rachel's church, proclaimed her love for Lester on the altar, and caused nothing but chaos after that. Mary told anyone who would listen that hers was Lester's baby. Turns out he wasn't, but by then, the whole church knew Lester had cheated on Rachel.

Mary had managed to get his body, but she could never get his heart, and at the end of the day, Lester and Rachel had overcome their problems and worked things out. Even Mary's baby hadn't been able to break them up.

Her heart dropped as she thought of her baby. Rachel had sent her pictures of Lester Jr. (they called him Lewis, but he would always be Lester Jr. to Mary). Her baby looked just like his no-good father, Craig, who was doing twenty to life for counterfeiting. She'd been sentenced to twenty-five years herself for all the cons and hustles she and Craig were involved in. It wasn't until Nathan and his prison ministry started coming to Huntsville that she realized she could turn her life around.

Nathan had done that. Then, he indeed had pulled some strings and gotten her case overturned on appeal. Now, she was ready to start her life anew.

There was a part of Mary that wished Lester Jr. could be with her. But in order to keep her son out of the foster system that she herself had grown up in, Mary had signed away her parental rights to Rachel when she thought she'd be spending twenty-five years in prison.

"Hey, what are you over there deep in thought about?" Nathan asked, gently rubbing her thigh.

"I'm just thinking about everything," she said, looking out the window. She ran her fingers over the plush seat of the rented Mercedes. "I'm just not used to all of this."

"Sweetheart, you are now a First Lady, so get used to the finer things. I've got big plans for us. For you." He looked over and grinned widely at her.

"For me? What kind of plans?"

"Can't tell you yet." He grinned like he had a major secret. "But if it pans out, it's gonna be huge."

Mary didn't need anything else. She had Nathan, and his eleven-year-old son, Alvin, whom she'd met while she was in prison. Alvin's mom had died of cancer and he'd taken a liking to Mary so she was looking forward to mothering him. Mary's own mother, Margaret, was reportedly clean and sober and living in Atlanta, but Mary hadn't talked to her in over a year. Margaret had been trying to make amends for being a horrible mother, but Mary had no interest in letting that woman back into her life. So Alvin and Nathan would really be the only family she had.

"Our church is about to blow up, baby!" Nathan said. "Just you wait and see. You're not only about to be rich, you're about to be famous, too!"

She just smiled, relishing in his excitement. Whatever Nathan's big plans were, Mary knew they'd be good.

For now, she just wanted to get to the airport, get on that plane, head to Atlanta, and begin her new life.

CHAPTER FIVE:
JASMINE

Jasmine nodded toward the young woman who'd led her and Mae Frances into the conference room. "Thank you," she said.

"No problem. Melinda will be right with you."

The moment the young woman closed the door behind her, Mae Frances *humph*ed. "Fancy," she grunted as she strolled past the artwork on the wood-paneled walls. Then, she turned to the conference table and pulled out one of the oversized chairs. She snuggled her hips into the leather as her fingertips caressed the polished grain of the mahogany table. "Isn't this a black TV station?"

"Uh . . . this is Oprah, Mae Frances. Oprah's not black, she's green. That's the only color people see when they look at her." Jasmine took the seat across from her friend.

"Humph!" Mae Frances rolled her eyes.

"Well, anyway, Jasmine Larson, you sure you really want to do this?"

Jasmine laid her palms flat on the table. "You can ask me that question a thousand times, and I promise you, a thousand times, I will give you the same answer."

"I'm just trying to make sure 'cause I can't see it."

"Would I be in these offices if I wasn't sure? Would I have asked you to call Stedman if I wasn't sure?"

"Stedman," Mae Frances whispered, then, her lips stretched into a wide smile. Her shoulders slumped and her eyes glazed as if she was suddenly in some kind of trance.

Jasmine frowned. "Mae Frances!"

Mae Frances blinked. Now, her shoulders squared. She sat straight, with her head up as if she was at attention. Clearing her throat, she said, "Well . . . uh . . . yeah. It was good talking to Stedman again. But . . . but this isn't about me. This is about you. And this here reality show. I just can't see it. You don't even watch reality TV."

"No, because I have respect for my brain cells. But I'm aware of the potential of these kinds of shows." Jasmine zipped open her tote and grabbed the folder of Internet articles she'd been collecting since Mae Frances told her that Stedman was going to take care of it all. "Do you know how much money these reality people make?"

Mae Frances turned up her nose and waved her hand in the air. "I don't know. I have brain cells that I respect, too. I don't watch any of that foolishness." She paused. "Well, *any* might be a strong word. Maybe I should say I don't watch that foolishness all that much. Well, not too much, you know, every now and then . . . and then some."

Jasmine frowned, dizzy from trying to figure out the circle of words that Mae Frances had just spoken. But she just shook her head and went back to making her point. Jasmine slid a paper across the conference table, "Well, both of our brains need to take a look at this." She paused just long enough to give Mae Frances time to take a quick glance at the page. "One of those housewives is taking her foolishness straight to the bank. She's making a million dollars."

"I may be watching a few of those shows, but I didn't know they had it like this. A million dollars?"

"A million dollars an episode."

Slowly, Mae Frances's eyes widened. "You mean to tell me that those women are earning one million dollars a week? Really?" Mae Frances turned toward the door as if she expected someone to walk in at any moment. "I wonder if somebody needs a new housewife. 'Cause I can be somebody's housewife. I know somebody's husband, so I can be somebody's wife."

Jasmine laughed as she leaned across the table and tucked the paper back into her folder. "According to what I've read, you don't even have to be married to be a housewife."

"Well, sign me up, 'cause I can use that kind of money."

"I know that's right."

"So, that's what they're gonna pay you?" Mae Frances asked. "A million dollars a week?"

"I wish. They haven't told me anything about pay yet, but I don't expect that much. That housewife didn't start off that way, but she's building a fortune now, and that's what I'm gonna do. I'm going to catapult this little venture into a financial windfall."

"So, that's why you're doing this? For the money?" Mae Frances asked, surprised.

Jasmine raised her eyebrows. "Why else would I do this? For fame?" She waved her hand. "I don't care who knows me or who knows my name. Just show me the money."

"You don't need any money," Mae Frances huffed. "Preacher Man is doing just fine," she said, referring to Jasmine's husband, Hosea, by the name that she'd given him years before.

"Of course he is, but what does that have to do with me and this show?" Before Mae Frances could respond, Jasmine added, "You know the saying . . . you cannot be too rich or too thin. I'm working on the rich part. This is how I'm going to help Hosea build our fortune."

"I don't think Preacher Man needs your help. Between the church and his TV show, you guys are more than fine. Plus, he's not the type to be thinking about building a fortune," she said.

"That's why he needs me. Because I will do the things that Hosea won't do. I care about the things Hosea doesn't care about. And with my forward thinking, our children's futures will be solid and set." When Mae Frances twisted her lips, Jasmine added, "How could it possibly hurt to add an extra million dollars a week to our bank account?"

Mae Frances's eyes brightened once again at the mention of that kind of money. "Well, when you put it that way . . . you sure they won't need me on this show?"

Jasmine grinned. "That's why you're here, Mae Frances! You got me in, now I'm gonna hook you up."

"You talking like you got this all worked out. What about Atlanta?"

Now, Jasmine sighed. Atlanta was going to be a problem. Hosea and his father had decided to open a satellite church in Atlanta, and although one of the associate pastors would be the lead pastor of City of Lights–Atlanta, Hosea wanted to be there with him for the first few months. The church had already rented a house and they were supposed to be leaving New York in two weeks, as soon as the kids were out of school for summer break.

"I know. Hosea is not going to be happy about me staying behind. But I'll convince him somehow." She paused and cocked her head a little, hoping it made her look just a little innocent. "You're gonna help me, right?"

"You know how we do this thing, Jasmine Larson. I have your back and you . . . well, you just live off the benefits of knowing me."

Jasmine grinned. "Thanks, Mae Frances, I can always count on you to help me with everything."

"Well, I'm gonna have to help you with something else, too, 'cause if you're really gonna do this show, then, you're gonna need a catchphrase."

"What the heck is a catchphrase?"

"A catchphrase is what's gonna help us get to that million dollars an episode."

"Then start talking."

"You're gonna have to come up with something cute and catchy, and then all the little followers out there in TV land will start walking around and saying your catch-phrase . . . and voilà, you're famous and you'll have a fortune."

"So, I say something on TV and then other people start saying the same thing?" Jasmine frowned as if she just didn't get that concept. "Why would they do that?"

Mae Frances shrugged. "I dunno. Maybe they don't have lives. Maybe they can't think of anything to say themselves. What-ever the reason, if you say what I'm gonna tell you every chance you get, we're gonna be well on our way to making that million dollars."

It was the second time that Jasmine no-ticed Mae Frances had suddenly changed the earning of a million dollars into a group effort, but that didn't bother her. In the years since they'd met, Mae Frances had become part of their family. She was the only grandmother that her children knew, and so any money that she and Hosea had would always belong to Mae Frances, too.

"Okay, so what am I supposed to say that's going to get *us* a million dollars an episode?"

Slowly, Mae Frances pushed back her chair, stood, and then made a show of straightening her mink. She glanced over her shoulder at Jasmine, batted her fake lashes and said, "That's what divas do and I'm done!" Then, she whipped around and strutted toward the door, swaying her hips in a way that Jasmine had never seen before.

At first, Jasmine sat there, staring blankly, waiting for something more. When Mae Frances turned around with a grin that stretched to her ears, Jasmine said, "That's it?"

Mae Frances pouted. "What do you mean, 'that's it'? That little catchphrase is gonna take you to the top. Just watch. Listen to me, Jasmine Larson, you'd better say that over and over again."

Before Jasmine could tell Mae Frances that none of that made any sense to her, the conference room door opened and an attractive, petite, cinnamon-colored woman stepped inside. Jasmine rose from her seat with a frown.

"Hello, Jasmine," the woman said as she walked to the end of the table.

"I know you." Jasmine almost sounded

like she was growling.

"We've met before."

Jasmine folded her arms. "Yes, we have."

Mae Frances's glance moved back and forth between the two like she was a spectator at a tennis match. "You know each other?"

"Like she said, we've met," Jasmine snarled. She spoke to Mae Frances, but she glared at the woman. "This is Rachel's friend Melinda. I told you about her, Mae Frances, when we were in L.A. This is the . . . lady who worked for the TV station and who wouldn't give me equal time after the interview she did with Cecelia and Rachel."

Melinda's eyes narrowed. "I told you then, equal time only applies in politics."

Jasmine ignored her. "She tried to embarrass me," Jasmine said as if Melinda hadn't spoken. "At first she wouldn't interview me, and then after I'd barely said my name, she turned off the cameras and said she had to leave for another story."

"Yes," Melinda said, putting her finger to her head, as if she was trying to recall. "I think we had to get to a story that was much more relevant . . . there was a house full of starving dogs that just couldn't wait." Melinda contorted her lips into something that was supposed to resemble a grin before she sat at the head of the conference table.

Jasmine stayed standing, still glaring.

"Well, let's get started," Melinda snapped, as if she hoped this meeting wouldn't last longer than two minutes.

"So, you're the Melinda I spoke to on the phone?" Jasmine asked.

Melinda blinked as if she didn't understand the question. "Yes, I'm the VP of Programming at OWN."

"Well, the person I spoke with was cordial and professional. But now, you seem different. Like you still have some kind of problem with me from L.A."

Mae Frances spoke up. "Oh, yeah, she's got a problem, Jasmine Larson, but it has nothing to do with L.A. This here attitude is due to the top."

Jasmine and Melinda turned to Mae Frances.

"What are you talking about?" Jasmine asked.

Melinda glared at Mae Frances as if she wanted to start a fight.

Mae Frances stared right back and with a smirk, said, "She got her orders from the top. Straight from Oprah. She was told to put you on the show and now she's pissed. Now, she knows that she ain't as important as she thinks she is."

Jasmine could almost see the heat rising inside Melinda as she asked Mae Frances, "And who are you?"

Jasmine said, "This is —"

But before she could finish, Melinda said, "Your mother. I can see the resemblance."

The smirk on Mae Frances's face turned upside down. "I am not her mother," she barked.

"You're not?" Melinda asked too innocently. "Oh, I'm so sorry."

There was nothing Jasmine wanted to see more than Melinda getting a beat down. Especially a Mae Frances kind of beat down.

But even though this woman was quickly making her way to the top of her enemies list, Jasmine didn't want to mess up her chances of being on the show.

"Mae Frances is one of my dearest friends," Jasmine said, "though I have an idea you knew that already."

"No, I didn't know. It's just that you look like you're about sixty and Mae Frances looks like she's eighty." Melinda sat back and chuckled as Jasmine and Mae Frances stared, shocked into silence. "Adding those numbers up, I just figured you were mother and daughter." Melinda pressed her lips together as if she was trying to hold back laughter, as if she'd just shown them who was truly in charge.

Jasmine couldn't believe this grown woman was coming at her like this. Mae Frances had to be right. Melinda was pissed about being forced to have her on the show. But to insult her like this? About her age? It seemed juvenile and over the top, especially for someone who was barely five feet two inches tall, and about one hundred pounds. Jasmine could take her out just by blowing her down.

Melinda was all wrong about that age thing anyway. Everyone knew Jasmine was much closer to forty than sixty, depending on how you did the math.

She had to think of something . . . something that would make Melinda scurry out of the room in complete humiliation. But before she could organize a thought, Mae Frances spoke up.

"Don't mess with me, little girl," Mae Frances whispered. "You don't want to end up like Paula Deen."

"Paula Deen?" Jasmine and Melinda said together.

Mae Frances nodded slowly. "You know what happened to her."

Jasmine tried her best to decipher what her friend was talking about. Everybody knew what had happened to Paula Deen. Her empire had fallen because of long-ago words she'd spoken and beliefs she'd had. But what Jasmine couldn't figure out was why was Mae Frances talking about Paula Deen now?

Mae Frances said, "Who do you think destroyed Paula?"

Neither Jasmine nor Melinda said a word or blinked an eye.

Mae Frances added, "I did." She sat back, giving them both a moment for her words to settle in. Then, she explained, "I knew her years ago and last month, she stole my grandmother's banana puddin' recipe. That was when my friend became my enemy. She messed with me, and ended up on the *Today* show crying her eyes out." Mae Frances paused just long enough to lean forward and put the threat in her body language as well as in her voice. "So, don't you mess with me, little girl, or you'll find yourself on the *Today* show and *Good Morning, America.*"

At first, Jasmine had the same shock on her face as Melinda. But then with a smile she turned and faced the VP. "So," Jasmine began as she settled back in her chair. "I guess *now* we can get this meeting started."

For a long moment, Melinda sat still and in silence, as if she was contemplating Mae

Frances's words. As if she was trying to figure out if Mae Frances was telling the truth. Then, the way her shoulders slumped, Jasmine could tell that Melinda knew she'd just made an enemy and now was trying to figure out if there was some way to turn that enemy back into a friend.

"Well," Melinda finally said with so much defeat in her tone, Jasmine almost felt sorry for her. Almost. "As you know, we'll start filming in the next few weeks. Will that be a problem?" Melinda spoke to Jasmine, but looked at Mae Frances as if she wanted to make sure Mae Frances was fine with it, too.

"No problem at all," Jasmine said, her pre–Mae Frances-beat-down-of-Melinda excitement returning.

"Like I told you on the phone," Melinda said, "we want to do something totally different with reality TV. We want to show smart women, women who have lives and their own things going on. Of course, we want the show to be hip and witty and entertaining overall, but each week, we want to leave the viewers with a message. We want to show First Ladies in a good light."

Jasmine was impressed. Melinda had recovered quickly. Her tone was once again professional, nothing but business, though the tightness of her expression and the stiffness in her voice let Jasmine know that Mae Frances's threat still rattled around in Melinda's head.

"We want a classy show," Melinda continued.

"Classy?" Mae Frances interjected. "Isn't that Rwanda chick going to be on the show?"

"Rwanda?" Melinda frowned. "The country? We're not filming in Africa."

"No," Jasmine waved her hand. "She means Rachel. Your friend Rachel Jackson Adams."

"Oh! Okay, yes," Melinda said. Then, she glanced at Mae Frances, but pressed her lips together as if there was so much more she wanted to say. As if she wanted to ask the old lady if she was coo-coo for Cocoa Puffs, but was smart enough not to say such a dumb thing to Mae Frances. Finally, all she added was, "Rachel is on the show, and it will be classy."

"That Adams girl and 'classy' together in one sentence?" Mae Frances laughed out loud.

Melinda continued as if Mae Frances were not cackling. "If we do this right, we'll be unique and we'll be able to ride this for several seasons."

Beneath the table, Jasmine slid her hands along the sides of her legs, trying to stop herself from shaking. She didn't care how much Mae Frances laughed; Melinda was already talking about several seasons and several seasons was exactly what she wanted to hear. Just enough seasons to get her to that million dollars an episode.

"There is one other thing I wanted to ask," Melinda said. She paused and looked at Mae Frances as if she needed permission to proceed.

Mae Frances nodded and Melinda cleared her throat.

"I know you work with Rachel with the American Baptist Coalition. . . ."

Jasmine didn't have a good feeling about where this was going.

Melinda continued, "Well, Rachel doesn't know that you're gonna be on the show. We're not sure how we're going to play it yet, but if you can . . . if you don't mind . . ." Melinda glanced at Mae Frances again and Jasmine realized her friend had traumatized her enemy. Now, Jasmine did feel sorry for Melinda. A little.

"We want to keep this a secret from Rachel. We want to get the two of you together during our first taping. Sort of as . . . a surprise for Rachel."

The reality of reality TV. Jasmine had read that most of the time, the scenes were scripted or set up by the producers. Well, she didn't mind this setup since it was Rachel who'd be on the receiving end of the surprise. In fact, this would be perfect, and play right into what Jasmine wanted. Rachel would be shocked to see her, would act like a fool since that was part of her DNA, and Jasmine would come off as the classy First Lady who deserved her own show or a million dollars an episode — whichever came first.

"That sounds good to me," Jasmine said. And then just to make Melinda feel a little bit better, she added, "In fact, I think that's a great idea."

Melinda smiled . . . kind of.

"Okay, then, I don't think there's anything else. As I told you on the phone, the contracts are almost completed and we'll get them over to you in a couple of days."

"That's fine."

"And you said no problem with the timing, right?"

"No, none at all." Jasmine paused. "I'm very excited about this, Melinda," she said, deciding that it was best for her to be cordial. She would have to work with Melinda for at least this season, so she might as well make it as bearable as possible. "This is going to be a great opportunity for me and my husband. I don't know if you're aware, but my husband is well known in the Christian community."

For the first time since Mae Frances had slammed Melinda's face to the ground, Jasmine saw a genuine smile on Melinda's face. And that made her frown.

"I know your husband," Melinda said. "Who doesn't? I've been following him and his father for years; I'm such a fan."

Maybe this cordial deal wasn't going to work out so well. Jasmine made a note-to-self: Don't let Melinda anywhere near Hosea.

"We're actually hoping to have Pastor Bush on the show, too," Melinda said.

"Well, Hosea and I haven't talked about the specifics of the show," Jasmine hedged. In fact, she hadn't said a word to Hosea since she hadn't quite figured out how to convince him that this reality show was as important as the new church.

He wouldn't be impressed with a million dollars the way Mae Frances was, so she'd have to think of something else to get him to say yes. Jasmine continued, "But Hosea and I will talk and we'll see. I can't promise anything, though, because he's really quite busy."

"I totally understand that," Melinda said, "And the fact that we'll be filming in Atlanta won't help, I guess."

"Wait a minute." Jasmine held up her hand. "Atlanta?"

"Yes, didn't I tell you?"

"Uh . . . no." Jasmine blinked several times, thoughts already clicking in her mind.

"I can't figure out how I missed that. I'm sorry," Melinda said, speaking to Jasmine, but looking at Mae Frances. "We were going to do the show in Houston, but now that we've added you, we didn't feel that it would be fair for you to move to Houston. And since Rachel was first, it wouldn't be fair to bring her to New York. So, we thought it best to film in a neutral location."

"Atlanta!" Jasmine said as her lips spread into a smile. This couldn't be anymore perfect. "Well, like I said, let me talk to Hosea. I think I'll be able to work something out."

"I'm sure you will," Mae Frances added, "now."

Jasmine shot her friend a look that was meant to keep her quiet, though Jasmine wasn't sure that was possible. "I'll talk to Hosea," Jasmine said again. "If we can work out the timing and the scene is right, I think he'll be glad to do it."

"Okay." Melinda looked down at her notes once again and added, "I guess the last thing is your son and daughter. Will they be on the show?"

Jasmine bit the corner of her lip. She hadn't thought about that. Did she want to expose Jacqueline and Zaya to all of this? "I'm not sure. I really wouldn't want my children involved in anything messy."

"Messy?" Mae Frances spoke up. "Didn't you hear what Melinda said? This is gonna be *class* all the way. Class. With you and that Adams chick. Class." Mae Frances laughed again.

Jasmine rolled her eyes at her friend. To Melinda she said, "Well, as long as I have editing approval for each episode, then my kids can be in."

Melinda shook her head. "That's not going to happen. We're not going to be able to let any of the principals have that kind of control. It doesn't work that way."

"Well, I'll have to talk to my husband then. Because we really believe in protecting our children."

Melinda nodded. "I understand. Especially with everything that your daughter's been through —"

71

"That is not going to be on the show," Jasmine snapped, wondering if Melinda was taking another shot at her. Because if she was, Jasmine was going to turn Mae Frances loose and by the time Mae Frances finished, forget about the *Today* show and *Good Morning America,* Melinda would be crying on CNN, MSNBC, and on FOX.

"No, no," Melinda said quickly. Her eyes widened as Mae Frances leaned forward in her chair again. "Definitely not. We would never exploit your daughter." Melinda paused. As if she needed to put in a little extra, she said, "I was just asking about her because I hope she's doing well."

Jasmine inhaled. "She's fine, thank you." Then, she exhaled. She was sorry that she'd gone off like that, but there was no way she could help it. That was now just a part of who she was. Anytime she was taken back to that dark place, that dark time, when her five-year-old angel had been kidnapped and taken away for weeks by a pedophile, she became crazy.

"Well, I'm glad that she's recovering."

Jasmine peered at Melinda. After a moment, she said, "Thank you."

Melinda closed the portfolio that held her notepad. "Well, I think that's all I have." She glanced at Mae Frances first, then spoke to Jasmine, "I hope I didn't upset you. I didn't mean to. I was just thinking about what happened to your daughter and how you turned something that was so bad into something so good." She took a breath. "I have to say that I really am impressed with the work that you're doing with Jacqueline's Hope and missing children. And maybe . . . maybe we can talk about Jacqueline's Hope on the show."

If this was just a ploy to get out of the way of Mae Frances's wrath, it was working. Jasmine smiled. "That would be great. I want more exposure for my foundation."

"Okay!" Melinda exhaled like she'd redeemed herself all the way. "I'm glad we're ending on a good note."

"Me, too." Jasmine pushed back her chair, stood, and Mae Frances did the same. "So, if we're done here."

"Actually, I was hoping for one more thing." Melinda glanced at her watch. "But I don't want to keep you waiting. . . ."

There was a knock on the door.

Melinda smiled. "Right on time." She stood. "I have a little surprise for you, Jasmine." Turning toward the door, Melinda yelled out, "Come in."

Jasmine watched as the door slowly pushed open. Then, her eyes widened.

"Melinda," Natasia said as she stepped inside the conference room.

"Yes, come on in." Melinda's grin was wide when she turned to Jasmine. "Surprise! The EP of the show is going to be . . . Natasia Redding. You two know each other, right?"

Melinda beamed as if she'd just brought two long-lost friends together. But she was the only one in the room feeling any kind of joy.

Natasia stared.

Jasmine glared.

And Mae Frances shouted, "Oh, lawd," as she fell back in her chair. "Up popped the devil!"

Chapter Six:
Rachel

"Mommy, where are you going?"

Rachel zipped the last of her Louis Vuitton luggage and set the suitcase on the floor. She picked up her four-year-old son, Lewis, and marveled at how big the little boy was getting.

"Sweetie, Mommy told you. I'm going to Atlanta to be a star."

"But you already a star," Lewis said with a big innocent grin.

Rachel toussled the little boy's hair. How she loved this little boy, as if she'd given birth to him herself. Her bond with Lewis was just as strong as it was to her biological children, Nia, Jordan, and Brooklyn.

Rachel and Lester had agreed that one day they would tell Lewis about his biological mother, Mary Richardson, but not until he was able to handle it. If Rachel had her way, she'd never say a word, but Lewis was biracial and would no doubt have questions once he realized his skin tone was different from his siblings. In the meantime, they would continue to shower the little boy with love and let him know that he was as much a part of their family as anyone else.

"So, you're really going to leave?" Nia asked, standing in the doorway with her arms crossed, a scowl across her face. Brooklyn stood next to her.

"Honey, we've already talked about this." Rachel motioned for her eight-year-old daughter to come sit on the bed next to her. "It's not going to be that long. I'm just going to go down, shoot some scenes, and maybe we'll even fly you all down and shoot some stuff with you."

"So, I get to be on TV, too?" Nia asked, finally breaking a smile as Brooklyn climbed on the bed next to her.

"Yes," Rachel replied.

"No," Lester interjected as he appeared in the doorway to their bedroom. "Rachel, we've already had this conversation. You doing this reality show is one thing. But you having our children on is another thing entirely, and where I draw the line."

"Seriously, Lester? It's just an innocent reality show." Rachel huffed.

"There's nothing innocent about those shows."

"Daddy, why won't you let me be on it?" Nia whined.

"Yeah, I wanna be a star like Mommy," Brooklyn added.

Rachel pulled both of her daughters close to her. "See, it's a Family Affair."

Lester narrowed his eyes at her. She knew he wasn't happy. He hated when she used the children like this, but he needed to see that what she was doing was for the good of their entire family. Lester had already carved a niche for himself as president of the American Baptist Coalition and she'd done well as the First Lady, creating programs and bringing some much-needed (and yes, a little unwanted) attention to the ABC. But this would take things to a whole different level. This would make her a power player. This would give her fame and a little fortune on the side. But it's the fame she wanted more than anything else. Although she liked the finer things in life — Coach, Michael Kors, an occasional trip to the Bahamas — Rachel didn't need a lot. But fame, that was a completely different ballgame. The fame would make people stand up and take notice. She had grown up as the preacher's daughter. Now, she was the preacher's wife. If this reality show went like she expected, she would be simply Rachel, the star.

"Nia, take your sister and brother and go play upstairs," Lester said.

"But Dad . . ." Nia cried.

"Not open for discussion," he said firmly.

Rachel kissed all of her children. "I'm not going to leave without coming to talk to you. Do like your father said."

As they scurried out, Rachel stood and glared at her husband. When she first met Lester, he was a pimply faced, red-mop-headed, shy boy. Now, he'd definitely evolved into a full-grown man with a backbone that sometimes worked her nerves. Even though Nia and Jordan weren't his biologically, he prided himself on being a good father to them, so Rachel knew that he was just trying to protect the kids.

Lester had gotten a lot more firm with her than he'd been in the early years of their marriage, but Rachel still knew how to win him over. She just chose her battles a little more wisely, and whether or not to have the kids on the reality show was not a battle she wanted to fight — just yet.

"Whatever you say, sweetheart. The kids won't be on the show. More air time for me." She planted a sultry kiss on him and he pulled her close.

"I'm going to miss you."

"I'm going to miss you, too. But I'll be back in a few weeks. They wanted my family to come down and shoot a few scenes but I understand you don't want to be on. I guess the producers will just have to hire me a family."

Lester's mouth gaped open. "What? They do that?"

"If they have to." Rachel knew that ultimately, Lester would never go for that kind of deception, so she wanted to plant that little seed so that it would fester and get him to agree with her eventually.

"Well, I guess I'd better get going," she said.

"Let me go grab my keys."

"Oh, no. I have a car service coming."

"A car service?" Lester balked. "What kind of sense does that make when I'm right here?"

"It makes a lot of sense because that's how we stars roll," Rachel tweaked his cheek before zipping her overnight kit. "Besides, Oprah is paying for it."

He laughed. "Oh, Oprah is paying for it?"

"Oprah, OWN, whatever. We're not footing the bill."

"Okay, babe." It was then that Lester noticed a package on the bed, next to a stack of flyers. "What's this?" He looked at the package, then at Rachel. "Addressed to Mary?"

"Just some pictures of Lewis." Rachel shrugged nonchalantly.

He looked at her in admiration. "I think it's great how you continue sending her pictures."

"Well, of course I don't want her getting any ideas, but as a mother, I'd want to see my child. Even if it was just a picture." Rachel had wrestled with that decision, especially because she couldn't stand that tramp, Mary. But Lewis couldn't help it that he was a product of that slug. And at the end of the day, Mary was essentially going to rot in prison, so Rachel saw no harm in sending her photos.

"Have I ever told you how awesome you are?" Lester asked.

"Not nearly enough." She kissed him, and then made her way over to the walk-in closet to get a pair of shoes she'd forgotten.

When she walked back out, Lester had picked up a flyer and was reading it. " 'Stay tuned for *The First Lady,* coming soon to OWN.' Wow, they've gotten flyers printed already?"

Rachel leaned over and examined the flyer. "You like?" It was a picture of her standing in front of Harpo Studios. Well, she wasn't actually in front of the studio. She'd just had it Photoshopped in the background but her graphic designer had done such an awesome job, it looked like she was right there.

"That's just a little something I had printed," she said.

"So, you had these printed?" Lester asked.

"Yes. You like?"

"How are you going to have something printed on your own?"

A mischievous grin spread across Rachel's face. "I just emailed one to Jasmine."

Lester shook his head. "Why would you do that?"

"Because since we're halfway cool now, I wanted her to hear about the show from me." Rachel expected to have heard from Jasmine by now. Everyone was talking about the *Access Hollywood* interview, but Jasmine still hadn't reached out to her.

Lester turned his lips up. "Really, Rachel? You're sending her a flyer?"

"Okay, there's a part of me that wanted to make sure she knew," Rachel admitted. "I wish I could be there to see the look on her face." Rachel laughed.

Lester dropped the flyer back on the bed. "You guys have some kind of friendship. And I hope you don't get in trouble when they see it."

Rachel put her purse strap over her shoulder, grabbed her carry-on, slid her sunglasses on, and said, "I keep trying to tell you, baby, it's better to ask for forgiveness than permission. Now, grab my suitcases, I'm ready to roll!"

CHAPTER SEVEN: NATASIA

"Ladies and gentlemen, as we begin to make our final approach into Hartsfield-Jackson International Airport, please bring your seat backs into the full upright position."

With her eyes still closed, Natasia pressed the button in the console next to her seat and eased herself upright. Those words had come much too soon. How could two hours have passed so quickly?

Her plan had been to get on this plane, find her seat in first class, and then sleep from wheels up to wheels down. But she hadn't been able to sleep a minute of the two-hour flight. Sleep had treated her like the enemy and had stayed away, just like it had all the nights since she'd been in New York.

She sighed and shook her head as that New York scene once again played in her mind.

Ambushed!

That was the only way to describe how Natasia had felt. The ambush-*er* had become the ambush-*ee*. And Natasia didn't appreciate being on the other side of someone's trick. A couple of weeks had passed, but the memory of that day at the OWN corporate offices still made her shudder.

Natasia stepped into the room, but the scene in front of her did not compute. Then, the old woman, wearing that mangled furry coat, spoke up.

"Up popped the devil!"

And in that instant, clarity came. She'd been tossed into the lion's den. Natasia turned her attention to the lion.

"Jasmine!"

At the same moment, Jasmine spoke, "Natasia!"

Then, simultaneously they said, "What are you doing here?"

Melinda answered for both of them. "Natasia, I told you that Jasmine was going to be on the show." Then, she turned to Jasmine. "And I wanted to surprise you. Reunite you with an old friend."

Melinda grinned like the Cheshire Cat and Jasmine and Natasia both growled. Jasmine turned her glare from Natasia for just a moment and shot daggers of hate toward Melinda.

The way Jasmine stared Melinda down, as if she wished she'd drop dead right there, made Natasia feel a bit better; she wasn't the only one who'd been set up.

Jasmine grabbed her bag from the table. "Are we done, Melinda?" she asked, though she didn't wait for an answer. Jasmine swept by Melinda and barely gave Natasia another glance.

Natasia frowned as the smile on Melinda's face widened, until the old woman stood up. With a slow stroll, the woman whom Natasia finally recognized as Jasmine's elderly friend moved closer to Melinda. The smile that the VP had worn from the moment Natasia stepped into the room faded and now a shadow of fear covered her face.

But the woman's attention went straight to Natasia. "Up popped the devil," she said again as she brushed past Natasia.

Natasia waited until the door was completely closed before she turned to Melinda. "I didn't know Jasmine was going to be here," she said accusingly.

Melinda simply shrugged. "I'm only in for the day and I had to set up back-to-back meetings." Then, her lips curved into a saccharine smile. "That's not a problem, is it?

I thought you and Jasmine were old friends."

Natasia crossed her arms. She had set up too many people, put together too many scenarios, played out too many schemes, not to recognize this game. She knew that Melinda was a smart woman who did her homework; who vetted the people she'd be working with. Surely she knew something about the history between her and Jasmine.

"You know that Jasmine and I were never the best of friends, right?" Natasia asked. Her question was a setup of her own, in hopes that Melinda's answer would give Natasia some insight into what was going on in Melinda's mind.

"No," Melinda said. "I didn't know that." *Liar!*

Melinda added, "But it's all business, right? You'll be able to handle this."

"Definitely," Natasia said as she finally took a seat at the conference table. At least now she knew where she stood with Melinda. This chick could not be trusted.

"Okay, well, let's get started," Melinda said.

Natasia pasted her own fake smile on her face and nodded as Melinda spoke about the plans for the show. But while she sat as if she was giving Melinda her full attention, her mind was on her own plans that had just imploded.

This was supposed to be a legitimate way for her to arrange a meeting with Hosea. But Jasmine being here messed all of that up. Because Natasia had no doubt that Jasmine would run home, tell Hosea, and block any chances of Natasia being able to contact him. Not only that, now that Jasmine knew Natasia was working on the show, of course she would do whatever she could to get Natasia dumped the way she had when Natasia had worked on Hosea's show.

She wasn't worried about that this time, though. Natasia came with high credentials, an impressive résumé. This reality show was lucky, no, *blessed* to have her name attached. Jasmine wouldn't be able to get to Melinda. At least not in that way.

Jasmine's poison would come in on the other side of her plan, the Hosea side. There was no way she'd be able to stay with her original plan of contacting Hosea. Not with the element of surprise now gone.

Well, she wasn't about to give up. She had to get to Hosea; she'd just have to be direct about it.

The forty-five-minute meeting with Melinda lasted forty-four minutes too long, and if Natasia had had the energy, she would've stood up and danced atop the table when Melinda finally said, "Well, that's all I have. Do you have any questions for me?"

"No, not at all," Natasia said. "You've explained it all clearly." She used the conference table to brace herself before she pushed back.

Melinda stood with her. "Your ticket for Atlanta has already been purchased. My assistant will email you the details. Oh, and we have reservations for you at Buckhead Tower, you know, the four-star, extended-stay hotel."

"I know it well," Natasia said.

"Well, we have a one-bedroom suite there for you."

"That's fine," Natasia said, glancing at her watch.

"I'm sorry," Melinda said. "Am I holding you from something?"

"No, I just want to make sure that I get back to LaGuardia in time."

"You're flying out tonight?"

Natasia nodded. "I just came in for the meeting with you," she said, looking Melinda straight in the eye. If Melinda could lie to her, then she could lie, too, with the same straight face, with the same sugary smile. "I have to get back to Chicago and close out my job."

"Is everything okay with that?"

"Oh, yeah. I'm taking an extended leave of absence. The network was glad to have me get this extra exposure on OWN."

Melinda nodded. "Well, it's too bad you're leaving tonight. I was going to ask if you wanted to go out for drinks. Or maybe even a quick dinner."

"Sorry, not this time," Natasia said, knowing that she would never break bread with this woman — at least not on a social level. Melinda had moved to the top of her skank list. "Maybe once we get to Atlanta we can hang out," she added anyway.

Melinda paused, stared at Natasia for a long moment. And in Melinda's eyes, Natasia could see Melinda was trying to figure her out. "Yeah, we'll get a chance to do that a lot in Atlanta."

With just a few more words of goodbye, Natasia walked out of the room with her head high and her back straight. It wasn't until she was in the hallway that she slowed her steps, giving herself time to gather her strength. Inside the elevator, she leaned against the panels and pushed the meeting with Melinda from her mind. It was time to focus on Hosea.

When the elevator stopped on the first floor, Natasia stepped out tentatively and looked around, half expecting to find Jasmine and her ancient, fur-covered sidekick waiting to pounce on her. But all was clear. She stayed on high alert when she stepped outside into the early evening madness known as Times Square.

With just a few steps to the curb and then a raise of her hand, a cab rolled to a stop and she slipped inside. "The Plaza Hotel," she said, and then leaned back on the cracked pleather seat.

Melinda may have believed that Natasia was on her way to the airport, but she wouldn't be doing that today. Instead, she had a two-night reservation at one of New York's premiere hotels, and she had hoped that she'd see Hosea at least one of those nights.

Her thought had been to wait until she was securely in her hotel room to make the call, but even though it was just a short ride to the Plaza, she no longer had that kind of patience. Seeing Jasmine had made her anxious, made her wonder if she could pull this off.

Her hand was shaking as she pulled her cell from her purse and scrolled through the names until she came to Darlin'. She pressed *67, then clicked on Hosea's number and closed her eyes as the phone rang.

"Please, God, please, God," she whispered.

And then, "Hello."

Natasia's eyes popped open.

"Hello?"

With a sigh, Natasia clicked off the phone. The voice was like nails on a chalkboard. Jasmine!

Jasmine had answered Hosea's phone. Jasmine was on to her. And even though she had blocked her number, Natasia was sure that Jasmine knew who was on the other end of that call.

There was no way Natasia would get to Hosea now — at least not during these two days.

"Miss . . ."

Natasia blinked.

"This is the Plaza," the driver said.

Natasia peered through the window; she hadn't even realized that the cab had come to a stop. "Oh," she said. And then, in the next moment, she added, "Would you mind waiting? I left my bag with the bellman and I just want to run inside and get it."

"Okay, where're you goin'?"

She paused for just a moment. "To the airport, LaGuardia."

"Okay," he said. "I'll be right here."

She pushed herself from the cab and

walked as fast as she could into the lobby, all the time thinking that she hadn't lied to Melinda after all. She was going home tonight. There was no need to stay in New York if she couldn't see Hosea.

She would just have to come up with another plan.

As the airplane descended and the Atlanta skyline came into view, all Natasia could do was sigh. In the time that had passed since New York, she hadn't come up with anything else. And now she was about to be in Atlanta . . . with Jasmine. Natasia didn't know if Hosea would be joining Jasmine, but from what she remembered about the man she still referred to as the love of her life, he wouldn't want any part of reality show madness. But he was also a man who loved his family and even if he wasn't on the show, he would definitely come to visit Jasmine and his children, who she assumed would be with their mother.

It wasn't going to be easy, but during one of his visits, Natasia was going to see Hosea alone. The only challenge was that it would have to be soon. It would have to be before her time ran out.

CHAPTER EIGHT:
MARY

This was where she was *supposed* to be. This was the life she was *supposed* to live.

As Mary sat in the second pew of Pleasant City Missionary Baptist Church, she couldn't help but smile at how far God had brought her. Gone were her cut-too-low blouses and cut-too-high skirts. She was dressed in a respectable, metallic jacquard suit that she wouldn't have been caught dead in a year ago.

Mary had longed for this life with Lester Adams, and at the time, couldn't understand why she couldn't have it. Now, she knew it was because God had something better in store. That something better was standing in the pulpit, straight showing out.

"Family," Nathan said, a huge smile on his face, "you'll have to excuse the extra pep in my step." He did a little jig. "The bounce in my ounce. But y'all know, the missus is home and let's just say, we've been like some bunny rabbits."

Mary gasped as the congregation erupted in laughter.

"But I come to you today to tell you that dreams do come true," Nathan continued, his voice rising. "When I came to this church, I took a leap of faith. I walked in that faith because I knew there was something great in store."

A chorus of amens rang out as Nathan talked about all of his plans for Pleasant City. It didn't escape Mary that not once had he preached the Word or referred to any scripture; he'd just spent the last twenty minutes talking about all the big things in store. And the congregation had been eating it up. Maybe this is what they did in church. Lord knows she didn't know. A product of the foster system, Mary never saw the inside of a church growing up and had only started going when Rachel's enemy hired her to seduce Lester.

Yet here she was, not only going to church, but sitting up as First Lady. If anyone from her past could see her now, they wouldn't believe the woman that she'd become.

Mary brushed a piece of lint off Alvin, who was sitting beside her. The eleven-year-old fiddled with his belt before scooting closer to her. They'd instantly bonded these past two weeks, almost as if Alvin longed for a mother figure. That was probably because his father was never at home. Alvin actually lived with his grandparents. Mary wanted him with her and Nathan, but Nathan had been adamant, saying, "Not yet" because Alvin was such a help to his parents.

"Church," Nathan continued, snapping Mary's attention back to the pulpit, "I told you all right before I went to pick up my wife that I had a blockbuster announcement." He smiled as he looked at Mary. Immediately, something didn't feel right. Nathan's eyes were dancing and though they hadn't spent much time together, she'd quickly learned that when he had something up his sleeve, his eyes gave it away.

"Well, I can't hold it in any longer. The missus doesn't even know about this yet."

That made Mary lose her smile. She didn't care for surprises, especially surprises in front of hundreds of people.

"Many of you know that reality shows are the hottest thing on TV right now. How many of you watch them?" There were some small rumblings, but only a few people raised their hands.

"Come on, you're in the house of the Lord, be honest." Laughter filled the room as several hands finally went up. "Um-hmm," Nathan sang. "You know you get your fill of Stevie and Mimi." A few more hands went up. "You can't wait to see NeNe and Kenya." Even more hands. "And some of y'all even find yourselves rooting for Honey Boo Boo. Let the church say amen?"

"Amen!" someone from the third row yelled.

"I'll admit it, I love Honey Boo Boo," someone shouted.

"I'm a *Basketball Wives* fan," someone else yelled.

Mary looked around, stunned. All these people were actually admitting to following that foolishness?

Nathan continued. "While many of these shows are degrading, millions of people are tuning in on a regular basis. And the Lord spoke to me and said 'Pastor, that's an audience waiting for the Word.' We can reach those people through the back door." He slammed his palm on the podium. "Y'all know we believe in reaching people by any means necessary here at Pleasant City."

Mary scrunched her face and peered at her husband. She definitely didn't understand where this was going. Why was he talking about reality shows?

"Well, I found a new way to spread the

gospel." Nathan turned to Mary and smiled again. "My wife is all set to appear on a new First Ladies reality show."

"What?" Mary found herself saying as a low rumble filled the room.

"I told you I have a big surprise for you, honey. One that was going to make you famous." Nathan was talking like he'd just announced they'd won the lottery. He ignored her glare as he turned back to the congregation. "While my wife will be the one featured, they'll show us," he swept his arm over the congregation, "and we'll be able to spread the Word and bring more souls to Pleasant City."

Reality show? Nathan had lost his mind. When she was locked up, her TV watching had been limited, but she hadn't missed the explosion of those stupid shows. A lot of the inmates watched them, but she wasn't one of them. She was trying to better herself and watching a bunch of ratchetness on TV wasn't the way to do it.

"We'll begin filming here in Atlanta next week so get ready, Pleasant City is about to go to the next level! And if you're doubting that we're going to the next level, let me add that my wife will be on the show with one of the premiere First Ladies in the country. You all know her as the First Lady of the American Baptist Coalition. That's right, folks, my wife will be starring with Rachel Jackson Adams."

Several people applauded and Mary felt sick to her stomach. Now she knew Nathan was working with half a brain cell. He knew her history with Rachel, so why he thought this was a good idea was mind numbing. Mary had been the submissive, obedient wife since she'd gotten out of prison, but he'd gone too far with this move and the minute he set foot off the pulpit, she would let him know. Mary had worked too hard to grow as a woman. Rachel was taking care of her child now and Mary had prayed long and hard to get over the hatred she felt for that woman. God had answered her prayers, so she needed to leave well enough alone. Rachel brought out the worst in Mary and she'd come way too far to turn back into the conniving, scandalous chick she once was.

After service, Alvin went with his grandmother and Mary headed straight to Nathan's office to wait for him. Twenty minutes later, his door opened and he must've known that she was about to go clean off, because before Mary could utter a word, he said, "Babe, hear me out."

"How could you do that?" she said.

"Look, I told you, everything I do, I'm doing for us." He took a step toward Mary and took her hands. "For the betterment of us and our family."

"Nathan, a *reality show*?"

"First of all, we need the money. Do you know how much money those people make?"

"Yeah, but at what cost?" Mary replied. "They're getting money to make themselves look like fools on national TV."

He dropped her hands like he was disappointed in her. "This isn't about you, Mary. This is about building up our church." He removed his robe and draped it across the chair. "I thought that's what you wanted."

"Don't do this," Mary said.

He pulled her close to him. "Come on, sweetie, you told me how you wanted the nicer things in life."

"Yeah, but I'm perfectly content now." Something else she never thought she'd say.

"But you don't have to be. You have a golden opportunity right here knocking at your door."

Mary let out a long sigh. "How'd this even come about?"

His eyes started dancing again. "I heard about the show, and I worked my magic. I had a friend make some calls. He knows the executive producer, Natasia something, and he got me into the studio. Once I met with her, told her our story, she was in."

Mary folded her arms and glared at him. "So, you gave her my history with Rachel?"

He smiled as he nodded. "I did. That's what sold her on it."

"Nathan, putting Rachel and me together is going to be toxic."

"And toxicity makes for good TV," he said matter-of-factly.

"But I'm not the same person. I've grown," Mary protested. "And Rachel, she's the mother of my child now."

Nathan pulled back, then walked around his desk. "I'm glad you brought that up." He reached in a folder on his desk and pulled out what looked like a Christmas card. "Here," he said, handing it to Mary.

Mary took the card and her heart dropped. *Happy Holidays from The Adams Family* was embossed across the top of the card. Below those words was a picture of Lester, Rachel, their two daughters, their son, and Mary's precious baby boy. Seeing Lester Jr. brought tears to her eyes.

"They're touting that baby like he's theirs," Nathan said sternly. "He's not. He's *yours.*" He stepped closer to her. "He's *ours.* And he belongs here with us."

Mary didn't look up from the card. "I signed away my rights." She sniffed, touching a finger to the image of her baby's face.

"There is nothing the right amount of money can't undo." Nathan wrapped his arms around her waist. "Do this show. We'll drum up support, get people behind you, make some money for a good attorney, and make it a public relations nightmare for the Adamses. Then, we will convince a judge to return Lewis to you — his mother."

That gave Mary pause. Could it be? Could she really get her son back?

"You paid for your mistake. It's time for our son to come home," Nathan said.

"How are we going to get him back?" Mary said, her voice soft and filled with hope.

"You leave that to me. You just do your part. Get the people" — he brushed a tendril of hair away from her face — "to fall in love with you. Give the camera what it wants, and I'll take care of the rest."

Mary glanced down at the card again. She'd never in a million years thought she had a shot at getting her child back. But now that it was a real possibility, she'd be willing to do whatever it took to make that happen — including star in a ratchet reality show with Rachel Jackson Adams.

CHAPTER NINE:
JASMINE

Jasmine rushed down the hall, but then paused right at the landing. She stood at the top of the steps and surveyed the sprawling foyer below.

This was the life, their temporary Atlanta home, or "baby mansion," as she'd been calling it for the last week. When Hosea had told her that the church had found a house for them, she'd been leery. Her plan had been for her and Hosea to make the trip to the Peach State and find their own home. But Jasmine had to admit that Mrs. Whittingham and Brother Hill, two of Hosea's father's most trusted assistants, had done the doggone thang.

This five-bedroom, six-bath, forty-two-hundred-square-foot home with a family room, library, backyard pool, and jacuzzi not only had enough space for Jasmine, Hosea, and their son and daughter, but their nanny, Mrs. Sloss, and Mae Frances both had their own bedrooms, too.

Jasmine placed one Gucci pump on the step below, then the other, and slowly descended down the curved stairway. This was exactly the home she'd dreamed of when she was growing up in that little two-bedroom cottage in Inglewood, California. Jasmine, her mother, her father, and younger sister, Serena, had been squeezed into eleven hundred square feet that had felt like a closet. She'd been so jealous of her best friend, Kyla's, Ladera Heights home that she'd vowed long ago to live a grand life. And she'd made it!

Jasmine so wished that Kyla could see her now. But of course, that wasn't possible. She and Kyla hadn't really spoken since Jasmine had slept with Kyla's husband. Jasmine didn't understand why Kyla couldn't just let that go. After all, she'd been so different then; coveting everything that Kyla had. But now that Jasmine had more than Kyla (and everyone else she knew), she'd been delivered from coveting.

Letting go of that sin was probably the reason why God had bestowed so many blessings on her — including this upcoming one. Jasmine was so ready to become the million-dollar-a-week reality TV star that she was born to be.

At the bottom of the stairs, Jasmine decided that they would definitely have to shoot a few scenes here at her home. And every time, she'd have to make her grand entrance just this way. Of course, they would only be able to do that when Hosea was away. It had been easy enough to convince him that her doing this show was fine, but she hadn't told him about Natasia — and she didn't plan to!

Jasmine's heels clicked against the foyer's marble floor, but then she quieted her steps when she pushed through the French doors that led to the family room.

"There you are, darlin'," Hosea said, jumping up from the sofa. "I was beginning to worry." He glanced down at his watch. "You're running late."

"Sweetheart, don't you know that every star has to make an entrance? We cannot be the first ones there."

Hosea chuckled. "I still can't believe you're doing this." He looked over his shoulder at Mae Frances, who was sitting in one of the burgundy wingback chairs. "Nama," he said, calling Mae Frances by the name that Jacqueline had given her when she first learned to talk, "was just trying to talk me into going to the restaurant with y'all."

Jasmine's eyes widened when she looked at her friend. Was Mae Frances really starting to lose it? Her talking to Hosea about this made Jasmine think that maybe she really was coo-coo for Cocoa Puffs.

Mae Frances's face was masked with innocence when she said, "Yeah, I was telling Preacher Man how that Melinda VP lady kept asking about him."

"Yeah, I told you that, honey," Jasmine said to Hosea. "But I told her that you were quite busy with the church and probably wouldn't have time —"

"I won't have time. I'm not going to be on the show, but I would've gone down there with you today to check it out," Hosea said, making Jasmine hold her breath. "If I didn't have to watch the kids."

She exhaled. "That's right, the children," Jasmine said, not able to recall a time when she loved her children more. "Someone has to stay with them. Speaking of that, Mrs. Sloss's plane lands at seven in the morning."

Hosea chuckled. "I know that's way too early for you, but don't worry. I'll be there to pick her up."

"I was just going to send a car."

Before Hosea could respond, his cell phone rang. Picking it up from the side

105

table, he glanced at the screen, then said, "I've gotta take this." Kissing Jasmine on the cheek, he added, "Have a good time and don't hurt nobody. Between this house and our place in New York I don't have a dollar left for bail, so behave yourself."

When Hosea strutted out of the room, Jasmine whipped around to face Mae Frances. With her hands on her hips, she hissed, "You were trying to get Hosea to come to the restaurant?" She didn't give her friend time to answer. "You know he can't be there."

Mae Frances pushed herself up from the chair. "Why? 'Cause you haven't told him about Natasia?" She grabbed the lapels of her mink and pulled the coat tighter around her.

Jasmine rolled her eyes, grabbed the chained straps of her purse, and stomped from the room. She had a few things to say to Mae Frances, but Jasmine didn't say another word as they passed through the hall, to the kitchen, and then out the back door to the garage. She didn't open her mouth until they were both seated in her rented BMW and she'd driven several streets away from her home.

Only then did Jasmine say, "You know I haven't said a word about Natasia being on the show. So, why would you invite Hosea? If he saw her —"

"Jasmine Larson, when are you going to learn the rules of deception." Mae Frances shook her head and sighed. "I've been trying to teach you all these years, but you always operate on emotions." She leaned forward, pressed the button for the air conditioner, then blasted it on high.

The air conditioning made Jasmine shiver right away since it was a cool sixty-two degrees outside. In her mind, Jasmine screamed, *If you'd take off that daggone mink . . . it's June, for God's sake.* But she said nothing. Saying something about the coat that her friend loved so much would set Mae Frances off and right now, she needed Mae Frances's help.

When the temperature in the car was probably about fifty, Mae Frances said, "Okay, that's better." She leaned back in her seat and continued, "So, about Preacher Man. First of all, I knew he had to stay home with Jacquie and Zaya today, and I also knew that if you weren't bugging him to come, he would get suspicious. He would think you didn't want him at the restaurant."

"I don't."

"But if he knows that you don't want him

there, he'll wonder why. And if he wonders why, he's gonna ask questions, and if he asks questions . . ."

"Okay," Jasmine relented. "Good point."

"But you're gonna have to say something about Natasia sooner or later."

Jasmine was shaking her head before Mae Frances had even finished her sentence. "My plan is to have her fired before Hosea finds out anything."

Mae Frances raised one of her penciled-on eyebrows. "And you think that's gonna keep her away? How do you know she hasn't tried to call Hosea again?"

Jasmine had to admit there was always that chance and that was always her fear.

The day she'd seen Natasia at the OWN offices, Jasmine had rushed home, taken Hosea's cell from their home office where he'd been working, and answered it for a couple of hours. There was that one hang-up, which she knew for sure was Natasia, but after that, nothing. Of course, she'd had to sneak the phone back to Hosea and then just leave it up to God. But she'd been pretty sure that Natasia wouldn't try to reach Hosea again . . . at least not that way.

Knowing Natasia, she would go for the gold — forget about calling and try to see Hosea in person. Jasmine had no idea how she would prevent that, but she was going to try. That snake was back for a reason, and this time, Jasmine had to make sure that she chopped off the head so that Natasia would never appear again.

"So, what's your plan?" Mae Frances interrupted Jasmine's thoughts. "When are you gonna tell Preacher Man that the first woman he ever loved is back?"

"Why you gotta say it like that? He doesn't love her."

"I said *loved*. He *loved* her. He *loved* her first."

"Dang, Mae Frances . . ."

"He had to really love her since he gave her that big ole engagement ring. Yup, it had to be true love. The kind that lasts forever."

"Mae Frances!"

"What?"

"I'm Hosea's wife. There's no need to talk about his past. We all did dumb stuff back in the day. What I need to be concerned with now is the future. You have to help me figure out a way to get rid of her."

"I thought you'd never ask." Mae Frances grabbed a folder from the tote that was still on her shoulder. She shifted through a pile of papers. "So, I made a few calls and found out that Melinda offered the position to Natasia *after* you were put on the show."

Jasmine banged her hand on the steering wheel. "I knew it! Melinda set me up, but why? Just for drama? But Natasia's not on the show so it can't be that." The questions and answers rolled off Jasmine's tongue. "Did she do it just to get on my nerves?"

"Probably. She wanted to get back at you for going to Oprah. But I don't think that was the only reason. Melinda's really been given the charge to produce a classy reality show." Mae Frances shook her head. "That's an oxymoron if I ever heard one. But anyway, Natasia has been brought on to add a newsworthy element to the show."

"News? What does news have to do with a First Ladies reality show?"

"Look, I'm just telling you what Stedman told me."

"Well, whatever the reason she was brought on . . . do you have a plan to eliminate her?"

Mae Frances cocked her head to the side and smiled. "Eliminate her? Like permanently?"

Jasmine frowned. What in the world was her friend offering? She never wanted to have to testify in a court of law. She'd learned that more than twenty years ago when another friend had "eliminated"

110

someone on her behalf.

"By permanently, do you mean permanently from Hosea's life?" Jasmine asked.

"That's exactly what I mean."

"But she'd still be alive, right?" Jasmine just wanted to make sure since she'd been down this road before.

"Do you want her to be?"

"Mae Frances!"

"What?"

"Can you just help me get rid of her so that she never calls Hosea again."

"Yes."

"But I want her to still be breathing."

Mae Frances grunted as if she was disappointed, but finally she growled, "All right. Let me see if I can work on getting her fired . . . we'll start there. But it's gonna be tough 'cause they really like her. I'll see what Stedman can do."

It was only about a ten-minute ride from their Buckhead home to Serendipity, one of the premiere restaurants in the city. Jasmine eased the car into the lot and pulled in behind one of the OWN vans. There were few cars scattered throughout, but Jasmine knew that was because of the early hour.

Jasmine turned off the car, then peered through the windshield at the glass panels at the front of the building. She'd been

111

pleased when one of the show's junior producers had told her that this where they were going to have their first meeting. That let her know that Oprah wasn't going to skimp on the budget . . . not that she ever expected skimping from the Queen of Television.

Jasmine flipped down the visor, opened the vanity mirror, and checked her eyelashes, making sure that each individual mink lash was still in place. Next, she puckered her lips and used her pinky to make sure that none of her gloss was out of line.

"Ah-hem." Mae Frances cleared her throat. When Jasmine didn't respond, Mae Frances coughed again.

"Are you doing that for my benefit?" Jasmine asked with her eyes still on the mirror.

"Don't you think we need to get in there, Jasmine Larson?" Mae Frances tapped her fingernail against the dashboard and pointed to the digital clock. "We're already twenty minutes late."

"It's not twenty minutes late, it's fashionably late."

"It's colored people late," Mae Frances snapped. "And I don't want to miss one moment in front of the camera."

Jasmine laughed. "Okay."

She slipped out of the car, straightened the hem of the red St. John's jacket that she wore with black slacks, and slung her purse over her shoulder.

The producer had told Jasmine to come camera ready and dress casually, but there was no way she was going to do that. She had to outshine Rachel and whoever else was going to be on the show. They'd show up in jeans — or, knowing Rachel, leggings — and Jasmine would look like the class act that she was.

Thinking about Rachel made Jasmine smile. She had no doubt that once she saw her, Rachel would play her role. She would react in her typical, not-so-ghetto-fabulous way. She would annoy everyone and set the stage for Jasmine to be the star.

Just as Jasmine reached for the chrome handle, the glass-paneled door swung open. "Welcome to Serendipity," a man in a tuxedo greeted them.

"Thank you," Jasmine said and Mae Frances nodded.

Before she could say another word, Jasmine was blinded by white light.

"What the hell, I mean, heck?" she said, recovering quickly.

"Just walk in, Jasmine," she heard a voice behind the light say. "We're taping."

Oh, that's right. So, even though it took a moment for her eyes to adjust, Jasmine strutted as she followed the cameraman who was backing up through the restaurant, leading Jasmine the whole way.

"Are you getting me? I think Jasmine is blocking my light!"

She'd been so caught up in the moment that Jasmine had momentarily forgotten about Mae Frances. But Jasmine didn't turn around, didn't miss a step. The light was shining on her and she wasn't going to miss a moment.

Then, a click and the light disappeared. Jasmine blinked, focused, and took in the white man balancing a camera on his shoulder, and Melinda and Natasia standing on either side of him.

"Mae Frances," Melinda said, moving her eyes between Jasmine and the older woman. "I . . . I didn't know you'd be here."

"Well, now you know," Mae Frances said, shrugging just a bit so that her mink hung off her shoulders.

"I think what Melinda is saying," Natasia jumped in, "is that you're not part of the cast." Natasia crossed her arms and looked Mae Frances up and down.

Mae Frances glared back at her. "The devil is a lie!" she said to Natasia. Then, to

Melinda, she said, "You don't have a problem with me being here, do you?"

It was a simple question, though it sounded like a threat. Every eye watched Melinda swallow hard. "Uh, no. No, of course we have to have a supporting cast."

"Yeah, that's what I thought and that's why I'm here," Mae Frances said, sauntering past the production team as if she knew where she was going. "To support all y'all." She slipped into one of the booths and snapped her fingers. "Okay, y'all can get back to filming me." Now, she completely shrugged the mink off her shoulders, leaned a little to the side, tilted her head, and smiled.

"Ah . . . excuse me."

Everyone in the restaurant turned the other way.

"Oh, my goodness! Rachel!" Melinda called out.

"Roll the cameras, quick!" the director, Sonny, shouted.

The blinding light came on once again.

Rachel held up her hand, shielding her eyes, and blinked.

Jasmine turned to fully face Rachel and she smiled as she watched Rachel's eyes focus, scan the group, then settle on her. She could almost hear the questions rattling

115

around in Rachel's empty head.

Then, "What the hell, I mean, heck?" Rachel jerked down her hand. "What is she doing here?" she asked, pointing to Jasmine.

Jasmine's smile widened. "Rachel. Dahling," she said, glad that she was standing with her good side toward the camera. "It is so good to see you." She reached for a hug, but the moment she put her arms around her, Rachel slapped her arms away — exactly as Jasmine knew she would.

Jasmine stepped back, pressed her hand to her chest, and wished she'd worn pearls so that she'd have something to clutch.

"What are you doing?" Rachel directed her question to Jasmine when no one answered her. "Why are you here?"

In the next moment, Jasmine was sure that Rachel was going to stomp her foot, throw a tantrum.

But then there was another "Ah . . . excuse me."

And again, everyone turned to the new voice, a white woman whom Jasmine didn't recognize.

"Oh, my God!" Rachel shouted.

Jasmine could tell that Rachel was so filled with fury that if she'd been a few shades lighter, her skin would've been beet red.

Whipping her head toward Melinda, Rachel shouted, "What is she doing here?" But this time, her finger was pointed at the white woman. "Do you know who she is?"

The cameras rolled, but no one responded to Rachel. Now, Rachel screamed, "Somebody call the police. This woman is an escaped felon!"

As murmurs rumbled through the group, Jasmine slipped into the booth next to Mae Frances. "This is turning out to be even better than I expected," she whispered. "Rachel is acting like she's lost her mind."

Mae Frances nodded, and she and Jasmine watched Rachel stomp from one producer to the other, demanding answers and that the police be called.

"I wonder who that white woman is? And why does she have Rachel all riled up?"

"You don't know?" Mae Frances asked.

Jasmine twisted to face her. "And I guess that means that you do."

"I do. 'Cause I know everything." Mae Frances said, "That there woman is Mary Richardson. She's Lester's baby's mama!"

Jasmine frowned. "Baby's mama? I didn't know . . ."

" 'Cause I didn't tell you. But Lester had an affair, and now everyone in America will know about it." Mae Frances tilted her head back and released a howl of a laugh that stopped everyone in the restaurant. "Guess you could say the devil made him do it . . . literally. 'Cause that woman there? Any second now, you're gonna see her horns." Mae Frances's shoulders shook with her amusement.

Now, Jasmine laughed, too. This was all working out perfectly. It wouldn't even take her a season to get her own show. Her fortune was on its way.

Chapter Ten:
Rachel

God was testing her. That's the only reasonable explanation that Rachel could come up with as to why she was standing here looking at the woman she despised most in this world. Up until recently, that title had belonged to Jasmine Cox Larson Bush. But she and Jasmine were cool now. At their worst, she didn't despise Jasmine nearly as much as the woman standing in front of her.

"Rachel, it's good to see you," Mary casually said.

"What. Are. You. Doing. Here?" Rachel repeated for what felt like the hundredth time.

The left side of her brain wanted to haul off and smack Mary, pop Melinda in the eye, and stomp anyone who had anything to do with this. But the right side of her brain told her she needed to calm down because her television debut didin't need to go this way. Out of the corner of her eye she saw the cameraman zoom in, so she tried every-thing in her power to compose herself.

"I guess you hadn't heard," Mary said with a big stupid grin. She was dressed in a tacky-looking church lady suit; her long blond hair was twisted in a bunch of curls. She looked absolutely ridiculous. "I'm the third First Lady on the show."

"How in blue blazes are you on a show for First Ladies?" Rachel questioned. "I don't . . . wait, what do you mean, *third*?"

That's when Rachel's eyes made their way over to the booth where Jasmine and Mae Francis were sitting. Jasmine did a brief finger wave as she smiled confidently.

"Awww, hell naw!" Rachel said. "Cut, turn the camera off!" She pushed toward the cameraman, but he stepped back. "I'm not playing," Rachel fumed. "Turn the camera off or I will walk up out of here right now!"

Melinda looked at her like she knew that wouldn't happen. Even still, she motioned toward the director, who rolled his eyes and said, "Fine, let's take five."

"We're going to need longer than five because someone needs to explain to me what in the world is going on," Rachel snapped as the cameraman removed the camera from his shoulder.

"Looks like you've got company on this

here show."

Rachel spun her head toward the booth from where that statement had come.

"Why are you even here?" Rachel yelled.

Mae Frances pulled out a fan from her purse, popped it open, and smiled as she began fanning herself.

Rachel gave her the hand. She didn't have time to deal with Methuselah right now anyway.

Rachel turned back to Mary. "What do you mean, you're the third First Lady? First of all, you're not a First Lady, and who is the second?"

"Raise your hand, Jasmine," Mae Frances said, lifting Jasmine's arm.

Rachel ignored her as she continued ranting. "This is my show!"

"Actually, Raquel . . ." Mae Frances said.

Rachel stomped over to the front of the booth. "Rachel! Rachel! Rachel! You know damn well my name is Rachel!"

Mae Frances frowned as she looked at Jasmine. "Can First Ladies say damn?" she snickered.

"Rachel, just calm down," Jasmine said. "It's not that serious."

"Not right now, Jasmine," Rachel said, jabbing a finger in her direction. "I'm going to get to why you're even here in a minute."

Jasmine smirked, then threw her hands up like she was out of it. "That's what divas do, and I'm done!" she said.

Jasmine was taking pleasure in this whole scenario. If she had anything to do with Mary being here . . .

Rachel turned back to Melinda, took a deep breath, and said, "Melinda, tell me what's going on."

Melinda shifted nervously. "Um, ah, I've always made it clear that the possibility existed that we may bring some other First Ladies on to the show."

"No, you didn't."

"Oh, I didn't tell you that?"

Rachel couldn't believe this woman — this woman who she thought was her friend — was standing here trying to play her. "No. You didn't. Really, Melinda? I thought you were my girl."

Before Melinda could reply, a tall stunner of a woman with light-brown, almond-shaped eyes and a fierce Halle Berry pixie-style haircut sauntered over and said, "Mrs. Adams, this isn't personal, it's business."

"And who are you?" Rachel said, not bothering to hide her disgust. "Are you on the show, too?"

The woman gave a big smile. "Natasia Redding. I'm executive producer of the show." She stuck her hand out. Rachel didn't take it.

"Rachel, we just felt like we needed to add several elements to the show," Melinda interjected.

"And no one felt like they needed to clear this with me?"

"Actually, that directive came from the top," Natasia said.

"The top?" Rachel looked around. "Someone give me a phone so I can call Oprah. I will talk to her myself." She'd never actually held a conversation with Oprah, even though she was confident that once she became O's biggest star, they would become the best of friends.

"Bwahahahaa," Mae Francis busted out laughing.

Rachel ignored her as Melinda said, "Oprah is kind of busy right now."

"And this is really *my* show," Natasia said, "if you want to get technical."

Rachel glared at her. "Look, lady. I don't know who you are or what rock you came climbing out from under. But this is *my* show. It's called *The First Lady*. I'm *the* First Lady."

Natasia actually had the audacity to look as though Rachel was starting to irritate her.

"Actually, the show will be called *First*

Ladies, Rachel," Natasia said. "*Ladies* is plural, as in more than one."

"She wouldn't know that because she only has a sixth-grade education," Mae Francis cackled.

Rachel didn't even look her way as she snapped, "And please explain to me why Miss Jane Pittman is here."

Natasia looked at Melinda, and Melinda's eyes shifted.

"I'm supporting all y'all First Ladies," Mae Francis answered for her.

"Whatever." Rachel didn't want to waste another moment of energy on Mae Frances. She spun back to face Mary. "How did you even get out of jail?"

Mary flashed a pleasant smile. "Rachel, I'm a different woman now."

"Oh, so you're no longer a conniving, low-down, home wrecking snake in the grass?"

"No, I'm not. I found the Lord," Mary said without losing her smile.

"Oh, give me a break," Rachel said. "I guess you Muslim now, too?"

"You can make a mockery of my faith, but I speak the truth," Mary said.

Rachel didn't know what kind of con Mary was running, but she knew this woman was up to no good. There wasn't that much changing in the world. Mary

Richardson was a con artist to the tenth degree.

"My husband," Mary motioned to a man standing in the corner, grinning like he was enjoying the unfolding scene as well, "Rev. Nathan Frazier from Pleasant City Missionary Baptist Church can attest that I'm a woman of God now."

"So, not only are you out of jail but you really are a pastor's wife?" Rachel was stunned. "This is unfreakinbelieveable." She looked at Melinda again. "Did you know anything about this?"

Melinda shrugged innocently. "No. I gave Natasia carte blanche to run her show. I can't possibly have my hand in everything."

Rachel couldn't tell if she was lying. She and Melinda went way back — her niece was one of the girls Rachel mentored back in Houston. But Rachel knew when it came to ratings, TV execs would sell their soul and it looked like her friend was no exception.

"Well, I'm not doing a show with her," Rachel announced. "Jasmine, I might be able to deal with because I'm used to her trying to steal my limelight."

"Excuse me!" Jasmine called out from her booth.

"Well, it's the truth," Rachel said.

Jasmine actually lost that smug smirk. "Little girl . . ." Mae Frances put her hand on Jasmine's arm to keep her quiet.

Rachel continued. "I can deal with Jasmine, but this heffa right here" — she jabbed her finger in Mary's direction — "not going to happen. I will not be in the same zip code as her."

"Well, I really hate to hear that." Natasia pulled out a manila folder, then removed a stack of papers. "You might want to take a look at section twenty-three point one of your contract."

"I don't need to look at anything." Rachel folded her arms defiantly.

"Okay, how about I refresh your memory." Natasia started reading. "According to the contract that you signed, Client — that would be you — understands that the producers have the discretion of bringing on board additional cast." She looked back up at Rachel. "And according to your contract, if you choose to abandon the project you will repay all monies advanced —"

"And?" Rachel cut her off. "I don't care about the money. I don't need your little funky money."

"And you will be in breach," Natasia continued, "facing potential lawsuits."

Melinda stepped toward Rachel and gently took her arm and led her to the side. "Rachel, let me talk to you real quick." She pulled her into a corner. "Come on, Rachel. It's not that serious. And do you really want to bail on the show and let Jasmine be the star? Yes, you may have costars, but all that's going to do is make you look better. If you bail, then Jasmine will be the one who has to be the bigger woman, and then ultimately, the one who becomes the star."

That made Rachel's blood boil. Every time she tried to give that troll, Jasmine, the benefit of the doubt, allow Jasmine into her friendship circle, she wanted to turn around and stab Rachel in the back.

"Fine," Rachel said, then raised her voice to make sure Mary could hear her. "All I know is you need to keep that so-called saved scallywag, Mary, away from me."

"I thought we had made our peace," Mary said, walking over to them.

"We had, when I thought you had twenty-five to life," Rachel replied.

Although Lester and Rachel had worked through their issues, Mary's presence on this show meant the whole world would know their drama and Rachel wasn't having that! No, Mary had caused Rachel months of grief. She would never be cordial with this woman.

Natasia closed her folder and walked over to where they stood. "Rachel, I understand you have issues with our newest cast member, but this show is all about growth. It's about serving as an example of a Godly woman who finds forgiveness in the most difficult of situations."

"I thought you said you didn't want fighting on this show," Rachel said to Melinda.

"And we don't. I am serious about that," Natasia said. "We will not be that kind of show."

"Then, I suggest you keep her" — she pointed at Mary, then cut her eyes at Jasmine — "and maybe even her, away from me. Ya feel me?" she added with serious attitude.

"Oh, Lord, now she's jacking lines from Lil Scrappy," Mae Frances muttered.

"Who is Lil Scrappy?" Jasmine said.

"From *Love & Hip Hop Atlanta,*" Mae Francis said.

"I'm mad that you even know that," Jasmine replied.

"Me and his mama, Mama Dee, used to have this beef —"

"Ugh!" Rachel screamed, interrupting them, "and especially keep her away from me!" she shouted, pointing at Mae Frances.

Rachel composed herself, fluffed her hair, smoothed down her burgundy BCBG wrap dress, then turned back toward the cameraman. "Let's just get back to fil—" She stopped when she saw the red light on the camera. This fool had been filming the whole time!

Rachel inhaled, balled her fists, then exhaled. She was definitely going to need Jesus to help her get through the taping of this reality show. But Melinda was right, she didn't need to let anyone — not Jasmine, not that Gremlin-fur-coat-wearing Mae Francis, not Natasia, and definitely not Mary — knock her off her game. She wouldn't be ratchet, but if any of them stepped to her the wrong way, they were definitely going to see a different type of First Lady. She was on the cusp of fame, and none of those bootleg chicks was going to take that away from her.

"I'm ready," Rachel announced. "Let's get this show on the road!" She turned directly to the camera. "You can bring on all the support staff you want. It's my world, my rules! Get it? Got it? Good!"

Chapter Eleven:
Natasia

Natasia rolled over in her bed and for what had to be close to the millionth time that night, she raised her head and glanced at the digital clock. 6:17.

Good! Morning had officially arrived. But even though day had finally broken through the night, Natasia let her head fall back onto her pillow. She had no plans to get up, even though she wasn't supposed to still be in bed. She was supposed to be getting up and getting ready for church. And she would have been if it hadn't been for Jasmine.

Natasia had a plan. But then Jasmine had blown it up, just like she'd done the last time. At least with the plan she'd had in New York, no time nor thought had been put into it. After all, it was just a phone call. And a call could always be intercepted, exactly the way Jasmine had intercepted her call to Hosea.

But this time, Natasia had a good plan. A

sophisticated plan. A plan that was simple and obvious. Reality shows usually taped six days a week, Monday through Saturday, with Sundays off. But this was a show about First Ladies. So, didn't it make sense to tape a couple of segments with the First Ladies and their husbands during a Sunday service?

Not that Natasia didn't need today off after spending the last week with these ladies. Maybe if she had watched more reality TV, she would have been prepared for the nonstop brawls. So far, the fights had been verbal, but she knew they were one eye roll, one finger in the face away from something really jumping off.

It had started on Tuesday, when Natasia thought she'd give Rachel a chance to look better on camera. Her first appearance on Monday hadn't been so great; all about Rachel's temper tantrum after finding out Jasmine and Mary had been added to the show. So, Natasia had come up with an idea to do a little damage control.

Of course, Natasia had an ulterior motive. It had only taken her about five minutes to figure out that she didn't like any of the women chosen for the show, but she could say she liked Jasmine the least. And as the EP, she wasn't about to let Jasmine come off as the shining star.

But when Natasia took the idea to Rachel, she hadn't cooperated.

"What do you mean you want me to apologize to Jasmine?" Rachel had said with her head seemingly twisting in every direction. "I don't have to be sorry for nothin' and I'm not sorry."

If Jasmine hadn't been standing right there, Natasia would've clearly laid out her plan, but instead, all she could say was, "We're just trying to make sure that the people watching the show will get a fair view of all of you."

It seemed like Rachel got the hint, but then the cameras started rolling. Jasmine sauntered into the restaurant like there were no cares in her world. A minute later, Rachel stomped in, slid into the seat across from Jasmine, and with a sugary smile and tone, said, "So, you wanted to meet so that you could apologize?"

Chauncey had lowered the camera and asked Natasia, "Do you want to start all over?"

Natasia shook her head. "No, let's see how this plays out."

If Rachel had planned to throw Jasmine off with that little flipping of the script, she didn't. Jasmine went straight into her role. "Yes, Rachel," and then she'd clutched the pearls she was wearing. "I am so sorry that you didn't know that I was going to be on the show. You know, I would've called you if I knew that you hadn't been told."

"Yeah, well someone should've told me."

"I agree. But I'm glad you came here so that I could apologize. I don't want any problems with you or Mary. We're all just women who love the Lord and we love our husbands. There should never be any animosity among any of us."

"Oh, so you're the peacekeeper, huh?"

"I guess you can say I am. 'Cause you know what the Bible says in Matthew."

Rachel frowned, looking like maybe she'd never read that particular book in the Bible.

"It's one of the beatitudes," Jasmine said, reaching across the table and patting Rachel's hand. "Blessed are the peacemakers for they shall be called children of God."

Rachel nodded her head slowly. "Well, I guess it's only right that you're the peacemaker."

Jasmine smiled and nodded.

"I mean, being that you're the matron of the group. Were you there when Matthew wrote that book of the Bible?"

Before Rachel was even finished, Jasmine's smile was gone.

Rachel kept on, "How old are you anyway?" Before Jasmine could answer, Rachel continued, "Never mind. No one should ever ask an old woman her age." She chuckled just a bit as Jasmine fumed. "Just tell me this. If I were to add my age and Mary's age together, would we come close to how old you are?"

Not a beat passed before Jasmine said, "I don't know, Rachel . . . do you know how to add?"

Now, Rachel was the one without a smile. "Yes, I can add," she said with major attitude.

"I'm just askin' 'cause I know you didn't graduate from the sixth grade."

"Yes, I did," Rachel shouted.

"Oh, I'm sorry. I know you had your first baby when you were ten or eleven . . . or were you twelve?"

Rachel put her palms on the table, pushed herself up, and leaned across it. "You'd better take that back," she threatened.

But Jasmine did not back down. She moved closer to Rachel so that their faces were just inches apart. "What? You don't want people to know that you started having sex when you were eight?"

"Oh, my God," Rachel screamed, looking at the camera. "Cut! Cut! I don't want her lies on TV!"

"That wasn't a lie. I was only telling the truth. 'Cause that's what divas do . . . and I'm done!" Jasmine stood, pirouetted, and then glided out of the restaurant.

Natasia sighed and told Chauncey to turn off the camera.

It didn't get any better on Wednesday, Thursday, or Friday. After a week on this show, all Natasia could say was that she'd finally found something positive about Jasmine — Jasmine Cox Larson Bush wasn't nearly as ghetto as Rachel Jackson Adams.

But even with the pettiness and the bickering and the close-call beat downs, it was worth it because of her plan.

It was clear that God was all up in her life the way this had worked out. She'd been so worried about how she would get to see Hosea, and he was in Atlanta with his new church all along. Once she put this in place, Hosea would *have* to see her, and once she was in his presence, she'd be able to steal a little bit of his time.

But just like with the last plan, Jasmine had torpedoed this one, even though she had waited until the very last minute to tell her.

"My husband is not part of the deal," Jasmine had said two days ago when Natasia had finally shared the plan with her.

Natasia had been prepared for that response because while she didn't like Jasmine, there was one thing she couldn't deny. They were very much alike, which was probably why Hosea had loved them both. And if Hosea had been her husband, she wouldn't let any ex-fiancées anywhere near him.

Natasia knew that she'd stand a better chance of seeing Hosea by just walking into his services on Sunday. But she couldn't do it that way. Her production team needed preparation time. Plus, whether she liked it or not, she needed the approval of the pastor. So, the door to Hosea had to be opened by Jasmine.

But Natasia's plan was multilayered. Anticipating Jasmine's reaction, she'd drawn out the big guns.

First, after Friday's filming, she'd had one of the production assistants ask Jasmine to stay behind, which had almost turned into an ordeal because of Rachel.

"Nobody asked me to stay," Rachel had pouted. "What do you want with Jasmine? What're y'all trying to pull here?"

Jasmine had shaken her head, rolled her eyes, and watched as the production assistant had pulled Rachel to the side. Then, the assistant told Rachel the words that Natasia had given her. The assistant whispered, "All I know is that Natasia isn't happy. That's why she wants to speak to Jasmine alone."

From across the room, Natasia had watched a grin fill half of Rachel's face. She'd jumped up and before she rushed out, Rachel said, "Bye, bye, Jasmine," with a laugh that let Natasia know Rachel hoped to never see Jasmine again.

If Rachel's hope was that Jasmine was going to be fired, she was going to be one disappointed First Lady on Monday afternoon when they had their brunch. Instead, when they were alone, Natasia asked Jasmine to join her and Melinda at one of the tables in the restaurant where they'd just finished filming. That was when Natasia had gone into her plan.

"It's time for us to bring your husband into this," Natasia had said, purposely not mentioning Hosea's name.

Jasmine had stared at her as if she had two heads that were speaking two different languages. "No," was all she said.

Natasia had sighed, rubbed her hands together, and then held them up, surrendering and turning the conversation over to Melinda.

"Jasmine," Melinda said, "this is a show

137

about First Ladies. How are we gonna have a show about pastors' wives and not have the pastors be part of it?"

"That sounds like your problem, not mine. You knew the deal when I signed up for this. I told you, my husband is very busy building his new church. I told you that he wouldn't have time" — Jasmine paused and looked straight at Natasia — "for any foolishness."

"Foolishness?" Natasia and Melinda said together. And then Melinda added, "Well, you were the one who contacted the powers that be so that you could be a part of this . . . foolishness," Melinda sniped.

Natasia was surprised at Melinda's snarkiness. Usually, she seemed to bend over backward, forward, and sideways to please Jasmine and her mongrel-wearing sidekick. But Mae Frances hadn't been with Jasmine on Friday, apparently too sick to show up for the filming of a show that she wasn't supposed to be a part of. And without Mae Frances, Melinda was aggressive and Jasmine backed down, just a little.

"Look," Jasmine began again, a bit calmer this time, "I'm just telling you what I told you before. Hosea can't do this." She spoke as if Melinda was the only one sitting at the table with her.

"No, that's not what you said," Melinda told her. "I believe your actual words were, 'If we can work out the timing and the scene is right, I think he'll be glad to do it.' "

But no matter what, Jasmine still said no.

It had been a devastating blow to Natasia because this was the plan that was supposed to work. So, what was she to do now? The question had kept her up all of Friday night. But then yesterday, Jasmine had really slashed Natasia's heart.

After they'd wrapped the day's filming, Jasmine had walked up to Natasia, grabbed her arm, and jerked her around to face her.

"I know your game," Jasmine snapped.

Natasia looked down to where Jasmine still held her elbow, and then her gaze rose to meet Jasmine's. It was only when she stared Jasmine down that Jasmine finally let go. Still, Natasia took a few steps back from Jasmine before she asked, "What game, Jasmine?"

Her eyes had narrowed as she said, "What you're trying to do. How you're trying to get to Hosea."

Natasia sighed as if she thought Jasmine's words were so middle school. "Paranoia is so unattractive, and such a character flaw. You really should have that checked out because all I'm doing is my job."

"Yeah, right." Jasmine folded her arms and peered at Natasia as if she was searching inside her, trying to read her motives. "Why did you decide to do this reality show anyway?"

"It's none of your business, but if you must know, I'm not doing it because of you. The world doesn't revolve around you and Hosea."

"Well, your world seems to because you're always trying to find your way into our lives."

"Always?" Natasia laughed. "Please; I'll say it again, I'm just doing my job."

"I thought your job was news. I thought you were a serious newswoman."

"I am."

"Well, reality TV doesn't seem to be the place for you," Jasmine said. "You can't even handle me and Rachel, not to mention Rachel and Mary. I think you need to go back where you came from."

"See, there you go again, Jasmine. Thinking . . . it doesn't work for you, so maybe you should just give it up. Give up thinking for Lent or something."

"You *think* you're funny, don't you?" Jasmine didn't wait for Natasia to respond. Instead, she took a step closer and warned, "Stay away from Hosea."

Natasia hadn't even blinked.

Jasmine said, "When I told him that you were here —"

Natasia blinked. "You told him?" she asked. Natasia had never been sure if Jasmine would or wouldn't talk to Hosea.

"Of course," Jasmine said, with wide eyes. "He's my husband. I tell him everything. I told him the day I saw you at the OWN offices. And when I told him you were here, he was as disgusted and as furious as I was." She paused and lowered her eyes, then bit the corner of her lip as if a new thought had just come to her mind. "In fact, you're the reason why he won't take part in the show."

"What?" Natasia asked, unable to hide her shock.

"Yeah. Melinda was right. I did say that Hosea would do it, but when he found out you were part of it, he decided against it. Because he knows what I know . . . that this is just a trick to get next to him."

Just those words had weakened her knees.

"So, give it up, Natasia, once and for all. Hosea and I have been through a lot together. You . . . and then . . ." Jasmine had stopped, but Natasia knew what she was thinking about. Their daughter, Jacqueline, and the kidnapping.

Hosea had contacted her during that time. She'd still been so angry at him for having her fired that all she'd done was hang up on him. If she'd only known then what she knew now.

"We've been through a lot," Jasmine repeated. "And we're still together. And we will be, no matter what you try to do."

Natasia had chuckled lightly, then walked away from Jasmine, as if nothing she said mattered. But she'd had to pray that her knees would hold up and not betray her. Not show just how much Jasmine and her words had shaken her.

She'd been rattled for real. Natasia had seen every hour go by last night, and now it was — she lifted her head again — 6:24 and she still had not closed her eyes.

It was the battle that was going on within that had kept her awake. During the first hours of the night, Natasia had started to believe that maybe she should do what Jasmine had said. Maybe she should go back to Chicago and not even try to bring Hosea into this.

But by the time the clock had ticked past three in the morning, her heart overcame her thoughts. Why should she go away without seeing Hosea when she didn't have any other choices? She could never go through this alone.

Then, it came to her. The solution was as clear as this new morning seemed to be.

When Jasmine had said no to a crew coming to her church, Natasia had settled on sending the cameras to Pleasant City with Mary and Nathan. But just because she wouldn't be filming Hosea, that didn't mean that she couldn't go to his church.

Natasia pushed herself up and swung her legs over the bed. Another quick glance at the clock told her it was 6:32. She was moving much slower these days, but getting up this early meant that she didn't have to rush. Two and a half hours. That was enough time to make it to the Sunday services at City of Lights–Atlanta. Two and a half hours was all that separated her and Hosea.

There were so many signs that this was where Natasia was supposed to be. Like when the usher escorted her to the seventh row, on the right side of the church. That's the row she used to sit in when she'd first met Hosea at Crystal Lake Cathedral in Chicago during his early days as a pastor.

Then, the praise team came out and sang her favorite song, "My Help," written by a childhood friend, Jacqueline Gouche. Natasia had raised her hands and proclaimed the words of the song. "All of my help cometh from the Lord," she'd sang.

But the most powerful sign was Hosea's message.

It had been hard enough to listen to him. From the moment he had strolled onto that altar, with all of that Godly swag, he'd taken her breath away. She'd stared at him, mesmerized as if she'd never seen him before, but of course, she had. She'd known Hosea in the most intimate ways. And if she'd had her way, she would've grown old with him by her side.

But somewhere in the middle of their wonderful relationship, not too long after he'd given her an engagement ring, he'd told her that all that they'd had; that the life they'd lived together, the love they'd shared, had been a lie. He'd told her that she wasn't the woman God provided for him.

That was the biggest lie of all. Of course, she was the woman he should've been with . . . and now, there were all these signs to prove it.

"And the peace I give," Hosea's voice boomed through the cathedral, "is a gift that the world cannot give. So, don't be troubled or afraid."

The tears were already in her eyes, but now they flowed like a faucet as Natasia wrapped her arms across her chest and rocked back and forth.

"No, church," Hosea shouted. "There is no reason to let your hearts be troubled. There is no reason to have fear in any part of you! I'm telling you what I know, the Lord will handle it if you give it to Him."

Natasia had to hold her breath so that she wouldn't begin to sob outright. That was the only way she could hold back all of this emotion.

She couldn't believe that Hosea's words were getting to her like this. After Hosea had left her, she'd left God. But the recent developments in her life had driven her back to the Lord's house, and God must've been pleased. Because in church in Chicago, she'd been receiving the strength she needed to make it through the days.

But though she'd heard many great messages over the last few months, nothing compared to Hosea's, which was music to her ears now. He had just preached from her favorite chapter in the Bible — John 14.

They had studied that chapter word-for-word when they'd been engaged, and whenever Hosea read any of those words aloud while holding her in his arms, she knew there was not a more spiritual place to be. She was with God. And she was with the man she loved.

That had been a long-ago feeling, but sitting in Hosea's new church, she felt that today. She felt that Hosea had reached out into the congregation and put his arms around her even though he didn't know she was there. Or maybe he did know. Maybe because they had once been so connected, he knew in his heart that she was there.

"And now, saints," Hosea said, "I feel like I need to open up the doors of the church right now. I feel like there is someone here who really needs to know that his or her heart must not be troubled. They should not be afraid." Hosea took two steps down from the altar and held up his right hand, beckoning the congregation. "Come to me," he said. "I want to pray for you. I want to pray and let you know that the Lord is with you. The Lord will give you a gift that the world cannot give." He paused and peered out into the sanctuary. "Come, let me pray with you and for you."

Then, Hosea stood silent, though his hand was still raised. He motioned to the director of music and before the first three notes were played on the keyboard, Natasia stood and stumbled over the three people to her left. Now, she was sobbing — it was hard to walk and hold her breath at the same time.

146

But her tears, her snot, her bawling did not shame her. Because this was where she was supposed to be.

Even though she was almost completely blinded by her tears, she could see Hosea waiting at the foot of the altar for her. And she was halfway to him when she saw the recognition register on his face.

His one arm was in the air, but now he raised the other, holding both arms to her, summoning her to come closer, letting her know that he was waiting for her. By the time she staggered to him, Natasia's cries were louder than the music that filled the sanctuary and she fell into his arms.

Behind her, Natasia was sure that many in the congregation were standing, holding out their hands, reaching toward her and praying. But it was the gasp that was almost as loud as a scream behind her that let her know there was one among them who wouldn't utter a single prayer on her behalf.

She hadn't thought about Jasmine since she'd walked into the church. And really, she wasn't thinking about her now.

"Natasia," Hosea whispered into her ear, even as he held her. "What are you doing here?"

She trembled and he held her tighter.

"Natasia," he called her name again. It

wasn't until he put his gentle fingers under her chin and lifted her face that she looked at him once again. He was so close, this felt so personal. She stared into the face of this sweet, gentle man.

"Hosea," she gulped out his name. "Hosea, I need you to pray for me," she cried.

"All right," he said. "You know I always pray specifically. So, what is it you want? What is it you need? What prayers do you want me to speak on your behalf?"

"I need to you pray, I need you to ask God . . . to give me peace. Because Hosea . . . I'm dying."

Chapter Twelve:
Mary

Nathan's plan was falling right into place. Mary still didn't feel good about this whole scenario, but the look on her husband's face told her that for Nathan, this was the next best thing to Heaven.

"And church," Nathan said, pounding the podium, "Let me tell you that the Word of God is almighty."

Nathan was on fire. And this was more than his usual blaze. He was doing it up for the cameras.

Mary glanced over to one of the cameramen, who had zoomed in to her husband. She was just happy to have the stupid thing off her. Personally, Mary had been hoping they'd go to that uppity ATM-in-the-sanctuary, helicopter-in-the-garage, new megachurch Jasmine and her husband, Hosea, had just opened here in Atlanta. It made sense for the show to get their church footage from there, because Mary still wasn't completely on board. But Jasmine had shut that idea down. Mary didn't know what it was, but something about that producer lady, Natasia, seemed to get under Jasmine's skin. So, when Natasia had suggested shooting at Hosea's church, Jasmine wasn't having it. And of course, Nathan, who had been hanging around the set every single day, stepped up and quickly offered up Pleasant City.

"It's no megachurch," he'd told Natasia. "But we do have a few celebrities that attend and you'll get some great video."

Mary had wanted to protest, but Nathan reminded her of the bigger picture, the goal that they were working toward — bringing Lewis home. In fact, that's what he called it: Operation Bring Lewis Home.

Mary smiled. She wasn't a fool. She knew her husband was playing this up for his moment of fame, but she was willing to do whatever it took to get her baby back.

"It's time for Take It to the Altar!" Nathan exclaimed.

Take It to the Altar? Now, he'd given altar call a name?

"Come lay your problems at the feet of the Lord," Nathan exclaimed, motioning toward the altar.

One by one, several people started filing

up. Mary knew some of them were just trying to get on TV because she had never seen
this many people come up during altar call.

The madness of it all was unsettling.

"Sister Frazier," Nathan said, waving
Mary up, "can you come pray for these lost
souls?"

Really, Nathan? She wanted to say. But
she slowly stood and made her way to the
front. She did the obligatory smile since she
saw the camera zoom in on her.

"Yes, yes. Come one, come all, bring your
problems to the altar," Nathan continued.

Nathan motioned for Mary to stand next
to a young woman who was one of the first
to come forward.

"Sister, what's your story?" he asked,
walking over to where they stood.

The woman wiped the crocodile tears that
were streaming down her face. "I come
today, standing in the need of prayer," she
began to a chorus of "amen"s.

She sniffed and continued. "I'm in love
with a married man and he's in love with
me."

Several people shook their heads as chat-
ter filled the sanctuary.

"We know it's wrong, but we can't help
it," she continued. "And the bad part is he's
a man of God." She looked around the

church. "Not anyone at this church, though," she added, managing a faint laugh.

Mary tensed at her words because they mirrored the ones she'd said the first time she had attended Lester Adams's church.

"You are in the right place," Nathan said as the camera panned over to him. He took Mary's hand and put it in the woman's. Something about this all seemed so wrong. It's like they were putting on a show for the Lord.

"Sister, I'm going to let my wife, Sister Frazier, handle this because she has lived your story." He threw his hands up. "Hallelujah! She was once where you are, crawling in the depths of despair, chasing after a married minister."

Mary struggled to contain her expression. Was Nathan really about to put her on Front Street like this?

He ignored Mary as he continued. "My wife chose to share her shame on the altar just like you." He turned to face the church. "Because where else should you shed all shame? Jesus says come as you are, flaws and all! Let the church say amen!"

The woman squeezed Mary's hand tighter and she had to struggle to keep from toppling over. She couldn't believe Nathan was doing this to her.

He turned back to the congregation. "We're not ashamed! You got to be tested to have a testimony and my wife has been tested." He took the woman's other hand and held it up. "She's like you, sister. Her blatant disrespect of someone else's marriage vows led her down a disastrous path and even landed her in prison. But guess what? The devil is a lie! God reached down in the gutter and pulled her up. And He'll do the same for you!"

If Mary could have reached over and slapped her husband at that very moment, she would have. She understood what he was trying to do but she definitely couldn't appreciate him doing it at her expense.

Nathan looked at Mary. "Sister Frazier, I'm not gonna ask you to speak out because I know how painful that time was, but I'm gonna just ask you to pray with God's child here. Just pray that she can be delivered just like you were."

Mary saw both of the cameras zoom in on her. She bowed her head and closed her eyes, but only because she didn't want the cameras to capture her tears.

Nathan led the prayer, then took a few more "confessions."

Mary was all too thankful to go back to her seat after the altar show, because that definitely wasn't an altar call. That was a bona fide parade of fools. It's like everyone that came up tried to one-up the person who'd come before them. She'd never seen so many people claim to be in need of prayer. The whole scenario made her sick to her stomach.

Nathan finally wrapped up the service — and only after seeing the cameramen start to pack up. Mary was seething, so she didn't even bother waiting on the benediction. She rose and stomped back to Nathan's study. This time, she didn't wait for him to come into the office. Mary met him in the hallway. He had the audacity to look proud of himself.

"You know what?" Mary fumed as he approached her. "I don't need to worry about Rachel, because you are doing a pretty good job of turning me back into the fool that I once was!"

Nathan looked shocked, like he couldn't believe her anger. Prison had left Mary a shell of her former self, but Nathan was bringing her back to who she used to be, and she didn't want to go there.

"Babe, what's wrong with you?"

Mary knew that she had been passive over the past year, but this was enough to push anybody over the edge. "Are you seriously asking me that? After the way you just threw me under the bus?"

"Oh, that." He laughed. "Sweetie, that was all for the cameras. Shoot, that woman was an actress. Pretty good, don't you think?" He actually leaned in and kissed her on the cheek. "You know we have to play it up or else we will end up on the cutting room floor."

"So, you really hired someone to lie at the altar?" She was dumbfounded but Nathan didn't seem fazed.

"Yep, I figured it was a great way to weave your back story in. I know, brilliant, right?"

His ambivalent attitude was making her even angrier. "When I agreed to do this, I had no idea you were going to put my business out there like that," Mary snapped.

He shrugged indifferently, and actually seemed to be getting an attitude with her. "I'm sure you knew this was going to come out." He squeezed her chin, then pushed past her, dismissing her. Mary's anger got the best of her because she grabbed his arm and pulled him back.

"No! Don't walk away when I'm talking to you. We're not finished discu—"

Before she could finish her sentence, Nathan spun around, grabbed her by her throat, and pushed her up against the wall.

"Woman, don't you ever put your hands on me!" he hissed.

To say she was stunned would be a major understatement. She had never seen this side of her husband.

"Y-you're h-hurting me," Mary said, struggling to speak as she grasped at his arm.

He actually tightened his grip as he leaned in and, in a much calmer tone, whispered in her ear, "I found you in the gutter and I hand-picked you for my vision, so you will do whatever the hell I tell you to do."

"Pastor, is everything all right?"

Both of them turned toward the voice coming from the end of the hall. Nathan quickly leaned in and kissed Mary, then stood back and released her before turning toward one of his associate pastors.

"Sorry, Rev. Mills, you caught me and the missus making out again." He popped Mary on the butt and grinned widely. "I just have a hard time keeping my hands off this woman."

Reverend Mills relaxed and then chuckled. "Yeah, me and my lady like it a little rough from time to time, too."

Nathan pulled Mary closer into a hug. She was so scared she was shaking.

"Well, just wanted to tell you that was

awesome out there today," Reverend Mills said, his voice booming with giddiness. "You said you were gonna put Pleasant City on the map and you sho' are doing it!"

Nathan joined in his laughter. "Well, Reverend, I assure you, you ain't seen nothing yet."

Mary struggled to fight back tears, not just because of what happened, but because his words sent chills up her spine and for the first time since she'd left prison, Mary found herself asking who was this man she had married.

CHAPTER THIRTEEN: NATASIA

Natasia felt like she was still shaking, though as she held her hands in front of her, she could see that they were steady. Maybe she was fine now. Maybe the shaking she felt was all inside. Maybe she was just shaking because she was waiting for Hosea.

It had taken her a few minutes to calm down after her breakdown at the altar. She hadn't planned for her meeting with Hosea to go this way; she hadn't expected to be crying all over the place. But how she was acting wasn't her fault. She hadn't been prepared for the way her heart swelled when she saw Hosea walk into the sanctuary and stand behind the podium. And she certainly hadn't been prepared for this morning's message.

From the altar, Hosea had touched her with his words, and then at the altar, he'd held her in his arms.

Now, she tried to settle into the leather of

the sofa in Hosea's office as she waited, but she still felt as if she was shaking. It had to be the memory of what had happened just a few minutes ago that had her this way.

It had been such a release to finally say those words out loud to someone besides a doctor.

"I'm dying."

But then, the relief came in the way that Hosea had held her, stroked her hair, and whispered that she would be okay. His actions made her cry even more, but from happiness, not pain. Hosea hadn't known that, though, and that was when he'd rescued her, rushing her back here to the sanctum of his private office.

He'd made sure that she was sitting before he'd said, "I have to go back out there, but I'll be right back. I have to . . . talk to my wife. Are you going to be okay here?"

She'd wanted to tell him no, tell him that after what she'd just confessed, he should stay with her and forget all about Jasmine. But all she'd done was say, "Of course, I'll be fine." Then, as an added measure, she'd said, "Go talk to Jasmine."

So, he'd left her. But now he'd been gone for too many minutes. She didn't want to be anxious, but if he was talking to Jasmine, there was no telling what she would say. He could stomp back into his office, call her a scheming, lying harlot, and throw her out.

"Please, God. Please, God. Please, God."

She prayed that her whispered pleas would be heard and answered. He just couldn't allow Jasmine to throw another grenade into her plans.

Natasia leaned back, rested her head on the leather, closed her eyes, and took a deep breath. Then another and another, until she was filled with some semblance of peace. With a sigh, she sat up and with nothing else to do, she slowly surveyed Hosea's office. The dark, wood-paneled walls and built-in bookcases gave the office such a masculine feeling, but the picture frames that seemed to be everywhere added the warmth.

She didn't have to get up to see the faces that smiled back at her. Photos of Hosea's children — his daughter, or rather Jasmine's daughter, who looked like she was getting ready for some kind of modeling career with the way she posed in each picture, always camera ready. Then, there was the son — Hosea's natural son, whose pictures showed that he probably had to be shoved in front of the camera. There were dozens of pictures, chronicling their early years. And though each picture made her smile, there was a place in her heart that ached. Because these pictures should've been photographs of the children she was supposed to give birth to for Hosea.

When her eyes wandered to the frames on Hosea's desk, Natasia quickly turned away. There was no need to look at pictures of Jasmine. She'd rather look at a blank wall.

The door opened . . . she took a breath.

When Hosea stepped in and smiled, she exhaled and all her leftover anxiety dissipated.

"I'm sorry I took so long," he said.

"No, don't be. You didn't know that I'd be here today." She paused. "Is everything all right?"

In that roundabout way, she was asking about Jasmine. Making sure that Jasmine wouldn't be joining them anytime soon. But Hosea only responded with a nod. That was a good sign.

"So," Hosea said as he unbuttoned his jacket, then lowered himself onto the sofa. It surprised her when he sat so close, but then, it shocked her when he took both of her hands in his. "Tell me," he began again, "what were you talking about at the altar when . . ."

She waited to see if he was going to finish the sentence, but when he didn't, Natasia finished it for him. "When I said I was dying?"

He nodded.

Natasia sniffed, fighting back fresh tears that were threatening behind her eyes. "I'm dying, Hosea." She paused, giving those words a chance to settle. "It started a year ago. I was diagnosed with lupus. An advanced case because my kidneys have been affected."

He frowned. "Lupus? I'm sorry . . . I don't know much about that."

"Most people don't," she said, "because it's not a simple disease. But to explain it briefly, my immune system is attacking my organs, my kidneys, to be exact. What I actually have is lupus nephritis, stage four, but that's probably getting too technical, it's probably too much."

"No, it's not." He gently squeezed her hands. "I want to know everything."

She sighed. "Really, that's pretty much it. Even though I've officially known this for about a year, I've had symptoms for a while. But that's the challenge with lupus. It has so many symptoms, it affects people in so many different ways, you just never know."

"How did they diagnose you?"

"I'd been having swelling in my ankles and legs for a while. At first, I thought it was just bad blood circulation because I hadn't been exercising the way I used to."

Hosea gave her a small smile. "You?" he asked as if he couldn't believe it.

And in that moment, memories of the bike rides they'd shared on the trails surrounding Lake Michigan filled her mind. She'd been the one to get him up early to bike, or jog, or go for a leisurely walk — anything to keep moving.

But when he left her, that part of her life stopped. It was like there was no longer any reason to stay in shape without him.

"Yeah," she said. "I hadn't been active for a while and the swelling just kept getting worse and worse. It wasn't until I became concerned about my urine, which suddenly darkened, that the doctor was finally able to give me a diagnosis."

"And the prognosis?"

She shrugged. "Most people who are diagnosed live at least five years. Over seventy percent live over twenty years. What complicates my situation is my kidneys. The doctors have prepared me. This could suddenly get very serious, and when it does . . ." She paused and took a deep breath. "This is a death sentence for me."

Hosea shook his head. "No, we have to get a second opinion."

163

For the first time, the smile that had filled her heart since she'd first laid her eyes on him this morning, made it to her lips. It was the way he said, "we," that gave her joy.

"I've done that already. I went to a second and then a third doctor. And each told me the same thing."

"So, what are you supposed to do?"

"Well, they're managing my symptoms with all kinds of medications, but my doctor's main goal is to do everything we can to delay the degeneration of my kidneys. The thing is, it's inevitable. It's only a matter of time before I have kidney failure."

"Okay, so besides your medicine, what else can you do?"

"Take it easy, reduce stress, all the things that we should be doing anyway."

Hosea nodded, though Natasia could tell that he was deep in thought.

He said, "Wait, I forgot to ask. What are you doing here? Are you seeing doctors in Atlanta?"

She frowned deeply. "No, my doctor is still in Chicago, though I will need someone here. I'm in Atlanta because of the show."

"What show?"

And right then, she knew the truth. Jasmine was a liar, though the real truth was, she knew that already. "I'm the executive producer on *First Ladies.* I thought you knew."

"No!" Hosea shook his head repeatedly as if he was never going to stop. "I didn't know."

"Jasmine told me that she'd told you."

The way his eyes narrowed, the way his nostrils flared just a little, made Natasia want to jump up, throw her hands in the air, and give herself a high five. She wondered what else she could say, what could she add, that might take his anger up another notch.

But instead, she played it safe. "I'm sorry," she said. "I just thought . . . look, Hosea. I'm not here to cause any problems for you and Jasmine. It's just that I didn't have anywhere else to go." She lowered her head; at first, just for effect. But when she felt the tears ready to burst through, she let them flow. Because the tears and the words she'd just spoken were real.

She *didn't* have anywhere else to go. After her parents' death in an automobile crash when she was a teenager, and her first fiancé's death in a bungie-jumping accident, she'd promised herself that she was never going to take the chance of loving again. Clearly loving her back was dangerous — it meant death to anyone who did.

165

But then, she'd met Hosea. And that's when she knew that her parents and even her fiancé were up there looking down on her. They'd opened up heaven and sent her an angel. Someone to be with her forever so that she'd never be alone.

But forever hadn't lasted very long and when Hosea left her, it felt like death all over again.

That's why she'd never accepted him leaving and had worked so hard to get him back, setting it all up so that she was hired to work on Hosea's TV show, *Bring It On,* while it was being filmed in Los Angeles. But when Hosea rejected her again, Natasia had given up and in the six years since he'd had her fired, she'd lived life like she was on an island alone.

That life and these years had been fine with her. She was a strong, independent woman who didn't need a man nor friends, and not even God since He'd allowed so many bad things to invade her life.

But the prospect of death being so close quickly changed her perspective. She was no longer strong and she didn't want to be independent. She felt like the end of her life could very well be waiting for her right across the street, and she was afraid to face it by herself.

"Natasia!" Hosea raised his voice just a little, as if he'd been calling her name for a while.

"I'm sorry, what did you say?"

"I said, I know you're not here to cause problems for me. You don't have to worry about me thinking that." He paused and peered at her. "Are you all right?"

She nodded. "I am. It's just that I'm a little overwhelmed with it all." She lowered her eyes and looked up at him through her eyelashes, a gesture that she remembered he loved. "Thank you," she said as she fluttered her lashes.

He stared at her for an extra moment, inhaled, then let go of her hands before he looked away. He gave himself a couple of seconds to breathe before he turned back, all business once again. "Do you think you should be working? Maybe you should be taking it easy. Take some time off."

She shook her head. "I can't do that. I can't sit around and wait for death to come. I'm going to fight it, Hosea." She paused and read his eyes. "Especially now that you know. Especially now that I have you on my side."

Not even a second ticked by before he said, "You do have me, you know that, don't you?"

She nodded.

"I'm going to be here for you all the way."

"Thank you, because without you . . ." She stopped as if the words she wanted to say were stuck in her throat.

"Oh, Natasia," he said softly. "Come here." He wrapped his arms around her and pulled her close. "You never have to worry about being alone. You'll never be alone again."

His words, his arms made her feel safe, safer than she'd felt in years. But still she sobbed. Because she finally had someone. Hosea was going to be there for her all the way.

Just like she knew he would.

CHAPTER FOURTEEN: RACHEL

"Honeyyy!" Rachel squealed as she ran into her husband's arms at Atlanta's Hartsfield-Jackson International Airport. Yes, she was being a little extra for the cameras, but she really did miss her husband.

Lester hugged her tightly but lost his smile when he noticed the camera panning around, capturing their embrace. "Ummm, what's that?"

Rachel leaned in close to his ear and whispered. "Reality shows film everything. Just go with it."

Lester didn't bother hiding his displeasure as he pulled her to the side, out of the camera shot. The cameraman, Chauncey, must've sensed the tension because he lowered his equipment and motioned for the sound and lighting guys to do the same.

Rachel knew she probably shouldn't have ambushed her husband like this, but if she had told him, he would've nixed it.

"Rachel," Lester began. "You know I don't like this."

"Aww, come on, sweetie." She flashed a seductive smile at him. "It's no big deal."

He set his briefcase — an expensive leather attaché that Rachel had never seen before — down on a nearby chair. "Rachel, it's one thing for you to be on this show. I told you how I feel."

Rachel stepped toward him and adjusted his bowtie, something else that he'd taken up since becoming president of the American Baptist Coalition. "And I told you. I need you." Rachel had told her husband about Jasmine, but she'd wanted to wait to tell him about Mary face-to-face. She wanted to make sure they'd taped a couple of episodes. Because of all the drama they'd had with Mary in the past, he would try to put his foot down and demand that she not take part. Rachel used to be able to manipulate Lester and make him do whatever she wanted, but those days were long gone, especially now that he was president of the ABC. Now, in addition to an improved wardrobe, he was always trying to prove that he was "the man of the house." She let him think he was most of the time. It's not that she'd become completely submissive (never that), but in the ten years that they'd been married, she knew how to get what she wanted from her husband.

"Hosea's doing it," Rachel lied.

"What?" Shock registered across Lester's face.

Now was the time to throw on her pouty face. (Okay, maybe she did still manipulate Lester from time to time.) "Yes, Hosea wants to do whatever he can to support Jasmine. And sweetie, she is really trying to steal my thunder."

"Rachel," he sighed.

She shrugged, hurt that he didn't believe her. "Okay, you'll see for yourself."

"I just don't understand why you two can't just bury the hatchet and move on. It's like I don't know if you're friends or foes."

"You and me both," Rachel replied, sucking her teeth. She was definitely starting to believe Jasmine was not to be trusted. And to think she'd thought they'd developed some type of sisterly bond. "But the fact remains that Hosea is on board," Rachel continued. "I mean, he didn't talk or anything, but he is on camera."

Lester paused like he was thinking. He admired Hosea greatly, to the point that it was sickening. The first time they'd met, Rachel had been furious because Lester acted like he was meeting Barack Obama. But right now, she'd call Barack herself if it meant getting Lester on board.

"Okay, fine," he said, relaxing. "I trust Hosea's judgment."

Rachel put her hands on her hips and cocked her head. "But you don't trust mine?"

He smiled. "Okay, sweetheart. We both know sometimes your judgment is a little skewed."

She turned back to Chauncey. "You can continue filming."

"So, how was your flight?" Rachel said, her voice raising several octaves as she got into character.

Lester laughed as he shook his head. "It was fine."

"Well, the limo is out front."

Lester lowered his voice. "A limo, Rachel?"

She leaned in. "I told you to go with it. As long as the cameras are rolling, we don't drive ourselves anywhere. Although I did rent a gorgeous white Range Rover in the event that we do have to drive."

"What?"

"Oh, don't worry, OWN is paying for it," she lied again. She actually didn't like lying to Lester, but sometimes the lie was easier than the truth.

Lester looked like he didn't want to argue either, because he just grabbed his briefcase, then took Rachel's hand. "Look, I just came to see my beautiful wife, handle some ABC business —"

Rachel didn't let him finish. "Great, I was thinking I could come and take part in the meeting and we could film some of that."

"Absolutely not," Lester said sternly. He turned his back to block the camera. "You have your own agenda with the ABC and you're doing a great job. This is a financial board meeting and the last thing we're going to do is have cameras rolling."

She waved him off. Not a battle worth fighting. She'd just find something else to film. She scooted Lester back her side and smiled widely. "Okay, darling. Come on. I can't wait for you to see the house."

"I still can't believe you rented a house without me seeing it," Lester said once they were in the car and on their way to their North Atlanta–area home.

"I told you to come down and help me pick it out."

"Rachel, I run a national organization and I pastor a church, I'm kinda busy. I'm sorry I couldn't fit it into my schedule."

"Well, you're here now." Rachel scooted

in closer to Lester, snuggling up next to him. The last thing she was about to do was get into it with Lester in front of the cameras. "I can't wait for you to see our new home."

Twenty minutes later, they were pulling up to the palatial estate. When Rachel found out Jasmine had rented a four-thousand-square-foot home, she'd had to one-up her and get a seven-thousand-square-foot home. Of course, where Jasmine was from, four thousand square feet seemed like a big deal, but in Texas you could find four thousand square feet in the 'hood. No, real homes were Texas-size. Real homes were *this*.

"Really, Rachel?" Lester said as they got out of the limo.

He looked over at the camera, which was already set up and filming. "Don't look at the camera, baby," Rachel said. "Everything is supposed to be natural."

"Oh, good grief," Lester replied.

"Can you get our bags, Farnsworth?" Rachel loudly told the limo driver.

"Is his name really Farnsworth?" Lester whispered.

Rachel shrugged. "I don't know, but doesn't it sound regal?"

Lester laughed. "What am I going to do with you?"

"Love me," she said, grabbing his hand and pulling him up the walkway.

"Let us go in first," Chauncey said, as he and the sound and lighting guys scurried ahead of them.

Lester and Rachel waited a few minutes, then walked inside.

Lester gasped the minute he set foot in the massive foyer. "Whoa, this is bigger than our house in Houston."

"Yes, and as soon as our taping wraps up, we're going to have to talk about that." Rachel loved her home in Houston, but *this,* this was how stars lived. The grand foyer with a rotunda led to a large formal living area. The chef's kitchen featured two islands and custom finishes. The family room led to an exterior veranda overlooking an immaculately landscaped backyard and pool.

"Did you know this home used to belong to one of Evander Holyfield's baby mamas?" Rachel asked. "We're renting, but I personally think we need to make an offer and make this our permanent Atlanta home."

"Well, we won't *permanently* be here," Lester replied as he continued to look around in awe.

Another battle she'd deal with later, because in her short time here, Rachel had decided this definitely needed to be her second home. This was where the movers and shakers were, and since she was definitely about to be shaking some things up, she needed to be right in the mix.

"This is nice, hon, but I don't know why we need all this space. It's not like the kids are even here." He turned to face her. "I think you're getting a little too into the high life."

"Oh, you ain't seen nothing yet." Rachel took his hand and led him through the rest of the house, giving him the grand tour from the piano room to the guest house.

"Well, Rachel, I must say, when you do it, you do it big," Lester said as they descended the back staircase.

"That's the only way to do it." She paused, giving Chauncey and crew time to catch up. "Well, the chef is preparing us dinner."

"Chef?" Lester asked.

"What? You're the one who just said I do it big."

After the crew had gotten a few more shots, Rachel knew she could no longer put off the inevitable.

"Hey, Chauncey, you got enough?"

"Yeah, I think we're good." He motioned to the rest of the crew to wrap things up. Rachel walked them to the door, then stood, inhaled, and turned to go back to face her husband.

Rachel slid into the seat across the table from him. "Remember, I told you there were some other First Ladies that they brought in for the show." Lester nodded. "Well, Jasmine is one of them and you're not going to believe who the other one is."

"Who?"

"It has taken everything in my power not to tell you this earlier, but I wanted to tell you face-to-face." She took a deep breath. "It's Mary."

"Mary who?" Lester asked without skipping a beat.

"Your Mary," she said, trying not to get angry all over again.

"I don't have a Mary. I have a Rachel. That's all I have," he said defensively.

"You know what I mean, Lester."

Lester paused like he was waiting for her to burst out laughing or something. Finally he said, "Mary Richardson? That can't be. Mary's in prison."

"Not anymore," Rachel replied. "She's out and she got her a bootleg version of you. They have a church here in Atlanta and somehow they managed to finagle their way onto the show."

Lester fell back in his seat. "Wow. Rachel, that spells nothing but drama. We may need to rethink this show."

"Too late, we've already shot too many episodes and seriously, it hasn't been a problem. She keeps her distance from me and I don't punch her in the eye."

"Not good. Not good," he said.

Rachel wasn't trying to hear all that. "Well, I just didn't want you to be shocked. I'm not going to embarrass you."

Rachel planned to hold true to her promise. The last thing she was ever going to do was be on someone's TV fighting. She was too classy for that. Even though those hood-boogers, Jasmine and Mary, tried to push her, she was hip to their game and knew how to play it. So, while they'd had more than their share of verbal sparring, she hadn't laid a finger on anyone.

"Don't worry, Lester, everything will be fine. I promise." Rachel truly hoped that she could keep her promise. So far, so good, but they still had four weeks of filming left to go.

Chapter Fifteen:
Jasmine

Jasmine paced from one end of the master suite to the other. This time, she had to have the right words. This time, she had to convince Hosea that he had to tell her what was going on. Today had to be different from all the other times.

It had been a week and a day since Natasia had stumbled up to the altar and whispered something in Hosea's ear. Something that was enough to drain the color from Hosea's face. Something that was serious enough for Hosea to motion to his assistant pastor to take over while he took Natasia's hand and swept her from the sanctuary.

Jasmine had jumped from her place of honor on the front pew, but by the time she raced past the altar to the other side of the building, Hosea and Natasia could not be seen.

She'd rushed to her husband's office; the door was closed.

She'd twisted the knob; it was locked.

She was about to bang on the door like she was part of Homeland Security, but then suddenly the door opened.

"I was just coming out to see you," he said, stepping into the hallway, though he left the door open just a little bit.

"Hosea, what's going on?" she asked and at the same time, she tried to get a peek inside. She moved her head to the left, then to the right. She even stood on her toes, trying to peer over Hosea's shoulder. She could see that no one was in his outer office and that made her fume. He'd taken Natasia into his private office? Why?

She tried to take a step forward, but Hosea stood as stiff and solid as a tree, not giving her enough space to move an inch.

"I need just a little time in here," he whispered.

"For what?"

"Please, honey. I need to speak to Natasia." Then, he paused, and finally added, "Alone."

It was the word that had come after the pause that set her heart pumping.

"Why alone? You never speak to women alone."

Even though it had been the church's policy for the last few years not to ever have a male pastor alone with a female member, Hosea, who always played by the rules, didn't even hesitate when he said, "It's all right this time. I promise you, it's fine. Just let me do this, please."

Jasmine wondered which part of her expression had gotten to him — her fear or her anger. Either way, he added, "Trust me." Then, he'd stepped away from her and shut the door before she could protest anymore.

Jasmine had stood there, not knowing what to do. It wasn't that she didn't trust Hosea, it was that she knew Natasia was a direct descendant of the snake that first came to notoriety in the Book of Genesis. She couldn't be trusted because she was full of lies. But on the other side, Natasia also knew some truth.

It was the truth that Natasia knew, the truth that she'd been working on the show and Jasmine had never said a word to Hosea — it was that truth that made Jasmine knock on the door. She knew Hosea wasn't going to be happy, but he had to let her in.

She was right — Hosea was pissed when just a second later, he opened the door.

She was wrong — he was not about to let her inside.

"I'm doing what God's called me to do,

Jasmine. Just take the children home, and I'll be there as soon as I can."

This time, he'd slammed the door. And that pissed *her* off. Not because he'd done that, but because he'd done that with that witch in his inner office.

But without any choices, Jasmine had gone back into the sanctuary, gotten Mrs. Sloss, and together, they gathered Jacquie and Zaya from Children's Church. But Jasmine's thoughts stayed on Hosea and Natasia the entire time. From the time she got everyone into the car, until she finally curved her car around the circular driveway of their Atlanta home, all Jasmine could think about was what Natasia was saying to Hosea.

It was going to be a mess, she knew that. He wasn't going to be happy that she'd lied to him yet again . . . even if it was by omission.

Desperation made Jasmine jump out of the car the moment she turned off the engine, and over her shoulder, she'd yelled to Mrs. Sloss to take care of the children. Then, Jasmine had hiked up her pencil skirt and she'd taken the steps two at a time, before she barged into Mae Frances's bedroom without even knocking.

Even though her friend was wrapped

tightly under a bunch of blankets and was snoring, Jasmine shook her until her eyes snapped open.

Jasmine asked, "Were you asleep?"

"Not anymore," Mae Frances had wheezed, her cough sounding as if she had pounds of mucus in her chest.

In the eight years that Jasmine had known Mae Frances, she'd never seen this woman sick. But Mae Frances had missed a week of filming and two Sundays of church. Her friend was not playing about this because only sickness or death could've kept Mae Frances away from the camera or from God.

But Jasmine also knew Mae Frances was all about being in the mix. She'd want to know what was going on, even in her sickness. So, Jasmine had jumped into the king-size bed with Mae Frances and spilled out her story.

At the end, Jasmine said, "I knew we should've gotten rid of Natasia sooner."

With a voice that was soft and weak, Mae Frances responded, "I think you're in trouble now, Jasmine Larson."

Jasmine leaped from the bed and put her hands on her hips. "That's all you got, Mae Frances? I need some help."

Mae Frances released a long stream of coughs before she wheezed out, "I tried to get her fired, but Stedman wasn't having it."

"You did? When?"

Another round of coughs and then, "Jasmine Larson, I don't tell you everything I do. I just bring you the results. And I couldn't get the results this time."

"Well, then, we have to try something else. What else can you do? Who can you talk to?"

Mae Frances shook her head, rolled over, and flopped back down onto her pillow. "I'd help you if I could, but I'm dying!"

"Mae Frances! You just have a cold. Come on, I need you."

But when her friend didn't respond, Jasmine ambled out of her room. Without Mae Frances to hold her hand, she'd been left to wait alone for Hosea to come home from church. She'd counted the seconds that turned into minutes that became hours. It wasn't until the daylight began to fade to night that Hosea finally stepped into their house.

His face was filled with lines as if he was frowning and exhausted and sad all at once. And his shoulders were slumped as if he carried more weight than he was used to.

"Is everything all right?" Jasmine asked, trying to gauge the situation before she said anything more.

He'd only shaken his head, slumped down on the bed, and looked down at his hands.

She sat next to him and repeated her question.

He said, "I don't know how to answer that."

With an inhale, she said, "Just answer it with the truth."

He nodded. "The truth. You want the truth." He paused. "Well, why didn't you tell me the truth about Natasia."

Jasmine sucked in air.

"Why didn't you tell me that she was working on the show?"

She'd just asked him for the truth, so Jasmine decided to do something she didn't do all that often. She decided that she would tell *him* the truth. "I didn't tell you because I was afraid," she said. "The last time Natasia came into our lives, it wasn't very good. It almost . . . broke us."

The truth worked. Without saying a word, Hosea lifted his arm, wrapped it around Jasmine, and drew her close to him.

The move surprised her; she was relieved.

Softly, he'd said, "Nothing is going to break us, darlin'. You've got to know that, you've got to believe that."

"I *want* to believe that, but —" She

stopped.

"You can believe it. We've been through it all. There's nothing that can come at us now. Nothing that can ever come between us."

Her worry dissipated, lifting off her like a rising cloud. She felt so good, she wanted to cry. Hosea held her in his arms, and Jasmine knew that no matter what Natasia had said, it hadn't worked. Hosea was not upset with her; all was right with her world.

Until he said, "I have to go back out."

"Okay. Where are you going?"

It was an innocuous question. Jasmine had asked, even though she believed she already knew the answer. She expected her husband to say that he was going to meet with the assistant pastors. Or maybe even Frank Anderson, his new armor bearer.

But Hosea didn't say any of the names she expected. Instead, he crushed her with "I have to meet with Natasia."

"What! Why? You just left her."

He stood up, then knelt in front of her. Holding her hands, he said, "There's something that's happened, something that I can't talk to you about."

"Something about Natasia?"

He nodded.

"What's going on, Hosea?"

"I just told you, I can't talk about it."

"You're my husband. We're supposed to talk about everything."

"But she came to me in church, she came to me as a pastor, and I would never talk to you or anyone else about anything that I've been told in confidence. I can't do that. People have to trust me. Natasia trusts me."

As Hosea pushed himself up and sauntered into his closet, Jasmine wanted to scream some sense into her husband. She wanted to tell him that this was just a trick. She wanted to remind him of just how duplicitous Natasia was, and all the low-down, dirty things she'd done before. She wanted to ask how could Natasia expect trust from anyone when she herself could never be trusted?

But the shock of the whole situation kept Jasmine silent. She sat on the edge of that bed until Hosea had come out of his closet, dressed in a jogging suit and sneakers.

He leaned over, kissed Jasmine's forehead, then looked into her eyes. "I love you and only you," he said as if he was sure she needed to hear that. "Trust me."

Those words were wonderful, but they weren't enough. If he really loved her, he would tell her what was going on so that she could help him see that that woman was a liar and the truth was not within her, on top of her, beneath her, or anywhere near her.

She didn't say anything, though, and he left, leaving her to do nothing except sit and wonder and count the passing seconds until he returned a little more than ninety minutes later.

The rest of that Sunday evening was spent as if all was normal. They'd sat together with the children as they prepared for bed. They'd prayed with their son, and then their daughter, before they checked on Mae Frances, wished Mrs. Sloss a good night, then retired to their own bedroom where they spent the next hours like the lovers they were.

There had been no place during that time for Jasmine to interrupt their heaven and bring up the devil.

But first thing Monday morning, she did.

"Hosea," she'd began, "I'm not asking you to tell me anything personal about Natasia. I just think it's important that I know what's going on with her." When he'd stared at her as if he wasn't about to have this conversation, she'd added "Since I have to work with her."

"Your working with her has nothing to do with this, Jasmine."

"But —"

"Leave it alone!" he'd said before he'd stomped out of the bedroom.

And that had been the last of it . . . at least from Hosea.

Natasia was a different story.

On the Monday after she'd bogarted her way into their church, Natasia had swooped onto the set where they were filming with twinkling eyes and a bright smile.

"What happened to you since Saturday?" Jasmine had overheard Melinda asking Natasia. "Did you meet a man and fall in love?"

Jasmine had wanted to yell, "Cut!"

No, they were not filming that scene. Of course, Natasia and Melinda were never in any scenes. But Jasmine had wanted to shout, "Cut," to get Natasia to cut it out. Whatever game she was playing was never going to work.

Except, it was working . . . with Hosea.

Three more times that week, he'd told Jasmine that he had to spend some time with Natasia.

"It's nothing that you have to worry about," he always assured her. "I love you and only you. Trust me."

But nothing Hosea said could reassure her. If he was spending time with Natasia, that meant trouble, and with Mae Frances

189

still on the injured list, Jasmine had spent eight days filled with nothing but frustration.

There was no way that she could let this go on. Hosea just had to understand that with their history, she needed to know everything about Natasia — whether he'd been told in confidence or not.

When she heard the two beeps of the alarm indicating the front door opening, Jasmine scooted out of the bedroom and scurried down the stairs. Usually, the children met Hosea at the door before she could even get there, but today she was the only one home.

She'd never get her answers if Hosea was in any way distracted. So, she'd sent Jacqueline and Zaya to Chuck E. Cheese's, and she'd told Mrs. Sloss to let them stay as long as they wanted. Knowing her children, they might not return until the next day, but that's what she needed — time and space.

At the bottom of the staircase, Jasmine paused to give Hosea time to step into their home. "Hey, babe," she said as she wrapped her arms around her husband. "How was your day?"

"Pretty good," he said, grabbing the tie from around his neck. "I'm really happy about the way things are going. It's not going to take long to build this church."

"I could've told you that." She smiled and kissed his cheek.

"How's Nama?" he asked. "The doctor came today, right?"

She nodded. "Only Mae Frances could get a doctor to make a house call in a city that's not even her home. But anyway, he said she has a mild case of pneumonia."

He stopped moving. "Pneumonia? That's serious."

"It can be, but the doctor said her case is mild and she can be treated right here at home."

"So, what does she have to do?"

"Just rest. He's given her some antibiotics and, of course, she has to drink plenty of fluids. He said she'll be tired for a while, but he's sure she'll be fine. She talked him into coming back tomorrow."

He chucked. "Only Nama. I'll go check on her in a little while."

Jasmine followed Hosea into the bedroom and thought about her timing. Which would be the best way to get what she wanted? Should she wait until he undressed? Should she feed him first, wait until his stomach was full, and then demand answers? Or should she sex him and after she laid him out, he'd tell her everything over a little pillow talk?

Any of those options would've been fine, and probably would've been better — if she could've waited.

But she couldn't.

The moment they stepped over the threshold to their bedroom, Jasmine said, "I know you don't want to talk about this, Hosea, but I have to know what's going on with Natasia."

"Not again," he moaned.

"It's because of us working together. You should see how she's been treating me, Hosea. Like she has some secret world that she lives in with you, and I'm not invited."

"I'm sure you're exaggerating."

"I'm not. You can ask anyone. Even Rachel."

"I'm not going to talk to anyone about Natasia. I told you what I could tell you, and nothing more. This has nothing to do with you, Jasmine. Just leave it alone."

He quickened his steps as he moved toward the bathroom. Jasmine followed him, determined not to give up. But then he shut the door behind him . . . something that he never did.

She should have definitely taken him to bed before she said anything. But while he was pissed, she was mad, too. This was her life that Natasia was messing with and Hosea was just allowing her do it.

As she heard the shower turn on in the bathroom, Jasmine once again paced the length of the bedroom, exactly the way she'd been doing since before Hosea came home.

She needed to do something . . . something. She needed help from someone . . . someone. But what? And who?

Like a strike of lightning, it came to her.

She plopped down on the bed. She still didn't have all the parts of this equation, but one half, she could fill in. She could fill in the who . . . Rachel.

Rachel Jackson Adams was not her favorite person. At least not right now. Not with the way she'd been acting on this show. She was walking around like *First Ladies* belonged to her and Jasmine just felt like she had to put that child in her place.

Things had really gotten bad at yesterday's taping at a Delta Sigma Theta charity fashion show. The three First Ladies had been called in to be celebrity models for the chapter and as they were in the back room checking out the clothes, the president of the chapter came in to greet and thank them.

"We are so excited to have you," the chapter president said. "You know, this is our tenth couture fashion show, so it's very special."

Just as Jasmine was getting ready to thank the president for having them, Rachel jumped in front of her. "Oh, yes!" she said. "I've actually done some modeling. I modeled for him a few years ago."

The woman looked confused. "For whom?"

"For Couture," Rachel said.

There was a moment of silence and then Jasmine filled the room with her laughter. Even Mary snickered.

The Delta president still looked confused, and Jasmine was going to let it go until Rachel said to her, "What's so funny? You jealous?"

"Of you and Couture? No . . . but let me ask you something. Does your mother know that you're stupid?"

Rachel's eyes widened and filled with tears. "My mother's dead!" she cried. "How can you be so mean?"

Jasmine knew that half of that drama was for the cameras, but then a part of her heart instantly ached. Having lost both of her parents, Jasmine understood that pain and she wished that she could've taken back those words.

But she wasn't going to take all the blame. Rachel was always trying to act like more than she was. And Jasmine just felt it was her place to remind her that she'd only come up two minutes ago.

Thinking back on that now, Jasmine sighed. She and Rachel were almost back to where they were when they met two years ago at the American Baptist Coalition. During that time, Jasmine had done all she could to expose Rachel as the not-too-smart bumpkin that she was. She'd even had her arrested for shoplifting, and there were times when she wanted to have her arrested again.

But maybe she'd hold off on that. Because without Mae Frances, Rachel was the only one who could help her. As the idea brewed inside Jasmine's head, it made more sense. Rachel owed her and all Jasmine had to do was remind her of that. And then, of course, Rachel would help her. They'd work together the way they had to clear Rachel's name in Chicago.

Yes, once she got Rachel on board, Jasmine had no doubt that it would take little time for the two of them to get rid of Natasia Redding.

Jasmine smiled. She finally had a plan.

CHAPTER SIXTEEN: RACHEL

Rachel surveyed the scene. This was absolutely perfect, and she couldn't have envisioned a better scenario if she'd put it all together herself. Well, she had put much of it together anyway, but no one needed to know that she was the one who'd convinced Melinda that this community service activity was exactly what they needed.

It had been Rachel's idea to come with her backups, as she called Mary and Jasmine, to this youth facility to talk to at-risk girls. *First Ladies* had filmed scenes at Mary's church, which Rachel wasn't about to attend; at each of their homes; at brunch; hanging out; and at a charity event. The three of them did a lot of bickering on the first few episodes — some of which had almost led to blows — and since she always seemed to be the one right in the middle of the mess, Rachel knew she needed to change the viewers' perceptions. The most successful reality stars were ones who brought the drama but who were also well liked. This would definitely make her well liked. Advising these kids, something she did already with her Good Girlz youth group, would show her soft side. And Rachel really did have a soft side. It's just being around those two brought out the worst in her.

"Hey, Rachel, I understand it was your idea to come here," Sonny, the director, said, looking around nervously. "Is this place safe?"

Rachel laughed nervously as she glanced around. She hadn't expected Melinda to tell anyone this was her idea, but oh, well. Rachel had purposely suggested Fulton County Right Track program because she knew these were the hardest of the hardcore girls around. Some of these girls had done time in juvenile facilities, mostly behind some guy. But there were a few bona fide criminals in the midst. A little ghetto chick never scared Rachel. But she couldn't wait to see how that siddity Jasmine reacted, she hoped they ate Mary alive, and of course, Rachel wanted it all caught on tape.

"Oh, yes," Rachel told Sonny, "these girls are harmless."

No sooner had the words left her mouth than Cara, the makeup artist, came stomping over.

"Unh-unh, Sonny. Y'all don't pay me enough for this!" she barked. "These girls want black eyeliner around their lips. I don't do black eyeliner around lips! And I know one of them stole my MAC brushes."

Sonny let out an exasperated sigh. "Can you just try to work with them?"

Cara threw her arms up. "It's not just me! They are giving Jeffrey the blues." She pointed to the horrified hair stylist, who was shaking his head while one of the girls shook a handful of blonde weave at him. "She wants him to put that dollar-store weave in her pitch-black hair. You know Jeffrey will slice his own wrists first."

Sonny looked like the last thing he wanted to do was go at it with the hair and makeup crew and since this was Rachel's idea, she decided to step up.

"Let me talk to the girls. I have a way with them." Rachel looked around. "But where's the production crew? They need to be rolling on this."

"They have fifteen minutes to call time," Sonny replied.

"Well, call somebody to come on right now so they can get this on tape!" Rachel had tried to get as many stolen solo moments as she could over these past two weeks, but it had been hard with Jasmine and Mary constantly trying to step into her limelight.

Sonny ran his fingers through his already tussled hair, then said, "Fine." He pushed the button on a little device clipped to his waist. "Can I get one sound and camera crew on set, stat?"

It didn't take but a minute for the two men to appear by Sonny's side.

"Grab your gear and film Rachel mediating this disaster," he said.

Rachel flashed a winning smile. This was why she always came camera ready. Whenever opportunity came knocking, she wanted to be prepared.

"Right this way . . ." Rachel's words trailed off when Mary and Jasmine appeared in the doorway.

"Umm, is someone about to film without us?" Jasmine asked.

Rachel rolled her eyes. Jasmine needed to change her name to Jasmine Always-Messing-Ish-Up Bush. She had the nerve to seem annoyed with Rachel. Rachel actually hated that this reality show seemed to be pulling her and Jasmine further and further apart. After that fiasco in Chicago, Rachel thought they stood a real chance of being close, but since Jasmine acted like she didn't know her place, it looked like that wasn't possible.

"So, are you guys taping already?" Jasmine asked. "Without us?"

"Yeah, I thought call time was ten a.m.," Mary replied.

Mary had done good in terms of not talking to Rachel outside of filming, and when her overbearing husband wasn't around, Mary actually tried to keep her distance from Rachel.

"It is," Sonny replied nervously. "We were just going to get this shot of Rachel helping out the girls."

"Oh, I don't think so," Jasmine said, pushing her way past the cameraman and standing next to Rachel. "If she's helping, I'm helping."

"And if *she's* helping, I'm helping," Mary added, pointing at Jasmine as she followed suit.

"Whatever," Sonny said. "Can we just do something before Jeffrey has a stroke?"

Rachel huffed again as she spun around and marched over with Jasmine and Mary close on her heels.

"Hi," Rachel told the girl arguing with Jeffrey. She looked like she couldn't be more than fifteen or sixteen. "What's your name?"

The girl was severely overweight, but her

clothes apparently didn't know it. Her outfit appeared about six sizes too small, and she had on some loud gold earrings and wore a necklace that said "Hood Chick" like it was a badge of honor. She stopped, looked Rachel up and down, then said, "Who wants to know?"

Rachel flashed a warm smile. "Oh, I'm just the star of this show, Rachel Jackson Adams, but girl, I just came to tell you those sheer jeggings are fierce."

The girl slowly smiled. "Yeah, it's the American flag." She held out her leg, which looked more like a tree trunk, and wiggled it.

Of course, Jasmine had to angle her way into the camera shot. "Hi, I'm Jasmine. One of the other First Ladies who stars on this show."

The girl hesitated, but then said, "I'm Quita."

"Quita, what's up? Is there a problem here?" Rachel sweetly asked.

"Yeah," the girl wiggled her neck ferociously. "I want my bangs to be blonde and this he/she won't do it!"

Jeffrey balled his fists and looked like it was taking everything in his power to keep his temper in check. "Look, you little thuggette . . ."

Rachel put her hand on Jeffrey's arm to calm him down. Jeffrey gritted his teeth but turned to Rachel. "I'm not doing it," he whispered. "I have been known to drop kick kids."

"Your hair is black. Don't you think it's a bit much to put blonde hair in?" Mary said with a terse chuckle.

Both Rachel and Jasmine stared at her. Rachel knew Mary had grown up around black people so she could hold her own, but she'd been locked up for a while. She wasn't ready for this new breed of kid.

Quita and another hoodrat-looking girl who had appeared next to her each took a step toward Mary.

"What did you say?" Quita asked.

The other girl, who had apparently mastered the art of chewing gum and talking, said, "I think she said your hair too nappy to be trying to put in that good hair like hers."

Mary looked confused. "No, no. That's not what I said. I was just —"

"How 'bout I snatch some of your hair out and have him put that in my hair instead?" Quita said, reaching out and grabbing a fistful of Mary's hair before anyone could react.

Mary yelped as security quickly moved in

and grabbed Quita before she could do anymore damage.

"Let me go!" Quita screamed as they pulled her away. "You betta tell Mary Poppins to recognize!"

"What in the world is going on here!"

Everyone turned to see Natasia standing next to Sonny, a horrified look on her face. Mary leaned against the wall as she nursed her head.

When no one answered, Natasia said, "Someone better explain to me what is going on!"

Rachel took it upon herself to step up. "One of the girls just got upset but it's all good."

"All good? That little delinquent attacked me!" Mary cried.

"I got your delinquent!" Quita called out from the corner where the center director had appeared and was trying to calm her down.

Natasia inhaled, briefly closed her eyes, then exhaled. "I told you all," she said, glaring at Rachel, Jasmine, and Mary, "there will absolutely be no violence on this show."

"I wasn't fighting," Jasmine and Rachel said simultaneously.

"And I wasn't fighting either. I was attacked," Mary added.

Natasia held up her hand to stop them from talking. "I'm just happy the three of you finally agree on something!" She turned to Sonny. "Can you take five? Especially since it's not even call time yet?"

Sonny looked relieved that someone else was here to take charge. "Take five," he told the crew.

Natasia motioned toward the women. "Ladies, can I speak with you for a minute?"

Rachel and Mary immediately followed her, but Jasmine stayed behind, her arms folded across her chest. This had been the scenario whenever Jasmine and the EP were anywhere near each other, and Rachel was trying to figure out what in the world was going on.

Rachel's eyes went to Natasia, then to Jasmine. Jasmine had a look in her eyes that Rachel had only seen directed at one other person — her. Jasmine's eyes were filled with . . . Rachel struggled to find the right word — *hate.* She looked like she hated Natasia. But why? Then, as if a light bulb had gone off, Rachel remembered.

"No," Rachel found herself muttering. Rachel didn't know much about the woman, but when Hosea and Lester were running for president of the American Baptist Coalition and she'd tried to help Lester out by digging up dirt on Hosea, Rachel had discovered that Hosea was once engaged to a woman named Natasia. "Are you . . . are you Hosea's Natasia?"

Jasmine spun on Rachel like she was the new star of *The Exorcist.* "Hosea only has one woman," Jasmine snapped. "And it ain't her!"

Rachel couldn't help it, she busted out laughing. Oh, this show had just gone to a whole other level.

"And what exactly is so funny?" Jasmine hissed.

"You. This." Rachel motioned between Jasmine and Natasia. "The irony." Rachel held her stomach, she was laughing so hard.

"I'm glad you find this amusing," Natasia said, "but can we get down to business?"

Rachel let her laughter die down, but this was good stuff. Jasmine and her decrepit old friend had taken little digs at Rachel over the past few tapings. They'd done that knowing this Natasia chick was here. Oh, it was about to be on. Now, Rachel just needed to figure out how to bring it up when the cameras were rolling. That might be a little challenging since Natasia wasn't actually on the show. But if there was anyone up for a challenge, it was Rachel.

CHAPTER SEVENTEEN: NATASIA

Natasia was a long way from being a school-girl, but that didn't stop her from feeling giddy.

She peered through the camera, taking in the scene that was unfolding before her. Jasmine, Rachel, and Mary sat in a circle with a dozen girls from the Fulton County Right Track facility.

From the moment Melinda had brought this idea to Natasia, she'd thought it would be a good scene for the show: these three First Ladies, who each had such shady backgrounds themselves, talking about their tests and giving their testimonies to young ladies who needed to hear words of inspiration and wisdom. Surely, Rachel, Jasmine, and Mary were capable enough to handle this.

But then, maybe not. Instead of being inspired, the girls were just . . . bored.

It had started with Rachel. When she'd

scooted forward in her chair and began to tell the girls how she became a teenage mom, but now she was a First Lady of a major church, the girls had exchanged glances, then slumped back in their chairs as if they knew this was gonna be a long day.

When it was Jasmine's turn, she told the girls about her life and how she'd been delivered from envy, jealousy, and coveting. But when she ended her talk with "That's how divas do it . . . and I'm done," the girls looked at each other and shook their heads like they'd never heard anything so ridiculous coming out of the mouth of a grown woman.

And now Mary was talking. Most of the girls had thrown their heads back and were actually sleeping.

Then, Quita, the girl who'd almost beat the mess out of Mary, let go a snore so loud she sounded like a bear coming out of hibernation.

Everyone laughed, even Natasia.

Chauncey asked, "Should I keep filming?"

"Yes!" Natasia exclaimed. "We can always edit that out." Or then, maybe not. She'd have to see if it helped to make for great TV.

Natasia couldn't believe how she was

really getting into this show. Often, she felt more like a referee than an executive producer, but she was getting the footage she needed to push the show to the top. She was sure of that. And with this being her first gig in this genre, that made her happy.

But what had her giddy had nothing to do with reality TV. What had her giddy was the reality of her life . . . and Hosea.

It had been more than a week since she'd walked into City of Lights and told Hosea everything and her heart still filled with joy when she thought about how it had all gone down. Not only had Hosea promised to be there for her always, but he'd even come to her home and then that night, had come back and taken her out to dinner.

They'd just had a quick bite at Captain D's. Hosea explained that he had to get back home to his family. For the second time that day, she'd held back what she really wanted to say — that she needed him more than his wife and children did. Instead, she'd let Hosea know how grateful she was for his help.

In the past week, he'd continued to be there for her. He'd spent five of the last eight days with her. He'd come by to check on her, bring her dinner, give her scriptures to read, and pray with her. Then, sometimes, they would just talk.

But he never stayed for more than an hour or two. Though Natasia cherished that time, she noticed that he didn't touch her, he hadn't held her the way he had on Sunday. That's what she yearned for; she just hadn't been sure how to make that happen again.

But then there was last night. Just thinking about that made her smile now.

Hosea had called just as she sped away from Copeland's, where she'd had a quick dinner with Sonny, Chauncey, and a couple of other guys from the crew.

"I'm just leaving church," he said. "Have you eaten yet?"

Natasia had looked in her rearview mirror at the restaurant's flashing blue sign.

"No," she said, even though she'd just stuffed herself with the pecan-crusted catfish, her favorite Copeland's dish. But she'd eat an elephant if it gave her a chance to go out with Hosea. "What do you have in mind?"

"I was gonna pick up a pizza . . . or do you want something else?"

Something else, she thought. Aloud, she said, "A pizza will be fine."

It wasn't the sit-down, candle-lit dinner that she'd been looking forward to, but she was sure that was coming. When that happened, she was going to make sure that Jasmine knew about it; maybe she'd even capture it on tape. But for now, sharing a pizza with Hosea at her apartment was a good thing — and actually, it might even be better than going out; this way, they could be much more intimate.

Just a little more than thirty minutes later, he'd shown up with the vegetarian pizza.

"I hope you're hungry," he said the moment he stepped inside her apartment.

"I am."

"Well, good. 'Cause I got a large for you." He'd followed her into the kitchen.

"Great!" She reached for two plates from the cabinet.

But then he'd said, "Oh, no. This is for you. I have to get home."

The look on her face must've told him that she'd expected more.

"I'm sorry."

"No, of course. I just thought a pizza, and a large . . ."

"Well, you can freeze some for later."

"Yeah, that's what I'll do," she said, trying to maintain her enthusiasm.

"Oh!" Hosea pulled a piece of paper from his pocket, unfolded it, and handed it to her. "I made some calls and found a doctor."

"Really?'

"Yeah, Dr. Ginsberg. He's supposed to be one of the best rheumatologists here in Atlanta."

"Thank you. I really do need a doctor here. I'll call tomorrow for an appointment."

He nodded. "And if you want, I'll go with you to see him."

"Are you kidding me?" she asked, and then, without thinking, she'd jumped into his arms. "Thank you!" All thinking was tossed aside when she leaned back from her embrace and pressed her lips against his.

At first, the kiss shocked even her. But when Hosea didn't pull back, Natasia pressed her body into his.

That contact awakened him and Hosea stepped away.

"Oh, my God," Natasia said, as she tried to catch her breath. "Hosea, I'm so sorry. I really am. I didn't mean —"

He held up his hands. "No, I get it." With his fingertips, he wiped her kiss from his lips. "It's fine."

"I just don't want you to think that this is anything but what it is."

"I know it was just the moment. I know you've been going through all of this by yourself and to now have a little bit of help . . . it must mean a lot."

"Yeah, that's what it is," she said, looking straight at him, hoping that he would believe her lie.

"So, we're fine," he said.

"Yeah, we are."

"Well . . ." He waited as if he expected her to say something else.

"Well . . ." She stalled, hoping that once he thought about it, he would want to turn that kiss into more than it was, into what she wanted it to be.

But Hosea had just turned away and with a curt "Good night," he left her standing in her kitchen.

It wasn't all that she'd hoped for, but Natasia got way more out of last night than she could've wanted. She had not been fooled by the way Hosea had left. Yes, she'd been the one to kiss him, but he hadn't pulled away. That's what she remembered. And that's why she knew that he wanted her as much as she wanted him. The thing was, he was such an honorable man. She would have to be the one to figure it out for both of them.

Not that Natasia had any false hopes about what could really happen with Hosea. Would he leave Jasmine? Probably not. Especially not with the medical death sentence that hovered over her. But that didn't mean that they couldn't have a relationship. She wanted it all — the time, the intimacy. She just wouldn't have the ring.

She shook her head slightly, a bit surprised that she was willing to settle for that. She never thought she'd be willing to just have an affair. But facing her mortality had changed her perspective on so much.

It took everything within her to turn her thoughts from Hosea and focus on the scene they were still filming. She let her eyes rest on Jasmine for a long moment, and for the millionth time, she wondered what Hosea saw in that woman. Then, she turned to Rachel and Mary, who still sat with Jasmine, all three women talking to the mostly half-asleep teen girls.

At least she wouldn't have to break up any fights today. The battles that they got into really amazed her.

It was a curious thing. Yes, Rachel always went to war with Jasmine, but their fights seemed to be all about the show. Each wanted to be the star and without that competition, Natasia could see the two being friends. Rachel had no class and Jasmine was only one step up, being the low-class chick that she was. That was enough to make them soul sisters.

But then there was Mary. Natasia could tell that if Mary was burning on a sidewalk, Rachel wouldn't even stop to spit on her. In the past, Natasia may have been curious enough to explore that drama on the show. But not right now. Right now, she had her own issues. She had her own drama and she wanted to use the show to play it out, to help her get what she wanted.

She had to get Hosea on the show. Of course, she could ask him directly, but she wanted to keep their conversations just about the two of them. She never wanted him to think that she was using him or had any other motives besides him helping her through this horrible time of her life.

But Hosea being on the show would give her just what she wanted — more time with him. And the secondary benefit was she'd be able to expose Jasmine for the mean fool that she was. It was horrible what Jasmine had said to Rachel the other day, asking if her mother knew that she was stupid. If Hosea had seen that, he would know the kind of woman she really was, and then Natasia would be right there . . . Jasmine's antithesis.

Natasia could think of a few scenes, a few scenarios that she could set up to expose

Jasmine to Hosea. But she'd need some help. First, getting Hosea on the show, and then setting Jasmine up. She needed someone who wanted to bring Jasmine down just as much as she did.

Someone like Rachel Jackson Adams!

Yes, Rachel was the most country-speaking, neck-rolling, Ross-wearing-thinking-she-was-fly woman she'd ever met. But today, Natasia had new respect for the woman she was sure could never pass a fifth-grade test.

It was Rachel's question, "Are you Hosea's Natasia?" that had Natasia looking at Rachel with new eyes. When Rachel had asked her that, "Yes," was right on the tip of Natasia's tongue. But she *was* smart enough to pass an elementary school exam, so she hadn't uttered a single word.

The question had made her curious, though. Why had Rachel asked? What did she know about her and Hosea? Had Jasmine been talking? Had Hosea been talking . . . about her?

She had no answers, but the fact that Rachel had asked let Natasia know that Rachel could be her ally.

When Sonny shouted, "Cut!" Natasia rushed to the circle of the First Ladies and the girls. Some of the girls were still asleep and had to be awakened, but Natasia left all of that for the producers. She headed straight to Rachel.

"This was such a brilliant idea," she gushed to Rachel. "Thank you for thinking of it."

It took Rachel a moment to respond, as if she couldn't believe Natasia was talking to her, and Natasia wished that she'd been a bit nicer to Rachel before now. Finally, Rachel said, "You think so?" and she grinned.

So easy, Natasia thought. "Yes. Because not only did you get to inspire the girls, but you know how much we wanted to bring a news element to this show? Well, this helps. I'm going to interview the administrator of this facility, and we're going to include that in this segment."

"That's fantastic," Rachel said, sounding like now she was the one who was giddy.

From the corner of her eye, Natasia could see Jasmine watching and seething. Jasmine was trying not to stand too close, but it was obvious that she was listening to every word Natasia and Rachel exchanged.

And so for the benefit of Rachel *and* Jasmine, Natasia said, "We should really have lunch very soon. I know this show is going to be a hit and when we get picked up for another season, I just might consider you as a producer . . . you have such great ideas."

"Oh, my God!" Rachel exclaimed and Natasia hoped that the girl didn't faint. Rachel already acted like she had fallen and bumped her head. "Really?" She clapped her hands.

Not a chance, Natasia said inside. "Yes! Let's talk about it soon."

"Definitely!"

Without giving a single glance to Jasmine, Natasia strolled to the back of the facility. Now, that she had Rachel in place, all she needed to do was talk to Melinda. Tell her that it made no sense that they'd filmed Rachel with Lester and Mary with Nathan, but they had nothing with Jasmine and Hosea.

With that, Melinda would be able to convince Jasmine. Really, Jasmine had no choice. This was Natasia's show, and she was going to make sure that Jasmine knew it. If Jasmine wanted to stay, she'd have to do it this way . . . or just leave the show.

And since Natasia knew that Jasmine wasn't going to do that, she was sure that Hosea would be on the set very soon.

Natasia sighed. Winning always felt so wonderful.

Chapter Eighteen: Mary

Every day, Mary was hating more and more that she'd allowed Nathan to talk her into this. Yes, Pleasant City had gotten some screen time, but she couldn't see how this reality show appearance would benefit them at all. In fact, if she were someone looking for a church home, she'd cross Pleasant City off the list for even participating in this mess. And Mary definitely couldn't see why so-called classy women like Rachel and Jasmine would be doing this foolishness.

Mary glanced over at the Christmas card again. Nathan had actually set it up on the credenza in their hallway as if to serve as a constant reminder. No, she may not know why Rachel and Jasmine were doing the show, but she knew why she was. And that's all she needed to focus on.

"What are you doing?" Nathan asked as he descended the stairs. "Why aren't you dressed?"

"I am dressed." Mary glanced down at her black chiffon dress that hugged her ample hips and cut low in the front, showing off just a tad bit of cleavage. Since Rachel had talked about her "matronly outfits," Mary tried to spruce her attire up a bit.

"Aren't you guys filming the brunch today?" Nathan asked, frowning in confusion.

"Yes." Mary nodded.

His eyes ran up and down her outfit again. "So, where are you going in *that*?"

It was her turn to be confused. "What's wrong with what I have on?"

"You look like a whore," he replied with disgust.

Mary bit her bottom lip in both anger and shame. Nathan was getting more and more crass every day.

"I . . . you agreed that I needed to revamp my wardrobe." She glanced down again. Yes, the outfit was a tad sexy but nothing like what she used to wear. "I was just trying to spruce it up."

"By looking like a harlot?" he shot back. Then, he paused. "Wait a minute, so are you wearing that for Lester?"

Today was slated to be the first scene they would film with all the husbands. And Nathan was more excited about it than she was. It's all he had been talking about for the past twenty-four hours.

"What?" she asked.

"That's exactly why you're wearing it." He nodded as if he'd convinced himself without any help from her. "You knew your little boyfriend was going to be here and you want to look nice for him. Is that it?" Nathan stepped toward her. She could see his nostrils starting to flare. Was he seriously about to get angry over this?

"Don't be ridiculous. I just put on an outfit." Still, Mary found herself wondering if subconsciously, she'd put this on for Lester. "I just —"

Before she could finish her sentence, Nathan reached out and slapped her across the face. She winced in pain as she grabbed her face.

"Wh-what was that for?" Mary managed to reply.

"Because I'm not being ridiculous and you're trying to play me and I don't take kindly to getting played," he hissed. He held up his hand like he was trying to calm himself. "I'm working my butt off and it's like you're fighting me every step of the way. I'm trying to get Lewis back for *us* and I can't do that if my wife looks like a cheap whore. Now, get your behind back upstairs and change into something First Lady worthy."

Mary sniffed as she scurried back up the stairs. If her old friends could see her now, no one would believe she'd been reduced to a submissive, whiny woman. The old Mary would have made Nathan the star of the new movie *The Burning Bed 2,* but this Mary was trying to walk with God and as Nathan was constantly telling her, that meant learning to be submissive and obedient.

Twenty minutes later, Mary was sitting in silence next to her husband as they rode to the church. Nathan was acting like nothing was wrong. In fact, he was actually humming along with the gospel song "I Am Worthy." At the stop light, he even closed his eyes and raised his hand to the roof as he gave God praise.

The whole scene was sickening, but Mary bit her tongue and remained quiet. She was all too happy when they finally pulled up in front of the restaurant where they were meeting for brunch.

She saw the attitude form on his face when he noticed they were already filming. "And we're late, because my wife thought it was okay to dress like she's on the pole," he snapped.

The pole? The dress had come to her

knees. How was he now making it into a stripper's outfit? Mary remained quiet as he eased the car up front to the valet.

"Come on," he said, throwing the car into park. "You see the cameras. Pull yourself together. Plaster on a smile."

Mary couldn't move. After what had just happened, she was now supposed to go in here and shin and grin like everything was okay?

Nathan glanced over at her and must've decided to take another approach. He took her hand. "Babe, I'm sorry, about earlier, okay? It's just that I'm fighting so hard for our future and you're fighting me every step of the way. We are a team, and I think sometimes you forget that." He smiled at her. "So, we're good?"

She nodded but didn't reply.

"There, that's better." He looked at the valet, who was standing there waiting to open his door. "Come on, babe."

"Hey, Mary," Sonny called out as they climbed out the car. "Just pretend we're not here and get on out and walk in. The others are already inside."

Nathan struggled to hide his irritation, but he plastered on a smile and gave a bunch of "hello"s and "bless you"s to random people as they made their way inside.

They had barely made it into the foyer area when Lester came around the corner and bumped right into Nathan.

Nathan grinned widely as he stepped in front of Mary. She couldn't help it, she lowered her head and tried to remain inconspicuous. She just wasn't ready to face Lester. She hadn't seen him since that day in court when she'd begged Rachel to take her daughter before they hauled her off to jail.

"Well, if it isn't the great Lester Adams," Nathan said. "I've heard several things about you."

Lester seemed confused. "I hope it's all good." He chuckled.

"Some of it." Nathan heartily shook Lester's hand.

"And you are?"

"Nathan Frazier." He stepped to the side and pushed Mary forward. "This is my wife, Mary. I think you know her."

Lester's smile faded and it looked like all the color drained from his face.

Mary wanted to crawl into a hole and die.

"Hi, Lester," she said, barely looking him into the eye.

"Um, hi, Mary."

Nathan put his arm around her as the cameraman panned back and forth among the three of them. "I know the last you heard, she was locked up. But I'm happy to say that my darling has paid her debt to society." Nathan was really playing it up for the camera.

Just then, Rachel came stomping toward them like a radar had gone off warning her that Mary was within five feet of her husband.

"Good morning, Lady Rachel," Nathan said as she approached.

"Lester, I need to speak with you," Rachel said, ignoring Nathan.

"Can't we all get along?" Nathan laughed as they walked off. "Nice to finally meet you in person, Rev. Adams," Nathan called out after him. "I look forward to great things."

"Okay, that's good," Sonny said. "Now, if you two can get on in, that would be great."

Mary could see that Rachel was not happy and she knew that Nathan was going to milk that for all it was worth to get more camera time.

Nathan happily took Mary's hand and led them to the table. There were four cameras shooting the long table from various angles.

"Okay, guys," Sonny said, "now that

everyone is here, we need you to just talk casually. Make introductions like you're getting to know each other."

"That won't be too hard." Nathan laughed. "Some of us know the others all too well. Ain't that right, babe?"

Mary couldn't believe Nathan was showing out like this. Rachel obviously didn't appreciate the humor either. She just rolled her eyes.

"All right, and action," Sonny said.

No one at the table moved or said a word.

"Cut," Sonny said, approaching the table. "Umm, yeah, when I say action, we'd kind of like some action."

Still no one moved.

"Look, Natasia will be here shortly and this scene needs to be done." Sonny ran his hands through his hair like he was frustrated. "Can we try this again? And action."

He stepped back and Nathan took the lead. "So, Rev. Adams, I've been following your career. The things you and Lady Rachel are doing with the ABC are phenomenal."

"Thank you," Lester curtly replied. Rachel didn't bother, so Nathan turned to Jasmine.

"And where is the esteemed Rev. Bush?" Nathan asked.

Jasmine looked over at Rachel, then back at Nathan, then over at Sonny. "What's the purpose of this scene again?"

"Ugh," Sonny yelled. "Look, take five. I'm going to talk to Natasia because I can't work like this." Sonny turned around and stormed off.

"I thought this was supposed to be a First Ladies show, anyway," Jasmine quipped. "Not First Ladies and husbands." She smiled at Lester. "No offense, Lester."

Lester finally smiled. "None taken. The only reason I'm here is because Rachel said Hosea would be, too." He eyed Rachel.

"Oh, Hosea won't . . . Ow!" Jasmine said when Rachel kicked her under the table. Jasmine looked like she wanted to reach across the table and slap Rachel but the pleading look in Rachel's eyes must've stopped her.

Mary couldn't help it, the corners of her lips turned up in a slow smile. Nathan wanted to be important so badly and they wouldn't give him the time of day.

He caught her smiling and cut his eyes at her. She immediately lost her smile and began toying with the salad the waiter had set down in front of her.

Mary paused when she noticed the expression on Rachel's face. Rachel was watching their exchange, almost as if she was study-ing them and Mary didn't know why, but she felt compelled to scoot closer to her husband and pretend that she was much happier than she actually was. Unfortu-nately, that was getting harder and harder to do.

CHAPTER NINETEEN: JASMINE

"Okay, that's a wrap," Sonny shouted and the smiles on all of their faces faded as fast as the bright lights from the cameras.

Nathan stood first, and Mary quickly did the same, looking like a trained puppy taught to follow her master.

Rachel and Lester remained seated, still chatting, and Jasmine scooted her chair back and scurried to the other side of the table before Rachel could get away.

Just as Rachel stood, Jasmine said, "Rachel, can I speak to you for a moment?"

Rachel paused for just a second, then looked over her shoulder before she turned back to Jasmine. "You talking to me?"

Oh, God, Jasmine thought. She didn't feel like having to deal with Rachel's middle-school attitude today. "You're the only Rachel in here."

"You don't have to get smart about it. First of all, you approached me. And secondly, I asked because you haven't said two funky words to me since we started this show."

Jasmine frowned. "What are you talking about? We speak to each other in every scene."

"Yeah, just for the cameras. And just so you can embarrass me. But now you want to get all friendly with me?" Rachel sucked her teeth. "Please! I need to go home with my husband."

Jasmine sighed. "Please, Rachel." She lowered her voice. "I really need to speak with you in private."

It must've been the word *private* that made Rachel face Jasmine once again.

With her voice still lowered, Jasmine added, "I need to speak with you away from the cameras."

If Jasmine wanted to speak to Rachel in private, there had to be something juicy going on and Jasmine knew Rachel would never resist juicy — Rachel was just that nosey.

"Okay," Rachel began in a tone that sounded like she was the one in charge of this conversation. "Let's talk in the bathroom. The cameras won't come in there."

As Jasmine followed Rachel, she replayed in her mind the words she wanted to say.

She had to get Rachel to join Team Jasmine.

Inside the bathroom, Jasmine stopped in front of the counter, but Rachel kept moving. She frowned as Rachel first peeked under each stall, and then pushed each door open. The bathroom was huge for a restaurant restroom, and Rachel did that for each of the fifteen stalls.

"What are you doing?" Jasmine asked.

"Just checking to make sure we're alone." Smirking, she added, "You ain't street smart at all. Don't you know that before you have any kind of private conversation in a bathroom, you should always check?"

"Okay," Jasmine said, trying hard not to roll her eyes. Who had private conversations in public bathrooms? "I'll try and remember that."

Rachel folded her arms and began tapping her foot. "So, what's up?"

Jasmine took a deep breath. These first words that she'd rehearsed were the hardest to say. "First, I wanted to apologize."

Rachel raised one eyebrow.

Jasmine continued, "You and I were in such a good space after all that stuff that went down in Chicago and the Virgin Islands last year. I actually thought of you as a friend after that." She paused. "But it doesn't feel like we're friends now."

"That's not my fault," Rachel said. "You're the one who's acting like you're the star of this show and I'm getting in your way."

"I haven't been acting that way by myself. I heard what you call me and Mary — your backups."

The corner of Rachel's mouth twitched as she fought to hold back a smile.

"And it really started before the show began. Before you even knew I was on the show, when you sent me that little funky email with that fake picture of you standing in front of Harpo Studios."

Rachel couldn't hold back her smile this time. "I was just trying to keep you informed since we're girls. And anyway, it didn't matter because you found a way to step in and steal my shine."

"Just like you stole mine when I was supposed to be on Oprah's show, alone."

"You know what?" Rachel began to move toward the door. "I don't need this. You always bringing up stuff from the past."

"Wait!" She paused until Rachel turned around. "Just listen to what I'm saying. This show has brought out the worst in us and I don't want that to ruin our friendship. Think about where we've come from. I got you out of that murder charge and —"

Rachel raised her hand, stopping her.

"Now, you wait. So that we're both perfectly clear, I never murdered anyone, I would never murder anyone, and there wasn't anyone even murdered."

"I know all that, but I'm just sayin', you were in a lot of trouble and I was there to help you. I put everything I had on hold; I could've gone back to New York to be with my husband and children, but I didn't. I stayed with you. I could've let you sit in jail when you were arrested, but I didn't. I made sure that Mae Frances got you out and got you an attorney."

Once again, Rachel folded her arms, and now she peered at Jasmine, trying to figure out where all of this was leading.

Jasmine kept on, "I just want us to get back to that place where we were before."

Rachel waited a couple of seconds before she said, "Okay."

"Okay!" Jasmine grinned, thinking how easy that was.

Rachel said, "So, what do you want from me?"

"What do you mean?" Her tone was filled with innocence.

"There is only one reason why you would come to me with all of this. You must need something."

Jasmine shook her head. She really needed

to reevaluate her opinion of Rachel. She always underestimated this girl, thinking she was just young and dumb. Well, for the most part, that's all she was. But there were times when Rachel surprised her.

"Well, now that you mention it . . ."

Rachel laughed, but then all the cheer left her face. "What do you want?"

"You're right, I do need something. I need your help." She paused, waiting for Rachel to say something. Then, "You were right about what you said earlier. Natasia Redding is the Natasia from Hosea's past."

Rachel busted out laughing. "I knew it! This is priceless. Hosea's woman is all up in this place."

"Yeah, just like Lester's woman is."

Rachel's laughter stopped and the way her face scrunched up, Jasmine was sure Rachel was going to start howling at the moon. Rachel said, "You know what?" Again, she turned toward the door. Again, Jasmine stopped her.

"Okay, I'm sorry I said that. It's just that both of us are dealing with these other women and we can't do anything about Mary. But I need your help to get rid of Natasia. I need her off the show, out of Atlanta, and out of the country, if possible."

Rachel tilted her head. "Why all of that?

You think Hosea's gonna step out on you with her again?"

"There is no *again,* Rachel," Jasmine said, trying hard not to snap. *"My husband never cheated on me!"*

Rachel paused, trying to figure out if Jasmine had taken another dig at her. But then she just asked, "So, what am I supposed to do?"

"Help me, like I helped you. We didn't exactly have a plan when I saved you in Chicago —"

"You didn't save me."

"But we got it done anyway," Jasmine continued, ignoring Rachel's comment.

Rachel pressed her lips together. "So, if I help you, what's in it for me?"

"Can't you do it because we're friends?"

Rachel laughed. "Yeah, right."

"I'm serious, Rachel. Just like what happened out there," Jasmine said, motioning with her thumb toward the door. "When I was getting ready to talk about Hosea not wanting to be here, and you kicked me under the table. I had your back."

"No, what you have is a big mouth!"

Now Jasmine wanted to be the one to turn around and walk out that door. But she needed this blockhead. So she just smiled and kept her growl inside. "Well, I stopped talking about Hosea, didn't I? I helped you out, and now I need you to help me."

Rachel paused, pursed her lips, stared Jasmine up and down. She did all of that, and said, "I'll think about it."

Jasmine wanted to scream. What did she have to think about? And didn't you need a brain to think?

But before she could go off and say all that, the bathroom door swung open and they both turned.

Mary stepped inside, but then stopped. She looked at Jasmine and then her eyes settled on Rachel. "Am I interrupting something?"

Rachel growled and Jasmine stepped back. Over the past few weeks, there were many times when Rachel and Mary went at it. But it was always controlled and in front of the cameras. Without the cameras, Jasmine had a feeling that Rachel was going to go off. And she wanted to see it. Something might happen that she could use.

When neither Jasmine nor Rachel spoke, Mary moved past them, but before she could go into a stall, Rachel grabbed her arm and swung her back around.

"You better get your hands off me," Mary said in a sister-girl tone that made Jasmine back up a little. This white girl sounded like she had some black in her.

"Oh, yeah," Rachel said, not backing down. "And if I don't, what you gonna do?"

Mary stared Rachel down, but then sighed and stepped back. "I'm not trying to go there with you. I told you, I've changed."

"So, is that why you were all up in Lester's face?"

Jasmine was mesmerized, but then, from the corner of her eye, she saw movement. She turned her head. Chauncey was tiptoe-ing in with the camera. Quickly, she turned back to the drama in front of her. Both Mary and Rachel were turned so that they couldn't see Chauncey right away, especially since he didn't have any lights on — none were needed in the bathroom. Though even with lights, Rachel and Mary probably wouldn't have noticed Chauncey; they were that caught up.

When they didn't notice, Jasmine turned back to Chauncey and nodded her head just a bit, letting him know that she wasn't go-ing to say a word. This was exactly the scene she needed, the scene that would show these two for the hoodlums they were. The scene that would show how far above both of them she was.

When Mary asked, "What are you talking about, Rachel?" Jasmine whipped her head around, getting back to the drama.

"I'm talking about you being the conniving snake in the grass that you've always been," Rachel snarled. "I'm talking about you always trying to seduce a man who doesn't belong to you so that you can get what you want."

"In case you haven't noticed, I'm married, Rachel. I have a husband and I don't do that anymore."

"You can try to sell that lie to someone who doesn't know you, but I know you haven't changed. And that bootleg preacher that you're married to —"

"He's not bootleg," Mary said. Her voice rose with anger. "Pleasant City is a growing church. You'll be hearing about us."

Rachel chuckled. "I'm sure I will. Hearing about how you stole money from the church, or how you slept with every man in there." She paused. "And now that you've been in prison, you're probably sleeping with the women, too!"

Mary looked like she wanted to punch Rachel in her throat so that not another word would ever rise up out of her again. But all she said was, "I know you don't like me," as calmly as if she was speaking to a child.

"What was your first clue?"

Ignoring her, Mary continued, "And you

don't have to like me. We're just doing this show and after that, you won't have to see me again."

"Yeah. Just make sure of that. Because if I ever see you sniffing around Lester —"

"I don't want your husband."

"Or coming anywhere near Lewis —"

"My son's name is Lester Jr."

Rachel balled her hand into a fist and Jasmine was sure that Rachel *was* going to punch Mary in *her* throat. She really wanted to see that happen, but then she thought about the talk that she and Rachel had just had. And in a little corner of her heart, she did care about Rachel. She didn't know why, but she didn't want her on TV beating down this white woman.

So, she jumped in. "Rachel, no," Jasmine whispered, grabbing her hand before it could connect with Mary's face. "You don't want to do this."

"No, I need to stop this heifer, right here and right now."

"Not with the cameras," Jasmine whispered.

"What?" Rachel whipped around just in time to see Chauncey clicking off the camera and stepping from the restroom. "Wait!" Rachel said, running behind him. "You can't use that!"

Mary rushed out behind her, as if she forgot that she needed to pee.

And while they ran, Jasmine turned toward the mirror. She pulled out her cosmetic bag, brushed the shine from her face, applied a little more lip gloss, then puckered her lips. Her work here was done. Rachel would surely help her now, especially once she convinced Rachel that Natasia was responsible for all of this.

Chapter Twenty: Rachel

No matter how hard she tried, Rachel couldn't reign in the side of her that was prone to acting a fool. That's because people were always trying her, pushing her back into her past, when she wouldn't hesitate to give someone a piece of her mind. But she'd worked to move on from being *that* chick. Things like that stunt in the bathroom, though, made her want to revisit that cut-some-tires persona.

Rachel knew how these shows worked. They thrived on the drama and loved to feature women going at it. Whether it was any of the Real Housewives series or *Mob Wives,* the numbers soared when the blows were flying. But while she definitely wanted to be a part of this show, it wouldn't be at the expense of her dignity.

"Honey, what are you doing?" Lester asked, approaching Rachel. "Jasmine just left and it looks like the others are leaving as well." Rachel couldn't help but notice that her husband took great care not to say Mary's name.

"Give me a second, babe," Rachel said. She'd been searching for Natasia, and finally spotted her in the back running her mouth on the phone.

"Excuse me, Natasha. I need to speak with you," Rachel said, stomping over to where Natasia stood.

Natasia cut her eyes at Rachel and said into the phone, "Winston, let me call you back." She ended her call and turned to Rachel. "First of all, it's Na-ta-si-a," she replied.

"Yeah, okay," Rachel said, waving her off. She couldn't stand bourgie black folk. That woman knew her mama named her *Natasha.*

"Secondly," Natasia continued, "it's very rude to interrupt someone on a phone call."

"I need to speak with you," Rachel demanded. "Now." She would've gone to speak directly to Melinda, but Melinda hadn't been at the last few tapings, almost as if she had completely turned the show over to Natasia.

"Yes, Rachel?" Natasia asked. "What can I do for you?"

Was that irritation she detected? Natasia

might think she was in charge, but she didn't need to get it twisted. Without Rachel there was no show. It was her idea and that afforded her certain liberties. What these people didn't know, what no one knew, was that tucked away on page eight of the contract no one thought she was smart enough to read, Rachel had gotten Melinda to agree to creative input. That meant the drama that was just filmed would *not* be airing.

"I don't know who sent that janky photographer into the bathroom to film me but I can't appreciate it," Rachel snapped.

"The bathroom?"

"Yes. I didn't stutter. Luckily, I wasn't sitting on the toilet, but that's a complete invasion of privacy and I'm going to need that tape destroyed." Rachel's voice was firm because she wanted this woman to know she meant business.

Natasia had the nerve to laugh. "It doesn't quite work like that, Rachel. But I will talk with Sonny because no one should be following you in the bathroom."

"You might need to read the fine print of my contract, because it *does* work like that. If I don't want it to air, it doesn't air," she said matter-of-factly. She had been trying to give Natasia her respect, but this whole sneaky filming had changed the game.

"Rachel, I really don't have time —" Suddenly, Natasia stopped, and as if a thought crossed her mind, her whole tone shifted, then a small smile crept up on her face. "Okay, I'll make sure it doesn't air. I just want to make you happy."

Her dramatic shift gave Rachel pause. "Well, ummm, thanks."

Natasia's smile grew even wider. "Well, since we've wrapped for the day, I was wondering if you'd like to go grab a coffee or something."

Rachel frowned. "Who?"

"You and I." The expression on Rachel's face must've belied her confusion, because Natasia's voice softened as she continued. "Look, Rachel, I know there's tension on the set. I'm not exactly on 'hanging out' terms with Jasmine, but you and I, I think we could be good friends."

Rachel cocked her head, studying Natasia, then said, "Okay, what are you up to?"

"I'm not up to anything. I'm here to do a job," she said innocently. Rachel wasn't buying it. She turned up her lip and folded her arms until Natasia finally confessed, "I need your help."

"Ha!" Was this some kind of joke? "My help? For what?"

Natasia released a long sigh. "You know the tension between Jasmine and me. You know it all too well." Natasia looked around. The crew was breaking down. No one was within earshot, but she lowered her voice anyway. "I've seen the way Jasmine looks down on you, the way she treats you like you're beneath her, and I don't think it's fair."

"I'm not worried about Jasmine."

"Well, you should be." She continued whispering, "She's trying to get you kicked off the show."

"What?"

"Yes." Natasia sighed like it pained her to continue. "I deplore gossip, but I just wanted you to be aware."

When Rachel's mom was alive she used to always say that a dog that brings you a bone will take one away. Natasia was up to something.

"Why are you making me aware? I know it's not because you just like me so much."

"Well," Natasia said, dragging out the word. "I do need your help in getting Lester to talk to Hosea and convince him to come on the show. That's all I want. And this has nothing to do with my issues with Jasmine. This is business."

"So, let me get this straight. You want me

to go behind Jasmine's back and get my husband to convince her husband to be on my show."

Natasia smiled, satisfied. "Exactly."

It was Rachel's turn to laugh. Game recognized game and Natasia was running a full court press on her. Rachel didn't know what this woman was up to, but Rachel couldn't appreciate Natasia trying to get her to stab Jasmine in the back. Rachel had her beef with Jasmine, but that was her own motive and Rachel didn't need anyone else fueling that fire. No, Natasia Redding was trying to use Rachel and Rachel didn't appreciate being played.

"The truth of it all," Natasia continued. "You help me out and I'll make sure your video doesn't air."

That definitely rubbed Rachel the wrong way. This heifer probably set it all up anyway. "Sweetie, it's *not* going to air. Again, check the contract. And furthermore, you need to watch who you threaten. I know that you want Hosea and no, Jasmine isn't my favorite person in the world, but I'm not about to help you steal her man."

Natasia glared at Rachel. "You have no idea what I'm trying to do."

"Yes, I do. You're trying to get with my friend's man." Rachel looked her up and down. "Matter of fact, why don't you get your own man? Trying to get with Hosea when he's made it clear that he doesn't want you, that reeks of desperation."

Rachel turned and summoned her husband. He was sitting at a table, typing away on his iPad, no doubt working on some ABC business. "Come on, Lester. It's time to go."

Lester stood, grateful that Rachel was finally ready to go. He followed Rachel to the exit, but just before she reached the door, Rachel saw Chauncey putting his gear into his bag. She knelt down next to him and whispered, "If I ever catch you sneaking and filming me again, you'll be lucky if you can find a job shooting YouTube videos."

She didn't give him time to reply as she stood and sauntered out the door. Chauncey had definitely better recognize. Everybody around here had better recognize. She was not the one. At least Jasmine was starting to get that. That's why she'd come to her, begging for help. Now, here was Natasia doing the same.

Rachel slid her sunglasses on as she climbed into the back of the limo. As they pulled off, her mind replayed her conversations with Natasia and Jasmine, both begging for her help. Yeah, it felt wonderful to be on top.

CHAPTER TWENTY-ONE:
NATASIA

Natasia was hot! And it had nothing to do with the flashes that often came because of her medication.

She was hot because of Jasmine Cox Larson Bush, Mary Frazier, and now especially, Rachel Jackson Adams. These diva wannabes had sent her blood pressure soaring.

Who did these women think they were? Obviously, they didn't know who they were playing with. These three cows were nothing more than fame-hawks and fortune-seekers who were never going to make it past the airing of this show. She was an award-winning journalist turned award-winning TV executive, and the First Ladies needed to bow down and recognize.

But it didn't seem like Jasmine, Mary, or Rachel cared about who she was, especially not Rachel.

Rachel's words still played in Natasia's

mind: *"Why don't you get your own man? Trying to get with Hosea when he's made it clear that he doesn't want you, that reeks of desperation."*

Rachel had said those words yesterday and still they played over and over in Natasia's mind like there was some kind of replay button in her head. She wasn't sure why Rachel's words haunted her so much. Maybe it was because without even knowing it, Rachel had spoken the truth — at least partially.

Natasia *was* desperate . . . desperate to stay alive. And she knew that Hosea could help her with that.

"Ugh!" she groaned out loud. Glancing at the clock, she put down her cup of coffee. She had to leave now if she was going to make it to her doctor's appointment on time.

The knock on her door made her moan again. Why were the housekeeping staff coming so early? When she'd moved in, she'd arranged for the morning staff to come around ten and the evening staff to arrive about eight. She was not in the best of moods and when she whipped the door open, her plan was to call whoever was on the other side incompetent and inept. But then her scowl went *poof!* In its place was a grin that revealed the joy in her heart.

"Hosea, what are you doing here?"

He leaned against the door jamb. "Don't we have a doctor's appointment?"

There was that *we* again, the word that made her feel like she could do anything, even beat this disease, as long as he was by her side.

"We do have a doctor's appointment," she said, laughing. "But I thought you were going to meet me there."

"I was, but only because I had a breakfast meeting. It was canceled so . . ."

"Well, let me grab my purse," she said.

He held out his arm and she hooked her arm through his.

"Let's get going," he said. And when he smiled down at her, she melted.

From the moment she stepped into the hallway, it didn't feel like she was on her way to a doctor's appointment. Never before had she felt any kind of happiness as she was heading to hear what she always knew would be dismal news.

Today, as she held on to Hosea's arm, as he led her into the elevator, then through the lobby to his car that was right out in front, she felt nothing but joy.

Inside the car, he turned to radio to 107.5, which surprised Natasia a little. She would have thought he'd only listen to gospel now.

And then, when Luther started singing, "Woke up today looked at your picture just to get me started . . ." Hosea blasted the music through the car.

"Do you remember," he shouted, "that little Thai restaurant we used to go to and they played Luther's songs all night long?"

She laughed. "Oh, my God! How could I ever forget it? It was our favorite food and our favorite music!"

"And those waiters would be singing right along, with their accents. We should've bought stock in that place."

Then, she asked him, "Remember our Friday nights?"

At first, Natasia wasn't sure that she should've asked that question. But when Hosea grinned, she exhaled.

"You mean our movie nights? How could I forget them? That's another place where we should've bought stock. . . ."

Then, together, they said, "Blockbuster!" and laughed.

Their conversation continued about the apartment they shared, their lakefront views, even the open-house estate homes they visited every Sunday as they dreamed about the home they'd one day buy to-gether.

Every bit of their talk made Natasia feel better, feel stronger. Every bit of it made her feel as if she'd live forever.

When Hosea kept talking about their life together, she was surprised. In the past, he'd wanted to stay far away from the subject of their past. When she'd come to work on his show in 2007, he made it clear that these types of discussions were off limits because he was married and loved his wife.

Today though, it was like he couldn't get enough of looking in the rearview mirror at their life. Maybe it was just that he knew this conversation was good for her soul, better than any medicine that could be prescribed.

But then he rolled his car into the parking lot of the Peachtree Medical Center, and turned off the radio. And all talking stopped.

Hosea squeezed her hand before he jumped out of the car and came around to her side to help her out.

It was like Hosea had been in the building before. Maybe he had scoped it out. He took her hand and led her straight to Dr. Ginsberg's office.

He checked in for her as she sat, and it wasn't until Hosea sat next to her that her knees stopped knocking.

"You okay?" he whispered.

She nodded. For more than a year now, she'd been going to these appointments, meeting with doctors, all by herself. With Hosea here, she really was okay.

They didn't even wait five minutes before they were called into the doctor's office, and he met them right at the door.

"I'm Doctor Ginsberg."

Natasia shook his hand, but even when she let go, she couldn't stop staring at the young Robert Redford look-alike. Surely, if this medical thing didn't work out, he could find some kind of employment in Hollywood.

"So, I have your records from your doctor in Chicago," Dr. Ginsberg said, getting straight to business. "You're going to be here in Atlanta for a while?"

"Yes," she said. "I'm working and even though the filming wraps up soon, I'll still be in Atlanta for probably another month or so."

"Maybe even longer than that," Hosea said to the doctor without looking at Natasia.

Natasia drew in a deep breath. What was Hosea saying?

"Well, we're going to take care of you while you're here," the doctor said. "What I want to do is get a list of all your medications, to make sure it matches up with your records."

Natasia nodded, working hard to keep her focus on the doctor when all she wanted to think about was what did Hosea mean?

"And we want to do some tests . . . are you ready to do that today?"

"Oh, no," Natasia said. "I thought you just wanted to meet me today; I have to get to my office."

"That's fine, that was the purpose of the meeting today. Just make an appointment with the receptionist before you leave. I'd like to get you in this week, though."

"Yes, definitely."

"Okay, well, do you have any questions for me?"

Natasia shook her head. "Not only have the doctors explained it well to me, but I've done a lot of my own research."

"That's a good thing," the doctor said.

"I have a few questions," Hosea piped in. "I don't know much about lupus, and I know even less about the type that Natasia has."

The doctor nodded. "That's understandable. Lupus is not a disease that gets a lot of attention."

As the doctor began telling Hosea everything that Natasia had already shared with him, she sat back and tried to glance back and forth between the doctor and Hosea. But what she really wanted to do was stop everything and make the doctor be quiet while she asked Hosea what he meant when he said that she might be in Atlanta longer. Was he thinking about a future with her already?

She let her mind wander and wonder and dream for the five minutes that the doctor spent explaining her illness to Hosea.

The doctor ended with, "We are going to do everything we can for your wife."

"Uh . . ." Hosea said.

"We're not married," Natasia said quickly.

"Oh, I'm sorry . . . I just thought . . . I assumed."

She shook her head. "We're just very good friends and Hosea is helping me."

He nodded. "Well, that's a good thing. While I'm a medical doctor, I'm also a Christian. And I believe that God is going to use my hands, but we all need to use our mouths and pray for His best."

"Amen," Hosea said, almost sounding like he wanted to give the doctor a high-five.

"I get in trouble sometimes when I talk to patients like this, but it's what I know. I believe in the power of prayer and the power of medicine. I also know that your mental state is going to be very important in this fight. So, keep your stress down, have as many positive people in your life as possible, and let's work this thing with the Lord."

They shook the doctor's hand, stopped at the front to make an appointment, and then Natasia almost bounced out of the medical center, feeling better than she'd ever felt before.

When they were back in Hosea's car, she wanted to ask him so bad about her staying in Atlanta. Did he want her to stay so that they could be together?

But when he turned on the radio and said nothing, she decided to do the same. It would come out soon enough. And if she could find a way to work her plan and get him on the show, she could make her dream happen right now.

By the time Hosea dropped her off at the OWN offices with promises to call her later, Natasia was floating.

But once she was in her office, and once she sat at her desk, and once she began thinking again about how to get Hosea on the show, she thought about Rachel Jackson Adams. If Rachel had just agreed to help her. Clearly, Hosea was ripe for it . . . he was so ready to be hers.

But Rachel had shut her down cold, which was so ridiculous. After all she'd done for that girl over the past weeks. After all she'd done to make sure that Jasmine wouldn't come off as the star. It hadn't been easy. Rachel seemed determined to play the fool; stupid just seemed to be one of the genetic instructions encoded on that child's DNA.

But still, Natasia had tried to help, setting up Rachel in the most positive of situations. And now, Rachel had no idea that she'd just made the dumbest decision of her life. Natasia was going to make sure that little bathroom scene would end up being the least of Rachel's worries. She had no idea what she would do, but she wasn't too worried about it. Dealing with someone with Rachel's limited intellectual capacity would leave lots of opportunities for Natasia to set her up.

With just a shake of her head, Natasia pushed aside all thoughts of Rachel — for now. She had to get working on next week's schedule.

Pushing herself up from her chair, Natasia took five steps away from her desk, when she felt it — the ache in her right leg. She glanced down. Her knee was swollen, again.

"Ugh!"

It had started out as such a good day, but

once she started thinking about Rachel, she had the onset of a flare.

She stumbled back to the desk, grabbed her medicine from her purse, popped two pills into her mouth, and swallowed without water, the way she always did.

She closed her eyes and leaned back. The knock on her door made her open her eyes, but she didn't answer. Even when the knock came again. She hoped her silence would give whoever was on the other side of that door a clue — that either she wasn't in, or she didn't want to be bothered.

But when the knock came again, and then again, Natasia finally called out, "Come in."

"I was beginning to think you weren't in." Nathan Frazier strutted in with a swagger that looked more like a stumble.

Natasia did everything she could not to roll her eyes. As much as she didn't like any of the First Ladies, when the right reverend Nathan Frazier was around, she felt like there were bugs crawling on her skin. He just seemed . . . what was the word she was looking for? *Slimy.* Yeah, he was slimy.

That was her thought from the very first time they'd met. He'd shown up to the OWN offices here in Atlanta, looking for "whoever is in charge of that new show for First Ladies." When he'd been directed to

Natasia, he'd told her all the reasons why she needed him.

"I have the best First Lady for you," he'd said that day without even saying hello.

"I apologize," she'd said. "And who are you?"

"Nathan Frazier. Reverend Nathan Frazier, to be exact. Head of the Pleasant City Church, the fastest growing church in Atlanta."

"And how may I help you?" Natasia asked, trying hard not to scratch the sudden itch on her arms.

"The real thing is how I'm gonna help you." The reverend grinned.

"Reverend Frazier, I don't have that much time."

"Oh, you'll want to make time for this 'cause I'm the reason why your show is gonna be a hit."

Oh, lawd, she'd thought. Was this what she had to look forward to working on reality TV? Real people showing up at her office saying crazy things?

She reached for the phone, but before she could dial the first number for security, the reverend started talking.

"My wife, Mary Frazier, is a different kind of First Lady," he'd said. "She's about to be released from prison . . . and she wasn't in there for traffic tickets."

Slowly, Natasia had let the phone down and listened to the story of Mary Richardson, who was now Mary Frazier, the con artist who'd been sent to jail for twenty-five years after she'd been found guilty of credit card fraud and theft. And so that her newborn son wouldn't end up in the foster care system, she'd signed away her parental rights to none other than Rachel and Lester Adams.

"So, you see," Reverend Frazier had said, "with my wife's past and her history with Rachel Adams, you're gonna have quite a show."

Natasia had hated to admit it, but she sure was glad that the reverend had walked into her office that day. He was right; his wife was gonna make for good TV. The only problem was whenever Natasia looked at the reverend, she couldn't stop itching.

Another problem arose as soon as they'd started filming. Nathan Frazier thought he was part of the show.

The reverend was always on the set, every single day, throwing out a suggestion here, tossing a critique there, as if he was one of the producers. The entire production team groaned when he came around. Natasia groaned, too. Groaned and scratched.

She itched right now, as the reverend settled into the chair in front of her desk, the way he had done that first day. "What can I do for you, Reverend Frazier?" she asked, as if she really cared. All she wanted to do was get this man out of her office so that she could lean back, close her eyes, and wait for her pain to subside.

"I think the real question is what can I do for you?"

You can get out of my office, she thought, feeling like this was the same conversation they'd had weeks ago. "Well, to be perfectly honest, I don't think you can do anything for me. And I'm really busy right now."

His lips spread into a smile. "Oh, there's lots that I can do for you, lady."

His words hung in the air and he grinned as if he'd just thrown out a playa-playa line.

See? Slimy! Natasia thought, wondering how did Mary live with this man? This wasn't the first time that she'd felt this reverend was making a pass at her. As if. But instead of calling him the sleazeball that he was, all she said was "Reverend Frazier, I have a lot of work to do, and —"

"Are you planning the schedule for next week?"

"Yes, and your wife will receive an email."

He held up a manila envelope. "I got your

show right here," and then he slid the envelope across her desk.

Natasia's eyebrows pressed together. She didn't have time for this, but she wasn't going to play games, either. The only way to get any peace was to take this envelope and then send the right reverend on his way.

"Okay," she said. "I'll take a look at this and get back to you."

He leaned back in his chair as if he planned to stay awhile. Shaking his head, he said, "Take a look now," as if he was the one calling the shots.

She wanted to scream. First Rachel and now the reverend? Somebody needed to send out a memo and let people know this was her show.

But the longer she delayed, the longer the reverend would sit in front of her and stare at her with those beady eyes. She snatched up the envelope, tore it open, then quickly scanned the papers inside. And then . . . she slowed down . . . and read the cover sheet again.

Petition for Sole Custody.

"What is this?" Natasia asked, though she was still reading.

"Exactly what it says. My wife and I are suing Rachel and Lester Adams."

Now, she looked up. "For custody of their son?"

"Mary's son."

"But when we met, you told me that Mary had given up her child. That it was her choice."

He shrugged. "That was then. This is now. Mary is out of prison and in a stable marriage with a pastor who's getting ready to blow up once this show airs."

You wish, Natasia said to herself. Aloud, she said, "Wow." Shaking her head, she added, "I wonder how Rachel is going to react to this."

The reverend leaned forward, placing his arms on her desk. "I don't know, but I know that it will make for good TV."

Natasia's eyes slowly widened. "You want her to be served on the show." It wasn't really a question. She was just stating his thoughts out loud.

He nodded. "Can you imagine how good that will be?"

No, she couldn't. But the scene started playing out in her head and if she'd had the strength, she would've gotten up and danced.

This was just precious. If Nathan had brought this to her yesterday, she would have turned him down. But now that Ra-

263

chel had basically told her to go to . . . anyway, Nathan's timing couldn't have been better. Natasia was looking for a way to make Rachel pay, and this was it for sure.

The grin on her face was as wide as his. "Well, it looks like we have our scene for next week."

Nathan sat back and nodded. "Now, I was thinking of the perfect way to film this," he said.

There he was again, playing the producer. But this time, Natasia let him speak. Nathan Frazier had earned the right to help with staging this. Especially since she had no doubt whatever idea Nathan had would make Mary look perfect and make Rachel look like . . . well, a fool.

Suddenly, she wanted to laugh out loud. Suddenly, she didn't feel so much pain.

She leaned forward and placed her arms on her desk the same way he'd done just moments before. "Tell me, Nathan," she said, calling him by his first name for the first time. "What do you have in mind?"

Chapter Twenty-Two:
Mary

Nathan was really beginning to worry her. As each day passed, he got more and more caught up in this reality show business. It didn't help that several church members had expressed excitement about seeing the final product. When Winston Rivera, the Academy Award–winning producer who attended Pleasant City, had told Nathan that he would be watching because he was looking for Christian content for his new production company, well, that only seemed to fuel Nathan's fire. So much so that Mary had arrived home a few days ago to find Nathan's attorney sitting in their living room.

He'd basically been summoned there to discuss Nathan's budding "entertainment ministry," and to begin the process of filing for sole custody of her son.

"Don't you think we should play this a little more slowly?" Mary had asked after the attorney finished his spiel.

Nathan had actually seemed exasperated as he'd replied, "When should we do this, Mary? When little Lewis is in college?"

She'd cringed when he said that. He knew that she hated that Rachel and Lester had changed her son's name. Sometimes Mary couldn't help but feel Nathan called her son Lewis just to get under her skin.

"Mrs. Frazier," the attorney interjected, "I assure you that if you hope to get custody of your son, now is the time to strike. We should get this in front of the courts around the same time your reality show airs, which of course will just generate unprecedented support."

"Yeah, babe," Nathan added. He sat behind his desk, his legs crossed like he was important. "We'll paint a picture of a woman who made a mistake and is now being punished by having her child taken away." Nathan was so excited, almost as if this move was the catalyst that would launch his career.

"Nathan . . ."

He stopped, giving her *that* look, the one that for the last month had made Mary slink back down in her seat. And so Mary did what she'd done since she'd become Mrs. Nathan Frazier — she shut up. Still, she hadn't been able to stop thinking about that.

Now she had a busy day ahead. They were supposed to be filming a scene at a Women's Day event at a local church and she hadn't even figured out what she'd be wearing.

Mary had just put the finishing touches on breakfast when her stepson, Alvin, came bouncing into the kitchen. She'd been so happy when Nathan agreed that he could spend the night last night.

"Good morning," he said. Alvin was the sweetest boy she had ever known. Mary couldn't help but wonder if that's how Lester Jr. would turn out.

"Good morning, sweetie." Mary set a plate down in front of her stepson. "Here's your breakfast."

"What is this?" Alvin chuckled as he slid into a seat at the breakfast nook.

Mary smiled proudly. "I made a happy face on your pancakes. The strawberries are the eyes and nose and the whipped cream is the mouth."

Alvin's face lit up, but then he said, "Aww come on, I'm eleven. This is for little kids."

She set a glass of orange juice next to his plate. "Well, humor me. I just felt like decorating today." She toussled his curly hair, a motion that he loved, though he would never admit it.

Alvin smiled and picked up his fork. She could tell he was trying to play it cool, but he was actually excited about the pancakes. "All right. I'll eat them just for you. Thanks." He stared at her.

"What?" she asked.

He shrugged nonchalantly. "It's just cool to have someone make me pancakes."

Mary knew Alvin's grandparents were old and pretty much left him to fend for himself when he was in their care, and Nathan, well, he never had time for anything but Pleasant City.

Mary resumed her cooking, scrambling eggs just the way Nathan liked them. It was almost eight o'clock, so he should be down any moment. She had just turned the fire off on the stove when he walked in.

"Hey, Dad," Alvin said.

"Good morning, son." Nathan kissed Mary on the cheek. "Morning, sweetie."

"I'm just finishing your breakfast," Mary replied, hoping he didn't get mad that it wasn't already on the table waiting on him the way he liked.

"Don't forget my game tomorrow," Alvin said.

Nathan grabbed a cup and began pouring himself coffee. "Oh, Alvin, I'm not going to be able to make that."

Alvin's mouth dropped open. "What? Dad, you promised," he whined. "It's the last game of the season. You haven't made any of my games."

"Son, you know my job is an important one." He shrugged like it was no big deal. "I can't make it and Mary has to tape her show tomorrow. But we'll be with you in spirit."

Mary's heart broke as Alvin fought back tears. "Man up, son. Life is full of disappointments." Nathan reached down and took a strawberry off Alvin's pancake and popped it in his mouth. "Sweetheart, can you bring my breakfast into my office?" He bounced out of the room without another word.

Alvin's bottom lip quivered as Mary eased over to him. "I'll be there, honey."

"Dad said you have to tape your show." He was struggling to keep his voice from cracking.

She flicked her hand. "That show will wait. They can live without me for one episode. I'm not about to miss you making the game-winning home run. I've seen you play. You're Barry Bonds, Jackie Robinson. and Sammy Sosa rolled into one. So, I'm not about to miss the last game of the season."

A soft smile spread across his face. "I wish you were my mom."

She squeezed his chin. "I am. Now, finish your one-eyed pancake. I'll be back." Mary kissed him on the top of the head and made her way to Nathan's office with his breakfast.

Nathan was already settled behind his desk, tapping away on his computer. Mary walked over, set his plate down in front of him, and just stood there.

It took a minute, but he finally looked up. "What's up?" he asked.

"You can't spare an hour tomorrow for your son?"

He sighed in frustration. "Mary, don't start that again. My son will be just fine."

"No, he's hurt by this," Mary said.

Nathan leaned back in his chair, obviously getting agitated. "Why are you always trying to start mess with me?" he asked. "All I do is work my butt off. Do you know where I was all day yesterday?" He didn't give her time to reply. "Setting everything in motion."

"Setting what in motion, and what could be more important than your son's last game?" Mary asked.

He glared at her, then finally grinned. "Your defining moment. You need to be grateful to me because I'm about to change your life forever."

Mary folded her arms and glared right back at her husband. It was such hard work being submissive and she just didn't know how much more of it she could tolerate.

"Nathan, what are you talking about?"

He paused, like he needed to make sure his words sank in. "Natasia was thrilled over the papers."

"What papers?"

He sat up in his chair. "I took the custody papers to Natasia."

Mary dropped her arms in shock. "What? For what?"

"To let her know what we were doing, in case they wanted to film it."

"Are you kidding me?" she screamed.

Nathan quickly stood up, which made Mary take a step back. "First of all, watch your tone. You know I don't play that." He relaxed, then continued, "Second, I told you from jump, we need to make you sympathetic to the viewer and we need to make Rachel look like a fool. Do you know how big of an impact this is going to have when she's served with these papers? She's going to go ballistic. And you're going to stand there" — he walked around the desk, stood in front of her, and cupped her cheeks —

"looking angelic, saying all you want is your baby."

Nathan took a step back, proud.

Mary felt sick to her stomach. Whatever disdain she had for Rachel was negated by the fact that the woman had helped her out in a time of need. When Mary was arrested, they were about to put little Lester in foster care, and since Mary herself had grown up in the horrible foster care system, she'd begged Rachel to take him in. Mary had caused major havoc with Rachel, lying by saying the baby was Lester's, so she hadn't expected Rachel to do it. But Rachel put aside all of her hatred and took Lester Jr. into her home as her own. It was bad enough that they were going to take him back, but Mary couldn't fathom that they were going to do it in such a public manner.

"I don't want to do that," Mary said softly. She hoped to appeal to his humane side. If he even had one, because more and more, she was starting to think he didn't.

"Too late, it's done." Nathan walked back around behind his desk. "You'll thank me later. Close the door on your way out." He sat down and started eating his breakfast while he looked at his computer screen, her cue that this conversation was over.

Chapter Twenty-Three:
Rachel

Rachel enjoyed being on neutral ground when it came to filming this show. They weren't at Jasmine and Hosea's church and they weren't at Mary and her bootleg preacher husband's church.

Rev. Moses Woodruff had invited the First Ladies to his church to honor them as part of a women's day program. Of course, he was probably just trying to get some publicity as well, but Rachel didn't care. She was in neutral territory.

Rev. Woodruff took the podium. "Church, we are honored to have in our midst today three fabulous ladies, including the First Lady of our very own American Baptist Coalition."

Jasmine rolled her eyes and Rachel stood and did a small pageant wave. Mary sat on the other side of Jasmine, because even in the Lord's house, Rachel wasn't trying to mask her disgust for that woman.

Reverend Woodruff continued, "I know some of you are wondering about the cameras, but if you read your emails, you'd see we are filming today. We are happy to be part of a new reality show. So, if you have a warrant or you're supposed to be at work, I suggest you move to the back of the church."

Chuckles filled the sanctuary as several people turned to look at the three cameras positioned throughout the church.

"And since it is Women's Day," Rev. Woodruff continued, "what better way to commemorate the event than to have an anointing word from the First Ladies."

Rachel looked around the room. *Were there some other First Ladies here?* Maybe he was talking about his wife, the portly woman who sat in front of them in the gigantic, fruit-filled hat (Who even wore those anymore?)

"Sisters?" Rev. Woodruff said, motioning for them to come up to the pulpit.

Jasmine leaned over to Rachel. "I think he's talking about you."

Rachel raised an eyebrow but didn't move.

"I see Satan is trying to keep you ladies in your seats." He laughed when they still didn't move. "Come on up."

Rachel turned to Jasmine. "He said *ladies.*

Plural. Come on."

"I'm not going up there," Jasmine replied.

"If I have to go, you're going," Rachel whispered, pulling Jasmine's arm.

"And do what?" Jasmine whispered as she stepped out into the aisle behind Rachel.

"I don't know," Rachel whispered back. "Maybe he just wants to give us a word of thanks for being here."

Rachel smiled again as all eyes were on them. She should've known they would have to speak. This was being taped, after all.

Mary stood and made her way out into the aisle as well.

"I'm coming, too," Mary said.

Rachel ignored her and led the way up to the pulpit.

"All right, family. I'm sure they're not as long winded as yours truly, but I can't wait to be blessed with the word from these women." Reverend Woodruff stepped aside and then pointed to the podium for them to step up.

Jasmine folded her arms and planted her feet firmly to let Rachel know she wouldn't be uttering a word. Rachel saw Mary move toward the mike and since she wasn't about to let that harlot steal the show, Rachel stepped forward.

But what word was she supposed to give?

Rachel took a deep breath. She could do this. As First Lady of the ABC, she spoke all the time.

"Greetings, family and friends," Rachel began. "We just want to thank you for opening your doors to us. We know that when you hear 'reality TV,' you might be a little worried, but we want to assure you that we are all about uplifting His holy name."

Rachel glanced back at Jasmine for help.

Jasmine smiled, then mouthed, "You got this."

Ugh. Rachel couldn't believe Jasmine was just gonna leave her out there like this.

She turned back to the crowd. "Our goal is to bring more people to Christ through this show and we hope that you will support it. Thank you."

Rachel was just about to step away from the podium when she noticed Reverend Woodruff sit down and open his bible.

"Well, go on, sister. Tell us what verse you're going to preach from today."

Preach? "You want me to preach?" Rachel yelled before catching herself and saying, "I mean, we thought we were just saying hi."

"Um, no. That's what Women's Day is all about." The reverend looked confused as he glanced out into the audience. That's when

Rachel noticed Natasia, who was standing in the back with a smirk on her face. Now, this all made sense. This heifer thought she was slick. She was trying to make Rachel and Jasmine look like fools.

Rachel turned back to the pastor. "Umm, well, ah, we weren't quite prepared."

"Nonsense," he said. "You're the First Lady of the ABC, you're always prepared with a word."

"Yeah," Jasmine echoed. "You're always prepared, Madame First Lady."

Rachel wanted to hit her in her Botoxed eye. She was standing there smirking, too, like she was enjoying this.

Rev. Woodruff tapped his watch. "We're ready for our word. The Falcons game comes on at two."

Rachel turned back to the podium as the congregation erupted in laughter. She could do this. Between her father and her husband, she'd listened to enough sermons to come up with something on her own.

She began. "The word of God says . . ."

"Tell us what it says, sister!" someone shouted.

I will if you'll give me a chance to talk, Rachel wanted to say. Instead, she just said, "The word of God says be faithful. What is faith? Faith is like taking that first step without seeing the whole staircase." She paused. Why in the world was she drawing a blank? "It's ummm, it's ah, it's about asking not what your country can do for you but what you can do for your country." Jasmine let out a loud cough. Rachel turned around and glared at her. *Was she trying not to laugh?*

Rachel took a deep breath. "We come to you today as women of faith, as women who had been through the storm. We love the Lord!" She looked around at the sea of faces just staring at her. Rachel had never in her life felt nervous. *You can do this,* she told herself. "Yes, we love Him," she continued. "And if loving God is wrong, I don't wanna be right!" That elicited some "amens" and eased Rachel's nerves some.

"And when your faith is wavering, just do what James Fortune says and hold on! Don't let anyone stand in judgment of you and your faith. Tell them you can do it all because it's the God in you! Let them know that what they can't see, is you on your knees, so the next time they ask you, just tell them it's the God in me!" Rachel was getting into it as her voice rose.

"God is faithful, he may not come when you want him, but he'll be there right on time." She held her hands up to the ceiling.

"Don't be ashamed to tell someone to take you to the King, even if you don't have much to bring." She smiled, relaxed, and looked back out at the congregation, many of whom were now looking at her crazy. That made her nerves flare up again.

"So, umm, just stay faithful," she continued, "As Jesus told Paul in the Bible, if you have faith as small as a mustard seed, nothing will be impossible for you."

Jasmine eased up behind her and whispered, "I think he was talking to Abraham."

"Like you know," Rachel hissed.

"Hosea just did a bible study on that," Jasmine replied. "That's how I know."

Rachel pointed to the podium. "Then you take over since you're a biblical scholar."

"Actually, ladies," Reverend Woodruff stepped in, "It was Peter that Jesus was talking to when He said that." He nudged them aside and stepped up to the podium. Rachel wanted to cry tears of relief. "Sometimes you have multiple interpretations of a particular passage, but that's the beauty of the word of God. His message never wavers. . . ."

A deacon stepped up and smiled as he held out his hand. "Ladies, I'll help you back to your seats."

Rachel couldn't hear the rest of the sermon, she was so furious — at Jasmine for leaving her out there like that, and at Reverend Woodruff for interrupting her when she was just getting into it. As she glanced back at the sick smirk on Natasia's face, her anger intensified. Natasia had tried, and almost succeeded, at making her look like a fool.

The next thirty minutes had to be the longest of Rachel's life. She couldn't wait to get out of there and hated that they had agreed to film the Women's Meet and Greet afterward.

" 'What they can't see is you on your knees'? Really, Rachel?" Jasmine laughed as they walked back to the room where the meet and greet was being held.

The cameras were getting set up in the back, so they weren't rolling yet and Jasmine was going all the way in. "You combined the New Testament with R&B, gospel, and presidential addresses," Jasmine said, cracking up.

"I'm just glad you find this amusing," Rachel snapped. "At least I didn't chicken out."

"Whatever. I know a setup when I see one, and I wasn't about to fall for it," she replied.

Rachel glanced around the room for Natasia. She wanted to give that woman a piece of her mind before the cameras clicked back on. "Well, Natasia is your girl and you need to get her in check."

"You're the one talking about it's your show. Check her yourself."

Rachel threw up her hand at Jasmine. "Whatever, Jasmine. Don't talk to me."

"Why, because every day you smile?" Jasmine laughed. "Or because the Lord will never leave nor forsake you, isn't that what it says in the Old Testament?"

"I don't know, you were there when they wrote the Old Testament. You tell me. And while you laughing, you know as much as me, talking about Abraham. He wasn't even alive at the same time as Jesus. Didn't y'all used to date, though?"

"Say what you want, when the show airs, I won't be the one looking like a fool in the pulpit."

"I just got nervous and I was caught off guard," Rachel protested. "Jesus taught in parables and that's what I was trying to do."

"Is that what you were trying to do?"

"Whatever, Jasmine. The godly may trip seven times, but they will get up again." Rachel cocked her head at Jasmine. "Proverbs 24:16. Bam!"

"Well, someone has been on BibleGate way.com," Jasmine quipped.

Rachel rolled her eyes. She was done with Jasmine. All she knew was that fiasco today could not air. She was better than that and her gut told her that wasn't a good look.

Rachel glanced around and spotted Natasia near the door. She was just about to march over there when Sonny announced, "Ladies, stand by. We're about to roll in five."

"I need a minute," Rachel told him.

"No can do," Sonny said, stepping out of the way as Chauncey began filming.

Rachel exhaled in frustration. She'd have to talk to Natasia later. She plastered on a smile as women started filing into the room. Rachel and Jasmine — Mary had disappeared — smiled as they greeted the women.

After a few minutes, Rachel saw Mary standing in a corner looking nervous. Why was she over there? But then, a tall, thin woman in a navy business suit stepped in front of Rachel.

"Are you Rachel Jackson Adams?" she asked.

Rachel stared at her, and out of the corner of her eye, noticed Chauncey zoom in. In fact, two of the cameras were positioned in her direction and the third was pointed at Mary.

"Ma'am, are you Rachel Jackson Adams?" the woman repeated.

Jasmine stepped up next to her. "What's going on?"

Rachel didn't answer her. For some reason, her stomach was in knots. Finally, she said, "I am."

The woman handed Rachel a brown envelope. "You've been served."

Rachel took the envelope, stunned. It seemed the room had grown silent and every eye was on her. Rachel slowly opened the envelope.

Petition for Sole Custody.

"What the . . . ?"

She scanned the document, not fully comprehending what she was seeing, but the words *Mary and Nathan Frazier, sole custody, and Lester Adams, Jr. aka Lewis Adams* stood out.

. . . Petitioners seek full custody of minor child . . .

Suddenly, Rachel forgot she was in church. She forgot cameras were rolling. She forgot all the progress she'd made in her walk with God. And she screamed as she bolted across the room toward Mary.

"I'm going to kill youuuuuuuu!"

Chapter Twenty-Four: Jasmine

Jasmine had no idea what happened. One moment, she was still chuckling inside about Rachel's little *Saturday Night Live* sermon, and the next, she was watching Rachel take flight — almost literally. Rachel leaped across the room with the ferocity of a lion ready to pounce on her prey.

All Jasmine had heard was that woman ask Rachel her name, then say, "You've been served," and seconds after that Rachel was screaming about committing murder.

But Jasmine had no time to think or figure it out. She sprang into action, knocking aside the pastor's wife to get to Rachel. She grabbed the hem of her jacket, right at the moment when Rachel's fist made contact with Mary's jaw.

Jasmine was impressed — Rachel didn't fight like a girl. She had socked Mary with an uppercut that would've had Floyd Mayweather shouting, "Well done." But Jasmine didn't stay around to admire Rachel's handiwork, nor did she stay to see just how much damage she'd done. At least Mary was crying, which meant that Rachel hadn't knocked her out cold.

"I'm gonna kill you," Rachel still hollered, even as Jasmine dragged her away.

Jasmine was breathing hard, using all of her strength to hold on to Rachel as she screamed, and kicked, and squirmed.

"I'm gonna kill you, you two-bit ho!"

Jasmine weaved through the church-women, ducking and dodging past the big hats with brims large enough to cause an eclipse of the sun. No one made a move to help her. They all stood frozen, staring and in shock.

And the cameras . . . still rolled.

"You ain't nothin' but a trailer-park tramp. And you think you're gonna get away with this? You're one dead slut!"

Oh, lawd, Jasmine thought. She had to get Rachel out of there before she incriminated herself any further on national TV.

"Please!" Jasmine felt like she could hardly take another breath as she looked at the women surrounding her, standing like statues. "Bathroom!" She had to yell over Rachel's screams.

At first, no one said a thing, then Reverend

Woodruff's wife, whom Jasmine had just knocked aside, stepped forward. "This way." She pointed toward the hall.

"Let me go," Rachel screeched.

It would've been easier if Jasmine had just knocked Rachel out. But then there would've been two violent acts in one scene. Jasmine shook her head. This was going to be some reality show.

It was a blessing; like Reverend Woodruff's wife said, the bathroom was just two steps across from the room. With her right foot, Jasmine kicked the door open, then tossed Rachel inside.

"What are you doing?" Rachel hollered.

"I'm saving your reputation and your life." She gave Rachel a gentle push, keeping her away from the door. "Get over there!" She pointed toward the corner and it must've been her tone that made Rachel do as she was told.

The bathroom was small, only three stalls. But like Rachel had taught her just a few days ago, Jasmine checked every one. When she was sure they were alone, Jasmine leaned against the door so that no one could get in and Rachel couldn't get out.

Rachel huffed and puffed like she was about to blow the whole church down. "You need to let me out of here 'cause I have a murder to commit."

Jasmine folded her arms. "Really? Haven't you had enough of murder? I mean, that was last year's story."

"I'm not playin', Jasmine, this is serious. Do you know what this is?" she cried before she tossed the papers in the air.

Jasmine caught the papers before they fell to the ground, and then scanned the pages to see what had set Rachel off.

"Oh, my God!" Jasmine exclaimed after a couple of seconds. "Are you serious?"

"Yes!" Rachel said, and then the floodgates opened and tears poured from her. "That gutter-punk trick is trying to take my baby!"

For a moment, Jasmine thought about mentioning that Lewis wasn't really her baby, but this was not the time to get technical. "Can they do this, though? I mean, didn't Mary sign over her rights to you?"

Rachel nodded and wailed, "Yes! But I know plenty of people who've adopted children and then had to fight the biological parents when they changed their minds. Oh, my God! I cannot believe this is happening." She sobbed so hard, she began to choke.

"Okay, Rachel, you've got to calm down,"

Jasmine said as she put her arms around Rachel.

But Rachel jerked away from her embrace. "How can you tell me that?" Her eyes were red from her fury and her fear. "How would you feel if someone tried to take Jacquie or Zaya from you?"

Jasmine stiffened, and that fire in her belly that she felt only at times like these began to rise within her. When Jasmine's fingers curled into fists, Rachel noticed.

She frowned at first, then, covered her mouth with her hand. "Jasmine, that's not what I meant. I wasn't talking about . . . what happened with Jacquie."

Jasmine had to take a couple of deep breaths before she responded, "I know."

"I'm sorry."

"I get what you were saying."

"So, that means you understand, right?" Rachel asked as she grabbed a couple of paper towels from the dispenser.

"I do, Rachel, I really do."

"Lewis is our son," she said before she wiped her tears and then blew her nose. "I can't lose him, I just can't."

"And you won't."

"How can you say that? How can you be so sure?"

Jasmine paused for a moment. She'd just

gone to Rachel asking for her help and Rachel had talked about needing to think about it. She could stand here and do the same to Rachel, but this was different. This was about a child, Rachel's child. And as much as she sometimes, kinda, sorta, really hated Rachel, she sometimes, kinda, sorta, really liked her, too. Jasmine wasn't going to let anyone get away with doing this to her friend.

Her friend.

Yeah, that's what Rachel was to her. It was hard to admit, but they were more friends than they were enemies.

"Jasmine!" Rachel called her name. "I asked you, how can you be so sure that we won't lose Lewis?"

"Because," Jasmine began, "You're Rachel Jackson Adams and I'm Jasmine Cox Larson Bush and together, has anyone ever been able to stop us?"

There was hope in Rachel's eyes when she looked up. "Really? You think we can stop Mary and her pimp-of-a-preacher husband?"

"Come on, Rachel. Look in the mirror." Rachel turned her head and stared at her reflection. "Don't forget who you are, and don't forget who I am. You've never let anyone get away with anything. Hell, you're always trying to go up against me and you know I can beat you anytime, any place."

"You wish," Rachel said, with just a hint of a smile.

"See what I'm talking about?" Jasmine said. "That's the attitude I need from you now. Okay?"

Rachel nodded tentatively, as if she wanted to believe what Jasmine was saying, but she wasn't quite sure.

Jasmine placed her hands on Rachel's shoulders and turned her so that they were face-to-face. "We're gonna take care of this. We're gonna take care of Mary . . . and we're gonna take care of Natasia."

Rachel nodded. "Yeah, Natasia, too," she said, suddenly all in with Jasmine's plan. "So, what are we gonna do?"

"First, we're gonna get you cleaned up," Jasmine said.

"Okay."

"Then we're gonna walk back out there with our heads held high, but we're not gonna talk to anyone!"

"Okay."

"And finally, we're going to see Mae Frances!"

Chapter Twenty-Five: Rachel

Rachel fought back the tears, held her head high, and opened the bathroom door. It helped that Jasmine was by her side, her arm draped through Rachel's. Although she didn't say a word once the door opened, Rachel felt Jasmine's support and it gave her strength. It reminded her that she was a First Lady. It reminded her of how far she'd come.

"Is everything okay?" Reverend Woodruff's wife said as she scurried over to them. She looked genuinely concerned. Rachel saw Natasia standing next to Chauncey, that smirk still across her face. Mary and Nathan stood in a corner. He looked cocky. She looked afraid. She should be because war had been declared and Rachel was ready to battle.

Rachel brushed a strand of hair out of her eyes, composed herself, and said, "Yes, First Lady Woodruff. I'm okay now." Out the corner of her eye, she noticed Chauncey, who had moved in close to her and had the camera pointed directly at her. "My sincerest apologies for the scene that just unfolded. By no means did I intend to mar your Women's Day festivities," Rachel continued, not focusing on the camera. She was sincere in her apology and she didn't want to diminish it by angling for the camera. But she did want Chauncey to get a good shot of her.

"What happened?" the First Lady asked.

"As a mother, I hope that you can understand." Rachel looked over at Mary. "The papers I received were from my costar, Mary Richardson Frazier, and her husband Rev. Nathan Frazier, announcing that she was suing me for sole custody of my son."

"What? How is that even possible?"

Rachel saw that a second camera had moved in and was getting her from another angle. She knew that nothing she said, no threat she made, would keep that fight off the air. So now, she had to clean up the mess she'd made.

Rachel took a deep breath. "A long time ago, my husband had a brief affair with Mary. She came into our church, seduced my husband during a difficult time in our marriage, then proceeded to try and take over my life. Through the grace of God, my husband and I moved past that indiscretion because I was pregnant. Only we found out Mary was pregnant, too."

The room was deathly quiet as everyone stared at Rachel in shock. Several of the women in the room were First Ladies themselves, so Rachel knew they could relate to her pain. The rest were most likely mothers, so Rachel hoped they could relate on that level as well.

"Mary said that she was carrying my husband's child," Rachel continued, to more gasps. Several people directed hate-filled looks in Mary's direction. She cowered behind her husband, who just stood there with that snarky grin on his face.

Reverend Woodruff's wife clutched her pearls in horror as Rachel continued. "Mary tortured me, made my life a living hell, to the point that I went into labor early. It turned out the baby was not my husband's, but when Mary was arrested for being a con artist, my husband and I adopted her child and raised him as our own in an effort to keep him out of the foster care system." Rachel glared at Mary and Nathan. "And now, for the sake of television ratings, they want to rip my child from the only home he has ever known."

By that point, several of the women were in tears as well. Many had gathered around Rachel and Jasmine.

"So, as you can imagine, getting those papers set me off." She glanced over at Jasmine, who nodded her approval. Rachel knew that Jasmine would've preferred that she not say anything, but Rachel couldn't go out like that.

"The devil is a lie!" First Lady Woodruff said, leaning in to hug Rachel. "You just remember that, okay?"

Rachel nodded, dabbing her eyes again. "I will." Jasmine touched her arm, the signal that they needed to go. "Again, my apologies. But now, I must go call my husband and explain to him the battle that we face."

Rev. Woodruff's wife hugged her tightly again. "My, Lord. You poor thing. I will be praying for you."

"We all will," another one of the women said.

"You're better than me," one of the women to the left of Rachel said. "Because I would've done more than just hit her in her jaw."

"I know that's right. She'd be rolling into the ER right about now if she tried to take my kid," another woman said.

Rachel squeezed their hands, comforted

that these women of God weren't judging her.

"Thank you, sisters," Rachel said as Jasmine took her arm and led her toward the door. They passed Nathan and Mary. Mary wouldn't look her in the eyes and that slimeball was grinning like he'd hit the jackpot.

"You won't get my son. Ever," Rachel said, as Jasmine lightly tugged her arm.

Chauncey followed them out the door and it was Jasmine who actually turned to him and said, "Enough."

It must've been the tone of her voice because he stopped, then glanced back at Natasia, who had walked out as well. Jasmine scowled at Natasia and repeated, "I said, enough."

Natasia did a small eye roll but gave Chauncey the cue to stop filming, which he did.

Rachel didn't know how she made it over to the waiting town car, but she did. Jasmine helped her into the car and the door had barely closed before she released another river of tears.

"Come on," Jasmine said, sliding in the other side. "You're better than this. Don't let them do this. You know it's all for the show. They will not get your child."

"They have money, too. What if they hire

top-notch lawyers?"

"But they don't have Mae Frances."

Rachel sniffed. As much as she despised that old woman, if anyone could fix this, Mae Frances could.

"Didn't you just get through preaching about faith?" Jasmine asked, a small smile across her face.

Rachel returned her smile.

"Heed your own words," Jasmine continued. "What's impossible for man, is possible with God. And Mae Frances."

Rachel finally managed a small chuckle. "I missed that addendum to the Bible."

"It's not in there, but it should be." Jasmine moved toward the door. "I'm going to go talk to Mae Frances now. She's still not feeling well, but I'm going to bring her up to speed. You go home, you talk to Lester, and then you meet me at my place at eight o'clock."

Just then, Mary and Nathan walked outside. He had the nerve to look jovial as he dragged Mary toward their car.

"You should've let me kill her." Rachel's hand reached for the door. "You know what? I'm just going to go talk to her."

Jasmine stopped her. "No, you're not. You're going to go home, talk to your husband, then meet me at eight o'clock. Okay?"

Rachel slowly let her hand fall off the door handle. "Fine."

"Home, Rachel."

"I said, okay."

They stared at each other for a moment, then Jasmine did the unexpected, and reached over and hugged Rachel. "Everything is going to be fine."

Jasmine had just opened the car door when Rachel added, "I'm sorry I didn't immediately help with Natasia."

Jasmine smiled. "It's okay. You're going to help now."

"I am," Rachel said. "We're going to help each other."

Jasmine exited and Rachel sat for a minute. Finally, the driver said, "Where to?"

Rachel leaned back against the plush leather seat. One part of her wanted to follow Nathan and Mary and have the driver run them off the road or into the path of an oncoming eighteen-wheeler, but instead she simply said, "You can take me home."

On the drive to her house, Rachel called her husband. Initially, he was shocked. Then hurt. And when he cried, she cried. They talked the whole ride home, with him trying to assure her that everything would be all right. But it was the shakiness in his voice that told her he wasn't so sure.

That's why when the driver dropped Rachel off at home, instead of going inside, Rachel pulled out her car keys, got into her leased Range Rover, and pulled out of the driveway. Yes, she had promised Jasmine she was going home . . . and she would, right after she had a serious face-to-face with Mary Richardson Frazier.

CHAPTER TWENTY-SIX:
MARY

That was a complete and utter disaster.

Mary nursed her jaw, still dumbfounded that Rachel had hit her. She knew Rachel could be ghetto, but she was a First Lady, after all. Mary assumed that Rachel would've taken that into account before getting violent. But Rachel had thrown all decorum to the wind and charged her like a raging bull.

Mary cut her eyes at her husband. He was on his cell phone, yapping away, telling one of his friends what had just happened. That bastard hadn't even asked if she was okay.

"Man, you should've seen the look on that woman's face when they gave her the papers. . . . Oh, you'll see it. It will probably be the number one YouTube clip once it airs." He laughed hard. "I love it!"

Mary glared at her husband and he finally noticed. "Yo, Deacon, let me call you back."

Nathan pressed the button to end the call,

then turned to face Mary. "What is your problem?"

Mary had been completely against serving those papers publicly, but Nathan had been adamant that they needed to do it this way. "Rachel will lose it and it will elicit more sympathy for you," he had said. Those women surrounding Rachel like she was their wronged daughter didn't seem to have an ounce of sympathy for Mary. If anything, she now felt like some kind of pariah.

"I just think this whole thing was unnecessary," she admitted.

"That's why I do the thinking in this relationship," he casually replied.

Mary noticed the driver pulling up in front of their home. "I thought we were going to get Alvin."

"Nah, we can just get him from my mom tomorrow." Nathan got out of the car and headed up the walkway, not bothering to help her out.

Mary sighed, then followed him inside. Nathan was already at the refrigerator getting a beer. That was another thing she wasn't feeling. She knew ministers drank occasionally, but Nathan drank a six pack a day. If he was such a man of God, shouldn't he limit his beer intake?

She decided against addressing the beer

issue — it's not like he listened any of the other times she said anything about it. "If we're a family now, Alvin doesn't need to be living with your parents. He hates it over there."

Nathan closed the refrigerator, then popped the top on his beer. "Oh, so now you're worried about being a family?" He took a swig. "You weren't worried when Rachel was being served."

Mary knew that was coming. He'd wanted to make that into a major show and she had flat-out refused. "What did you want me to do, Nathan?"

"I wanted you to do what we talked about. You were supposed to be right there next to her so you could've been in the shot together," he replied. "It's bad enough they didn't serve her during the actual church service, but you messed the plan all the way up."

She couldn't look him in the eyes. Nathan would be livid to learn that she had actually asked the process server to come during the reception. What they were doing was bad enough. She just couldn't see having the server walk up into the sanctuary and hand Rachel those papers.

"It's just wrong to make such a spectacle of someone's heartache," she said.

"I don't get you," Nathan said, leaning against the refrigerator. "When I met you, you were a washed-up criminal doing hard time."

"And you were the one that helped me turn my life around," she said. "You were the one that helped me find God. Your whole ministry."

He waved her off. "Whatever, Mary. If I had known you were going to turn into Dolly Do-Right, I would've left you in the pen."

That comment stung, but Mary was tired of arguing. "You could at least ask if I'm okay," she finally said.

"Please. That little punch couldn't have done you any harm." He laughed. "Although it did look like it hurt. If you could've seen if from my vantage point, whew! She knocked you out like Tyson did Holyfield."

"Glad you can find some humor in all of this." Mary folded her arms and turned her back to him.

"Come on, babe. Don't be mad." Nathan eased up behind her and wrapped his arms around her waist. "When you have your son back and we're all one big happy family and Pleasant City's membership is through the roof to the point that we have to build another church, then you'll thank me."

Mary doubted that but she didn't feel like discussing this with him anymore.

"I'm going to go work on Sunday's sermon," he said. "Maybe I'll preach on how sons belong with their mothers. That's a good idea, don't you think?"

She nodded. "Yes, it's a great idea." She would say anything just to get him to leave.

Nathan kissed her on the cheek — the sore one — and she grimaced from the pain and the contempt that was starting to fill her heart.

Mary made her way over to a drawer, pulled out a baggie, and filled it with ice. She used to think that her ex-boyfriend Craig, her son's real father, was bad. He was a serial con artist. If there was a scam to be run, Craig was the man to do it. His hustle and the life of crime they were leading had gotten on her nerves and they'd broken up. But she was starting to think that Nathan made Craig look good. At least Craig never claimed to be a man of God. At least Craig never put his hands on her.

She shook off thoughts of her ex. She hadn't talked to him since the day she testified against him in court.

Mary had just put the ice pack on her cheek when her cell phone rang. She pulled it out and frowned at the number she didn't recognize.

"Hello," she answered.

"Mary?"

Her heart raced at the sound of Lester's voice.

"Yes?" she said, lowering her voice as she opened the screen door and stepped out onto the back porch.

"It's Lester."

Mary's eyes darted over her shoulder. She knew she should just hang up, but her heart raced at the sound of Lester's voice. Mary didn't know if it was fear, or the fact that deep down, she knew that she still loved this man.

"I know who it is," she said. "What's going on?"

"You tell me," Lester replied. "Are you seriously trying to take Lester Jr.?"

The fact that he'd used her son's real name made her want to cry. "I'm so sorry."

"How could you do this?"

His tone wasn't accusatory or demeaning. That's the way Lester had always been with her. She'd been hired to seduce him and she'd fallen head over heels in love because he was the first man to ever make her feel worthy.

"It's just . . . Nathan . . . he's the one, he

thinks — he thinks my son belongs with us," Mary stammered.

"This is devastating to Rachel. To me," Lester continued. "Why are you doing it?"

"I don't mean to hurt you, Lester. I —" Mary turned around and dropped the phone at the sight of her husband standing right in front of her, glaring at her through the screen door.

Nathan didn't say a word as he opened the door, stepped out onto the porch, and picked up the phone. "Rev. Adams, how are you today?" he asked as he walked back into the kitchen. "Yes, I understand that, but in the future, if you have any correspondence whatsoever, you need to talk to our attorney. And if you can't get our attorney, you need to talk to me. What you *won't* be doing is talking to my wife. Got that? You have a blessed day." He hung up the phone and turned and glared at Mary, who had followed him back inside.

"I-I'm sorry. H-he just call —" Before she could get the word out, she felt the sting of the back of Nathan's hand across the same cheek where Rachel had just cold-cocked her.

"You're going to stand in my house and talk to another man?" he bellowed. "Have you lost your mind?"

Mary grabbed her face and slid to the floor. "I'm sorry," she cried.

"I don't want to hear your tired apologies." He kicked her. As his wingtipped shoe connected with her side, she let out an agonizing scream. "Don't you ever disrespect me in my own house."

"Y-you said you wouldn't ever put your hands on me again," she sobbed.

"That's before I knew you'd be talking to your ex in my kitchen." He paced back and forth across the kitchen, his fury on full blaze.

"I'm doing all of this for you, and this is how you repay me?" Nathan reached down, picked her up by her collar, and slammed her against the wall. "I should've left you on the dirty jailhouse steps where I found your trailer-park ass. The next time I come in here and find you talking to another man, will be your last time." He pushed his forearm against her throat. Mary thought she was going to black out. "Don't let the bible talk fool you. In my former life, I was a thug and I will fu—" He caught himself, then slowly lowered her as he adjusted her blouse. "See how you make me act. Whew!" He blew a tight breath. "Disrespect me again and see what happens." He tossed Mary to the floor like she was a rag doll.

She lay there weeping as she heard those awful wingtipped shoes click away. She was in a lot of pain, but she knew she needed to get up. She had to get dinner started before he acted an even bigger fool.

Mary reached up to grab the counter and pull herself up. That's when she noticed the figure at the screen door. Staring at her from the other side, her mouth hanging open in shock, was Rachel Jackson Adams.

CHAPTER TWENTY-SEVEN: JASMINE

"Darlin', are you still sure about this?" Hosea asked her.

With the phone pressed to her ear, Jasmine rolled her eyes. Maybe she shouldn't have told Hosea what was going on. "Definitely; the majority of the show has been good." That's what she said aloud. But inside, scenes where she and Rachel or Rachel and Mary had gotten into it scrolled through her mind. If this show wasn't edited right, *First Ladies* could end up looking as ratchet as any of the other reality shows. But she kept on trying to convince Hosea. "And you can't blame the show for what Mary and that SOB did to Rachel and Lester."

"Jasmine!"

"What?"

"Even though I don't approve of what Reverend Frazier did, that language . . ."

"What? All I said was SOB. That stands

for . . . son of a butcher. Yeah, that's what it stands for. I heard somewhere that Reverend Frazier's father was a butcher."

"Yeah, okay. But I have to agree with you; what the Fraziers did was foul. I'll give Lester a call after this meeting this afternoon."

"I know he'll be glad to hear from you. Anyway, enough about the show. I miss you. And so do Jacquie and Zaya."

He chuckled. "I just left this morning."

"I know, but it's been hours already."

"Well, you may miss me, but I don't think our children do. Are they going to be out all day?"

Even though Hosea couldn't see her, she nodded. "Mrs. Sloss said that she'll have them back from the CNN Center around six or so. We'll call you as soon as they get home, okay?"

"Okay, darlin'. Well, don't worry about Rachel and Lester. Just pray. God's gonna work it out."

With a final "I love you," Jasmine hung up and thought about Hosea's last words. *God's gonna work it out.*

Jasmine had no doubt about that; she was going to make sure that God worked it out exactly the way she wanted.

Now that she'd checked in with Hosea, it

was time to put the plan into action. First up, Mae Frances — she had to get her friend on board.

But just as Jasmine put her foot on the first step to go upstairs, there was a pounding on her front door.

Then, "Jasmine!" More pounding. "Jasmine!"

"What in the world?" Jasmine whispered as she turned around and rushed to the door.

She pulled it open and Rachel stumbled inside, breathing hard as if she had run all the way to Jasmine's house. But when Jasmine peeked over Rachel's shoulder, she saw her car. So it wasn't physical exertion that had Rachel hyperventilating.

"Rachel! What happened?"

"Oh, my God! Oh, my God!" she exclaimed, her hand pressed to her chest. "You're not going to believe what just happened."

"Come in here. Sit down," Jasmine said, leading her to the living room. It took a few seconds for Rachel's breathing to slow down so that she could speak. "Do you want some water or something?"

Still heaving, Rachel shook her head.

"What in the world is going on?"

"I just saw . . . Mary . . ."

Jasmine frowned. "She came to your house?"

"No . . . at her house . . . and . . ."

Jasmine groaned. "Don't tell me you went over there. I told you to go home."

"I know . . . I know . . . I did and I was going to stay at my place, but I got to thinking . . . and so, I went over there and . . ."

"You hit her again?" Jasmine moaned. She could imagine it. Rachel had probably given Mary a ghetto-girl beat down. If Mary was still alive, she might not ever be able to walk or talk again.

Rachel shook her head. "I didn't hit her."

"Good!" Jasmine breathed.

"But that punk-preacher that she calls her husband did."

An extra moment passed and Jasmine said, "What?"

Rachel nodded. "I was just going to go over there to reason with her. Talk to her face-to-face. But you should see her face now."

"You saw him beating her? What happened?"

"Well . . . wait." Rachel paused and looked around. "Where's Mae Frances? I might as well tell both of you at the same time."

"She's up in her room. I haven't even had a chance to tell her that we need to talk to her. I came home, changed my clothes, called Hosea, and I was just going to see Mae Frances now. 'Cause you weren't supposed to be here for another" — Jasmine glanced at her watch — "six hours, remember?"

"I know, I know. But after I saw Nathan beating Mary down like that . . ." Rachel shook her head and shuddered. "I got out of there quick. Mary saw me, but . . ." Rachel shuddered.

Jasmine grabbed her hand and pulled her up from the sofa. "Come on," she said.

With Jasmine leading the way, they dashed up the stairs and without even knocking, Jasmine burst into Mae Frances's bedroom.

"Mae Frances," Jasmine shouted.

Like most times when Jasmine had entered her room in the past weeks, the blinds were closed, darkening the room, and Mae Frances was hidden beneath a boatload of blankets.

"Is she asleep?" Rachel asked as she tiptoed behind Jasmine.

Jasmine stood at the side of Mae Frances's bed, peeked down at her, then did what she always did . . . she shook her.

"Mae Frances, are you awake?" She paused for a moment, then shook her and called out her name again. "Are you awake?"

This time, the woman stirred, lifted her head, and opened her eyes slowly. She focused first on Jasmine, then on Rachel standing right behind her. And with a groan that filled the silence in the room, she dropped her head back onto the pillow.

"I'm so glad you're awake," Jasmine said as she opened the blinds, then bounced onto the edge of the bed.

"I'm not awake!" Mae Frances growled.

"Yes, you are. And you have to hear what's going on."

"I'm sick, Jasmine Larson." Mae Frances covered her head with her pillow.

"Stop claiming that! The doctor said you're getting better. And you have to hear this, 'cause if you find out about this when you get better, you're gonna be mad at me for not having told you now."

"I don't want to hear nothin'! I want to sleep."

"Maybe we should go," Rachel whispered to Jasmine. "She's sick. And what did you say was wrong with her?" Rachel rubbed her hands over her arms as if she was suddenly cold. "She doesn't have some kind of infectious, third-world disease, does she?" she asked as she looked around the room.

"What?" Jasmine scrunched up her face. "Don't be so dramatic. It's nothing like that." Then, Jasmine mouthed, "Watch this." She cleared her throat and said, "Okay, Mae Frances, we'll leave you alone. Sorry to bother you. Just thought that you'd want to hear how Nathan Frazier is beating the crap out of his wife."

Mae Frances's head popped right up. "Nathan Frazier?" she asked. "You mean Mary's husband?"

Jasmine nodded slowly.

It took some effort, but Mae Frances rolled over, pushed herself up, then, as she leaned back against the headboard, she looked from Jasmine to Rachel with bleary eyes. "Start talking."

"Okay," Jasmine began, then she filled in Mae Frances on the earlier events of the day, from the Women's Day service, to Rachel being served with the papers, and how Rachel had knocked Mary to the floor with a single punch.

Mae Frances turned her eyes to Rachel and with just a little bit of a smile, told her that she was impressed.

Rachel smiled a little, too, as she began her story, "I was just so mad that I went right over there after we left that church. I wasn't going to do anything. I was just going to tell her that she and her gorilla-husband didn't want this fight. I was just gonna let her know that Lester and I were not giving up Lewis, and —"

Mae Frances released a long sigh. "Can you just get to the part where she got beat up?"

"I'm getting there," she snapped. When Mae Frances raised one eyebrow, Rachel softened, suddenly remembering that she needed this woman's help. "Anyway, when I got there, I didn't know what to do. I thought about walking up to the front door, but then I was thinking that her husband might answer and then I wouldn't get anywhere. So, I snuck around to the back —"

"Oh, lawd," Jasmine said, shaking her head.

"I was just trying to figure it out. I was thinking that if they were anything like me and Lester, Mary would be in the kitchen getting dinner ready and that phony preacher would be in his bedroom changing his clothes or in the family room watching baseball or something."

Motioning with her hands, Mae Frances asked, as if she was trying to rush the story along, "Is that when you saw her getting beat down?"

"No. At first, he was just screaming about her talking to another man while she was in

315

his house."

"What?" Jasmine and Mae Frances said at the same time.

"She's cheating on him?" Jasmine asked.

"I guess so, 'cause he went in on her. He knocked her to the ground, then kicked her while she was down."

"Dang!" Jasmine and Mae Frances sang together.

"Then he picked her up and choked her."

"Really?" Jasmine said with a smirk. She wondered if Rachel was telling the truth as the story got more outrageous.

"Yes, really. You saw how I was when I first got here. It was something. He cursed her and told her that if she ever disrespected him again, she'd come up missing!" Rachel embellished.

"Wow!" Jasmine said.

"Yeah, wow! But the good news is that I can use this against Mary," Rachel said.

"Use it for what?" Mae Frances asked.

"That's why we needed to talk to you," Jasmine told her. "We need a plan to stop Mary and Nathan from going to court and getting Lewis . . . and at the same time, we need to stop Natasia, too."

"Natasia?" Mae Frances frowned and crossed her arms. "What does she have to do with this?"

"You know she set this whole thing up," Rachel said.

"And she's still after Hosea," Jasmine said.

Mae Frances pointed her finger in the air. "You know, while I was lying here, I kept having a dream about her. She's not a problem, Jasmine Larson. I don't know why, but she can't get Preacher Man."

"What? You're having visions now?"

"I don't know what you call it, but you know that I know everything. She's not going to get him," Mae Frances said sternly.

"Well, that's not gonna stop her from trying," Rachel piped in. When Jasmine and Mae Frances turned to her, Rachel kept on, " 'Cause she came to me looking for my help to get to Hosea."

"What? What did she say and why didn't you tell me?"

"I was going to, but then all this happened."

"So, she told you that she was going after Hosea?"

"Not in those exact words."

"Well, what did she say? What did she want you to do?"

"I don't know; we didn't get that far 'cause I told her I wasn't going to do anything against you. I told her to get her own man," Rachel said, snaking her neck with each word.

Jasmine grinned and Mae Frances rolled her eyes.

"I guess this makes y'all friends again," the woman said, pointing to the two of them.

"We were always friends," Jasmine said.

"That's not what you told me," Mae Frances exclaimed. "When you found out that she was doing this reality show, you called her a —"

"Never mind, never mind," Jasmine talked over Mae Frances. "The only thing that matters is what's going on right now and what're we gonna do about it."

Rachel stared at Jasmine for an extra moment. As if she was trying to decide if she should question Mae Frances more about what Jasmine had said, or if she should just get on with what she'd come to Jasmine's house to do.

Her son won out. "Well, like I said," Rachel began, "I think we can use this against Mary and Nathan. Mary can't take care of herself, how can she take care of my son? It would be great if we could get Nathan beating her on camera."

"No," Jasmine said. She stood and paced from one end of the bed to the other. "That'll never happen. That would be too controversial for the show and Natasia ain't having that. Plus, she's only interested in making you and me look bad."

"Well, if we can't get it on the show, maybe we can get some pictures of Nathan actually hitting her."

"Oh, that would be good," Jasmine said.

"What're y'all gonna do?" Mae Frances jumped in. "Hide out in their bushes?"

"You say that as if we haven't done it before," Jasmine said. "Remember, we handled Chicago."

"Ha! Y'all would still be in Chicago if I hadn't gone there and rescued you," Mae Frances boasted. "Anyway, y'all are going about this the wrong way. You wanna go after Mary, but she's the victim. If this comes out, people will feel more sorry for her and they might want to give Mary her child as a consolation prize for losing the husband lottery. You don't want her to come out looking like the heroine. Just go after her husband."

"That's what I'm saying. If we show how he's abusing —"

Mae Frances raised her hand, stopping Rachel. "It will just be your word against his about the abuse. 'Cause Mary ain't never gonna tell anyone and I'm sure he hits her where he'll leave very little physical evidence. What you need to do is set him up in another situation where there are witnesses . . . more than just the two of you," she said, jutting her chin toward Rachel and then Jasmine.

Rachel glanced at Jasmine and when she shrugged, Rachel asked, "How are we gonna do that?"

Mae Frances tilted her head. "I don't know. I gave you what I got, and now I'm tired," she said, as she slowly slipped down in her bed. "Just set him up and bring him down."

"Wait, Mae Frances, don't go back to sleep yet . . . what about Natasia? I have to get rid of her, too."

Mae Frances just shook her head. "I can't worry about this right now. I'm too sick."

"So, what am I supposed to do?" Jasmine whined.

"Do the same thing. Set her up, set him up. Bring her down, bring him down. Now, y'all get on out of my room!"

When Mae Frances closed her eyes, Jasmine knew she was done . . . at least for now. She sighed. They needed Mae Frances, because when she got involved, life got handled.

"Come on," Rachel said. This time, she led Jasmine out of the room and they didn't exchange another word until they were settled once again in the living room.

"Well, that wasn't much help," Rachel pouted.

"I don't know," Jasmine said. "Mae Frances never wastes words or advice. She knows what she's talking about. We've got to set them up."

"How?"

"The first thing we need is information. On Natasia and Nathan. We have to find out something about them. Something they're hiding. Something they wouldn't want anyone to know."

Rachel nodded. "Yeah, everybody has something in their closet. Especially Nathan. The way he was acting this afternoon . . ." She shook her head as if she was remembering the scene that played out in front of her. "But Natasia, didn't you already research her?"

"Yeah, I mean, I didn't, but Mae Frances did a few years back."

"A few years back?" Rachel sucked her teeth. "Girl, please. People's lives change by the day." She gave Jasmine a sideways glance. "You must not know nothin' 'bout snoopin'."

"Well, what do you know?"

Rachel twisted her lips, grabbed her purse,

and stood up. "Everything I know about you I got from snoopin' . . . and I know a lot."

Jasmine frowned.

"I got this," Rachel said. "This is what we'll do. I'll get as much information on those two hussies as possible. And if I don't find anything, I'll make something up. While I'm doing that, you figure out what we're gonna do with the information once I get it all."

"Okay," Jasmine said softly as she led Rachel to the door. Before she opened it, she stopped, turned around, and faced her. "What do you know about me?"

Rachel sighed. "Nothing, I was just saying that. Dang! You take everything so seriously. I'll call you later." She shook her head as she bounced down the front steps with a different attitude leaving than she'd had coming in.

Jasmine stood at the door and watched as Rachel slid into her Range Rover, then circled the driveway and rode away.

She stood there and wondered, what Rachel meant. What did Rachel know about her? But then she closed the door. It really didn't matter. Rachel was on her side . . . at least for now. All Jasmine needed to be concerned about was what were they going to do with the information Rachel found —

or made up. It was all about bringing Natasia Redding and Nathan Frazier down!

CHAPTER TWENTY-EIGHT: NATASIA

As Natasia put her key into the door of her apartment, she had only one thought — it had been a helluva wonderful day.

"I'm a genius," she whispered to herself as she stepped inside the living room. With a few more steps, she was in the bedroom and she tossed her purse and the portfolio she carried onto the bed.

"I'm a genius," she repeated, though if she were honest, she knew that all the credit didn't belong to her. Nathan Frazier was the mastermind behind this wonderful day.

When Nathan suggested that they have Rachel served at the Women's Day event, Natasia thought that was brilliant. She had already planned to set Rachel up to look like a fool by having her preach without any advance notice. She was sure Rachel couldn't find Genesis in the Bible, so there was no way she'd be able to deliver a substantive message without a lot of preparation and coaching. But Nathan's suggestion had made Rachel look like a fool and a thug.

Rachel Jackson Adams behaved exactly the way Natasia had expected. A hood rat was a hood rat no matter how many discount designer clothes she bought from T.J. Maxx. What Rachel had done when she was served those papers today proved that theory. Natasia couldn't have scripted it better.

It was true that when the show first began, she didn't want any fighting. But then, with the way Rachel and Jasmine and Mary behaved, it was inevitable. She would never allow fighting every week, but this thing that happened today . . . this was going to be one of the scenes they'd use in the promotional trailer. With one First Lady knocking out another in the series teaser, the first episode was going to score record ratings for OWN.

Natasia pumped her fist in the air, then flopped down onto her bed. She was exhausted. Today, even though things had gone great, her aches and pains were taking their toll. She truly needed to rest. Especially since today had been stressful, though filled with anxiety really described it better.

When the processor hadn't shown up during the service, Natasia had tried her best not to fret, but it had been difficult. At least it had all worked out and for the rest of the afternoon, she'd be able to take it easy.

As she approached her closet, Natasia's thoughts had already moved away from this afternoon. She unbuttoned her dress and stepped out of it. She took her focus back to where it needed to be — on Hosea, now that she had put Rachel in her place.

Even though she had spoken with him every day since her doctor's appointment, Hosea had not repeated what he'd said in Dr. Ginsberg's office. Maybe he just needed a little push, a little encouragement to bring that up again.

Natasia slipped into a T-shirt and a pair of leggings, then grabbed her iPad and cell phone from her purse. She lay back against the headboard, opened the Scrabble app, set it to play against the computer, then she pressed Hosea's name on her phone.

Usually he picked up on the first ring, but tonight it rang a few times. She exhaled when she heard, "Hello?"

Right away, she pushed tears into her eyes and her voice. "Hosea!"

"Natasia, what's wrong?"

"Nothing . . . I didn't want to bother you."

"You're not bothering me. What's wrong?"

She sniffed back fake tears as she studied the letters on the Scrabble board, then set L-I-E-S on the tiles.

"Natasia!"

"I'm sorry, I just . . . I didn't get good news from the doctor."

"Doctor Ginsberg? You saw him today?"

"No, I didn't, but he called me about my tests . . . and it's not good." She paused as the computer placed H-O-P-E on the board. Then, she said, "The doctor said there's not much hope."

"What does that mean?"

"He didn't want to say it, I think. . . ." She placed the letters C-H-E-A-T on the tiles. "I think he's trying to tell me that my time is running out."

"I'm shocked. He sounded so positive when we saw him."

Natasia paused. She had to make sure that Hosea wouldn't call the doctor, though because of privacy, she doubted the doctor would speak to Hosea without her since they weren't married. "He is still positive and hopeful. And you know I'm not giving up, right?" She pushed the Scrabble board aside. "But it's hard."

"I know it is, darlin'," he said.

Natasia sat up and grinned. For the years when they were together, she'd melt whenever he called her that. That term of endearment was saved for only the people whom Hosea loved.

She wondered if he noticed, but then she thought he probably didn't. That was even better — he'd called her "darlin' " subconsciously.

She took a breath and took herself back into her role. "I'm just so afraid that I'll be thinking about this all night and I won't sleep, which will just make everything worse."

"I think you should stop working, Natasia. Jasmine told me what happened this afternoon . . ."

She inhaled a quick breath. Had Jasmine blamed it on her?

". . . and I think it's all too stressful for you," he finished.

She exhaled. "You may be right," she said. "I just don't know what to do." Then she sighed loudly. "Do you think, would you mind coming over?" Before he could answer, she rushed her explanation, "I'm only asking 'cause I don't have anyone else but you to talk to, and to help me get through this news that I got today."

"Natasia," he said, "you don't have to explain every time you ask me for something."

"I just don't want you to think . . . or Jasmine to think . . ."

"We're fine. You're fine. But I can't come over."

What? He had never turned her down before.

"I'm in New York," he explained.

"Oh." The emotion he heard in her voice was real this time. She'd just put on the show of her life, all for nothing.

"But," he added, "I'll be back in the morning and I'll come to see you before I go home."

That made her smile. He'd come to see her before he went to his wife? "Really?" she said.

"Definitely. I just want you to rest tonight."

"I'll try," she said, putting the sadness right back into her voice.

"Well, maybe I could help you with that."

Her smile was wider this time. What was he going to do? Would he really consider flying back tonight?

"If you can't sleep," he said, "call me and we'll talk. I'm sure I'll bore you so much you'll fall right off to sleep."

She laughed just a little. "That's one thing you can never do. You can never bore me."

"We'll see. So, call me, if you need me, okay?"

I always need you. "I will."

"And Natasia," he paused, "I'm praying for you."

"I know that. Thank you."

She hung up without saying anything more. She'd done enough. With what she'd just told him, Hosea was close to being ready to do all of her bidding.

She kicked her feet in the air and giggled before she settled down. And she thought about Hosea's wife. He hadn't mentioned Jasmine, and Jasmine hadn't said anything else to her about staying away from Hosea. That meant that he probably hadn't told Jasmine anything, not about her illness, not about her doctor's visit, not about the time they were spending together.

That was better, really. Sneaking around was always better. And when the time was right, she'd make sure that Jasmine found out that Hosea was spending all of this time with her.

That giddy feeling spread through her once again, and Natasia jumped up from the bed with more energy than she'd had in a long time. She needed to give Melinda a call, let her know what had happened on the set today before she heard the news from someone else. And she wanted to do that before the night housekeeping staff came into her apartment.

She took two steps away from her bed and paused. Her eyes widened and before she hit the ground, her world had already faded to black.

CHAPTER TWENTY-NINE: RACHEL

Rachel's mind had been churning since she'd left Jasmine. She had no clue how she would get to Natasia, but she was determined to help Jasmine bring Natasia down. She wanted to do this not just because Jasmine had helped her, but now her vendetta against Natasia was personal. The process server, the impromptu sermon, even the fight . . . none of that would've happened without Natasia's stamp of approval.

And now, Natasia was about to learn, like so many others, that Rachel was not the one to be messed with.

Rachel navigated her Range Rover onto Interstate 75. Lester's flight would arrive first thing in the morning, and Rachel knew that once he found out about the fight — which she conveniently had not told him about — he'd be ready to pull the plug on her reality TV debut and focus all of her attention on fighting for their son.

But Rachel was starting to feel that maybe Jasmine was right. Maybe the petition for sole custody was all for show and nothing would ever come of it. But regardless, she knew her fighting on national TV would not help her cause, so she needed to make sure that clip didn't air. She'd handle that first, then she would deal with Natasia.

Rachel reached into her hobo bag and grabbed her cell phone. She kept one hand focused on the steering wheel while the other scrolled through the phone until she found the number she was looking for.

"Hey, Rachel," Melinda said, picking up her phone on the second ring. "Make it quick. I'm about to board my plane."

"Hey, Melinda. Just wanted to see if you had heard what happened on set today."

The phone went silent, as though Melinda had stopped moving. "No. What happened on set today?"

"Well, there was a little altercation . . ."

"What? Somebody got into a fight?"

"It wasn't really a fight, but I did hit Mary in the jaw." Rachel debated telling her about what she'd later seen at Mary's house, but she decided she needed to keep that ammunition for when she really needed it. Part of her felt sorry for Mary, but if she wanted to stay in an abusive relationship, that was on her.

"Rachel," Melinda sighed.

Rachel used to really like Melinda, but now she didn't trust her as far as she could hear her. And quiet as it was kept, Rachel wouldn't be surprised if Melinda knew all about Natasia's plans. Melinda definitely struck Rachel as someone who would sacrifice her first child for ratings.

"Well, I was just calling to tell you that I don't want the altercation aired," Rachel continued. Silence filled the phone again.

"Hello, did you hear me?" Rachel repeated.

"Rachel, that's out of my hands," Melinda finally said. "You need to talk to Natasia about that."

"My contract says —"

"I am well aware of what your contract says," she replied, interrupting Rachel. "I'm the one you went back and forth to make that happen. But you know at the end of the day, the executive producer has final say. You have some creative control, but the EP has the final say."

What good was creative control if she couldn't call any shots? "I guess I need to just call Oprah myself," Rachel snapped.

"Yeah, Rachel, how about you do that?"

Melinda said, her voice full of sarcasm. "I'm sure Oprah will side with you after she finds out that yet again, you showed your tail."

Melinda had a point there. The last time Rachel had been in front of Oprah, the Big O had to cancel her show behind Rachel and Jasmine's drama. No, she needed to keep Oprah out of this.

"Look, I have to board my plane. All I can tell you is, try to appeal to Natasia," Melinda said, and Rachel couldn't help but feel her friend was blowing her off.

"Fine, I'll talk to Natasia," Rachel said, feeling hopeless. She had worked so hard to build up her image as a First Lady. She'd made strides not only with her own church, but as the First Lady of the ABC. Her dad would be so disappointed. Their members at Zion Hill back in Houston would be disappointed, and Rachel knew Lester was not going to be happy, especially since he hadn't wanted her to do the show in the first place.

Unfortunately, Natasia was the key. Rachel had to convince that battle axe not to air the show. How was she supposed to do that, and try to bring her down at the same time?

Suddenly, an idea hit Rachel. Maybe she could pretend she was going to help Natasia with whatever cockamamie plan she had to steal Hosea. Once Natasia thought Rachel was on her side, she'd nix the video, then maybe Rachel could get close enough to find some information they could use to get Natasia fired. It was a win-win for both Rachel and Jasmine.

Rachel smiled, proud of herself as she grabbed her phone and dialed Melinda's Atlanta office.

"This is Margaret Sims, assistant to Melinda Lawson," the recording said. "I am out of the office but please leave a message and I will return your call on the next business day. If you need to get in touch with me immediately, please call 770-443-7645."

Rachel memorized the number, hung up, then punched in the ten digits.

"Hi, Margaret," she said when the young administrative assistant answered. "It's Rachel Jackson Adams. Melinda is running to catch a flight."

"I know, she's on her way back." Margaret sounded like she wondered why Rachel was regurgitating her boss's schedule.

"Yes, and she asked me to get in touch with you and have you give me Natasia Redding's address. We have a meeting and I don't know what I did with her address."

Margaret was quiet for a minute, then

said, "Oooh, I don't know if I'm supposed to be giving out that information."

"Really, Margaret?" Rachel said, making sure she sounded super irritated. "You can call Melinda yourself."

"But I thought she was getting on the plane?"

"She is." Rachel paused. "Then, fine. Don't give me the address and when Oprah asks why I missed our very important meeting, I'll say because Margaret wouldn't give me the address like her boss asked her to."

Rachel could hear the fear through the phone. "You're right. I'm sorry. I'm just being careful," she quickly said.

Rachel heard some ruffling of papers and Melinda rattled off the address.

"I'll make sure and tell Melinda you did a good job. You're a doll." She disconnected the call.

"Buckhead Tower," Rachel mumbled, reading the address Margaret had given her. Of course, Natasia would be living it up in one of Atlanta's most exclusive long-term hotels.

Rachel made a U-turn and headed toward Buckhead.

Twenty minutes later, she was getting off the elevator and heading to Natasha's apartment. She had just turned the corner when she heard the scream for help.

Rachel raced to the door where the scream was coming from. Her eyes blinked in shock when she saw the apartment number and realized it was Natasia's apartment.

Rachel pushed the door open and eased inside. A woman in a maid's uniform was pressed up against the wall, her mouth open in horror.

"Oh, my God, she's not breathing," the woman cried.

Rachel's eyes eased toward the floor, where Natasia was sprawled out like she was dead.

Visions of the last time she'd happened upon a dead body immediately began to fill Rachel's head. That's why her first instinct was to turn and get the heck out of there, but the cleaning lady was a basket case and Natasia might still be alive.

"Did you call 911?" Rachel asked, dropping to Natasia's side.

"N-no . . ."

"Well, call them," Rachel snapped as she took Natasia's arm and felt for a pulse. A flutter of relief ran through her when she felt one.

Minutes felt like hours, but Rachel soon heard footsteps racing toward the room. Soon, paramedics and security personnel filled the apartment.

The paramedics immediately went to work and Rachel actually exhaled when she heard one of them say, "We've got her stabilized."

Natasia moaned as they rolled her out of the room on the stretcher.

"Ma'am, can I talk to you?" a man in a too-small gray suit asked Rachel. He had on a name badge so Rachel assumed he was hotel security. "Do you mind if I ask your relationship to the victim?"

"Victim? She's a victim?" Oh, Lord, Rachel didn't need anyone thinking she'd done something to Natasia. Rachel glanced around the room. Where was that cleaning lady? She needed to get over here and tell these cops that Natasia was like that before Rachel arrived. The last thing Rachel needed was to be accused of yet another crime that she didn't commit.

"Maybe that's the wrong choice of words," the security officer corrected. "She's stabilized, but we're trying to ascertain what happened." He pulled out a notepad and a pen. "So, again, you are?"

"I work for her. We, uh, we had a meeting. I just arrived and she was like that. But the cleaning lady is the one that found her. Talk to her. She'll tell you, I came in later." Rachel looked around frantically. "Hey, Cleaning Lady! Where are you? Come tell them you found her."

The officer held his hand out to settle Rachel. "Ma'am, we've already got her statement. We know she's the one who found her."

Rachel's shoulders relaxed just a little. "Good." She pointed to the man's notepad. "Make sure you write that down. Rachel Jackson Adams was not the one who found her."

"Ma'am, we got this." The security officer spotted an open bottle of pills on the nightstand and said, "Are those hers?"

Rachel shrugged. She could cooperate now that they were clear that she wasn't involved in whatever happened to Natasia. "I don't know."

"Hey, Jay," another investigator called out from the bathroom, "there's a lot of medication in here that may give you an idea what happened."

Rachel's mouth fell open as he appeared in the bathroom doorway with an armful of pill bottles.

The man held up one bottle. "This medication is for lupus. The only reason I know is because my sister is on some of this stuff. And the milligrams? This is heavy duty. She might be advanced."

Jay looked up at Rachel. "Did she have lupus?"

Lupus? Advanced? Oh, wow. Was Natasia sick?

"I told you, I don't know. I just came here for a meeting."

The security guard sighed, resolved that he wouldn't get anywhere with Rachel. "All right, ma'am." He closed his notepad. "We have your info. We'll be in touch if we have anymore questions."

That was her exit cue. Rachel couldn't wait to get out of there. Not just because the whole environment made her stomach turn, but now, she couldn't wait to tell Jasmine what she'd found out. The question now was, exactly what were they supposed to do with that information?

CHAPTER THIRTY:
JASMINE

"Okay, babe, I'll just see you later. Love you." Jasmine pressed End on her cell and then frowned.

"What's wrong?"

She turned to look at Mae Frances, who sat propped up in her bed with her arms folded across her chest. It had been weeks since she'd seen her friend this way — up and nosy.

But she was so glad that her friend was not only awake, but up to talking, that Jasmine was going to tell her whatever she wanted to know.

"Nothing's wrong," she said, sitting in the chair next to the bed. "That was Hosea."

"I figured that was Preacher Man. I didn't think you'd be saying 'I love you' to anyone else, at least not this early in the morning."

"Mae Frances! I'm not like that and I haven't been like that for years. You know that."

"Oh, yeah, I forgot. But don't change the subject; what's wrong with you? What did Preacher Man say?"

Jasmine shook her head. "I don't know. He just landed, but he told me that he's not on his way home. He said he had to take care of something important. And then he said, 'Trust me.' "

"What's wrong with that?"

"Whenever he's said that recently, it has something to do with Natasia."

Mae Frances shook her head. "You waste a lot of time thinking about that woman and I already told you —"

"I know, I know, you had a dream."

"Don't be poo-poohing how the Lord chooses to talk to some people. I'm telling you, she can't take him away from you."

Jasmine shook her head, thinking how much she missed the Mae Frances who would've shut Natasia down. Natasia Redding would've been living in the caves of Afghanistan by now if the old Mae Frances had taken over.

But then Jasmine had to pause and think about Mae Frances's words. Natasia had been here for weeks and if she was trying to get Hosea back, she didn't have much to show for her efforts. There were no late nights when Hosea was gone for hours.

There were no Saturdays when he was gone all day. There were no early morning disappearing acts — except for today.

Something was going on, but like Mae Frances said, it didn't feel like Natasia could do anything. It didn't feel like she was in a battle for her relationship the way she'd felt back in 2007.

Still, Natasia was a low-down, dirty trick, and a liar, and a cheat, and could never be trusted. So, Jasmine wasn't about to turn her back, especially because Hosea did love Natasia once. That's why she needed to be gone. For good!

"Well," Jasmine finally answered Mae Frances, "Maybe you're right. Maybe she can't get him. But I'm just tired. Tired of trying to figure her out. Tired of trying to figure out what's going on. Tired of trying to figure out what she's gonna do. It's too much. I have to think about her at home and on the show. What if this goes on for another season?" Jasmine shook her head. "I just need her out of our lives for good."

Mae Frances gave Jasmine a half-nod as if she only kind of agreed. "Okay, I get that. So, what're you gonna do? Have you and the hoochie come up with any plans?"

Jasmine chuckled. "Why she gotta be all that? Why you gotta call Rachel names?"

"I forgot; y'all girls now. Okay, I apologize and I'll rephrase . . . have you and the hoochie mama come up with any plans?"

Jasmine shook her head because she couldn't believe Mae Frances, and because she hadn't spoken to Rachel since she'd left last night.

Then, her cell phone rang and "Hoochie" showed on the screen. Jasmine jumped up so that Mae Frances wouldn't see the name that she'd had for Rachel.

But when she glanced at Mae Frances and saw the way her lips were twisted, Jasmine knew she hadn't moved quickly enough.

"What's up, Rachel?"

"I've been trying to call you all night!"

"Oh, I ended up having a slumber party with Jacquie in her bedroom. Kind of a girl's night in since Hosea was away."

"Well, I wish you'd had your cell with you 'cause I have some news."

"I hope it's good news."

"Depends on your definition of *good*. But it's about Natasia."

Jasmine perked up. "News that will get rid of her . . . finally?"

A pause, and then, "Yeah, you could say that," Rachel said softly. "I'm gonna come over."

"Why don't you just meet me on set? We

345

can find someplace to talk."

"You haven't checked your emails? What have you been doing all morning? I know Hosea is in New York, so you got some other man over there?"

Rachel laughed, but Jasmine didn't. "I told you; I've been hanging out with my children like you were probably doing — oh, wait. Your children are not with you."

"You know what?"

"Look Rachel, we shouldn't be fighting each other when we have so many people to go up against. Let's just handle our business, okay?"

"Well, you started it. But anyway, I'm going to come over to your house 'cause our taping has been canceled this morning."

"I didn't know that."

"That's what I was saying before you went in on me. Melinda sent out an email early this morning canceling the shoot and telling us she'll be in touch."

"I wonder what's going on?" Jasmine asked.

Rachel sighed. "That's what I've been trying to tell you."

"So, tell me," Jasmine said, hardly able to hide her curiosity now.

"I'll see you in a little while."

Rachel hung up and Jasmine stared at the

phone. That girl was evil. Just pure evil.

But Jasmine needed her right now. And she even liked her a little, 'cause what Rachel just did — hanging up without giving anymore information — was something that Jasmine would've done.

"What's going on?" Mae Frances asked.

"That's what I was trying to find out. Rachel's on her way over. She said she has some news but that's it."

Mae Frances was quiet for a moment. "Bad news."

Jasmine rolled her eyes. "Well, whatever, I just pray that Natasia will be dead to us soon. Once and for all!"

Jasmine stared at Rachel with wide eyes, as Mae Frances just shook her head.

"What is it with you and dead bodies?" Mae Frances asked as Rachel finished telling the story of finding Natasia in her hotel last night.

"I told you, she's not dead. She just looked that way."

"Oh, my God!" Jasmine held her hand to her pounding heart. "I've been wishing . . . I just prayed that she was dead!"

"Well," Rachel said, plopping down in the chair next to Mae Frances's bed. "God almost answered your prayers."

"Please, God doesn't work like that," Mae Frances said in a tone that sounded like she'd always been a sanctified saint. "The Lord don't pay attention to that kind of foolishness." She paused. "But I told you she wasn't going to be a problem anymore."

Jasmine's eyes opened wide. "You did say that!"

Mae Frances nodded slowly. "But what I want to know is what's wrong with her? Is she pregnant?"

"How she gonna be pregnant when she ain't got a man?"

"Well, you're the one who's been doing all the talking about her having yours."

"I never said that!" Jasmine snapped. "You need to stop —"

"Do you two wanna hear what I have to say?" Rachel jumped in.

Jasmine rolled her eyes at Mae Frances, but then nodded at Rachel.

"Dang! I do all this work and y'all act like you don't want to hear it." When Jasmine and Mae Frances stayed quiet, Rachel said, "Thank you." she sat back, crossed her legs, and said, "To answer your question, Mae Frances, no, Natasia is not pregnant, she's sick. She has lupus."

"Lupus?" Jasmine and Mae Frances said together, both sounding as if the word was foreign to them.

Rachel nodded and pulled her iPad from her tote bag. "I did some research and though I don't know what kind of lupus she has, it's serious. The medicine that was in her apartment was for advanced stage."

"Oh, my God," Jasmine said.

"Yup, she may not have been dead last night, but that chick could be dying."

"I can't believe it," Jasmine whispered. "I don't like her, but . . ."

"I know," Rachel nodded.

"Hey!" Mae Frances growled, making Jasmine and Rachel sit up. "There's no need to be sitting here worrying about her. Nothing you can do to save her. The thing now is, how are you going to use this against her?"

Rachel shook her head and Jasmine said, "Mae Frances, we can't do that."

"Why not? This is perfect. Obviously she didn't want anyone to know; she's been hiding it. And since you've been so worried about her, Jasmine Larson, you can use it as blackmail. Tell her that if she doesn't move to Timbuktu, you'll release the story to the *National Enquirer*. And by the time they finish with the story, lupus will be contagious, Natasia would've infected the entire set, and everyone associated with *First*

Ladies will be dying."

"Really?" Rachel said. "Is that what you really want to do? You want to go after someone who's really sick? Who could be dying?"

"Well, she ain't dead yet," Mae Frances said.

"Dang, old lady. You need to have a little compassion," Rachel said.

"Who you callin' old? Do you know what I will do to you if I get up out of this bed? I'll Django you all up in this place!"

"Come on, y'all," Jasmine jumped in before Rachel could even make a comeback. "We just got this news and you want to fight?"

"So, what do you want to do?" Mae Frances asked. "Pray for her?"

"I'm not sayin' all that. I'm just sayin' . . ."

"That your problem is solved," Rachel finished for her. "We don't need to do anything with this information because I seriously doubt that your husband will leave you for a sick woman."

"He was never going to leave me!"

"And not only that," Rachel said, ignoring her, "Natasia probably won't even be back on the show."

"Wow!" Jasmine sank onto the bed. "Just like that, it's over."

"It's not over yet," Rachel said. "It's just over for you."

"I do feel sorry for her," Jasmine said. "I bet that's why Hosea said he wasn't coming home this morning. I bet he went to the hospital."

"And that doesn't bother you?" Mae Frances asked.

Jasmine shook her head. "No, not now that I know what all of this was about. Hosea couldn't tell me what was going on. He did the right thing then, and my husband will do the right thing now." Jasmine sighed in relief. "It's over."

"Uh . . . excuse you." Rachel sat up and folded her arms. "It's not completely over. What about my situation? What about Mary?" When Jasmine looked at her blankly, Rachel said, "I helped you with Natasia, now you have to help me get rid of Mary and Nathan, 'cause I'm not giving them my son. So, what are we gonna do?"

Mae Frances sighed and threw her legs over the side of the bed. "Well, let me get up."

Both Rachel and Jasmine turned their attention to Mae Frances.

"Really?" Jasmine asked. "You feel like you're strong enough?"

"Yeah, and I have to be. 'Cause y'all need

my help. The way you're handling that Natasia girl . . . y'all have gone soft. And if you want to keep that baby, Rasheda," she pointed to Rachel, "you need me to get up, take a shower, get dressed, eat some breakfast, then sit back and figure this out for you."

"Okay." Rachel grinned, not even bothering to correct Mae Frances. "How long before you'll be ready to talk?"

"I'm gonna take my time," Mae Frances said as she ambled toward the bathroom. " 'Cause you know, genius cannot be rushed."

CHAPTER THIRTY-ONE: NATASIA

Even in the darkness, Natasia could feel, Natasia could hear. She felt the impact of her fall, but had no strength to scream out. She heard the scream of the housekeeper, but her eyes wouldn't open. And then she heard the voice of Rachel Jackson Adams.

She'd tried hard to wake up then. Wake up, get up and tell Rachel to get out of her apartment. She'd tried to come out of it, and that was when the darkness overtook her; she heard nothing, felt nothing, remembered nothing.

But now, once again in the darkness, she could hear, she could feel. And she felt the squeeze of her hand, over and over again. And a voice that sounded like it was a million light-years away.

"Natasia."

Then, another squeeze, and the voice came closer.

"Natasia."

More squeezes. The voice calling her name.

Her eyes fluttered open, but at first it felt like she was in a thick, white fog.

"Natasia."

Slowly, she inched toward the light and when she blinked again, she saw him, standing over her.

Her angel. Hosea.

Was she in heaven?

"Natasia, can you hear me?"

She blinked again and saw the white walls. With just a little twist of her head, she could see the machine next to her and the catheter bag hanging from the bed's railing.

"Natasia."

She turned her head back to him and when he smiled, she tried to do the same thing.

"I'm . . . in the hospital," she said through lips that felt so dry she could hardly part them.

He nodded, then reached over her and pressed the button. "I'm calling the nurse. The doctor told me that you would be waking up."

"What happened?"

"You fainted last night. And then when you came to, they gave you something to sleep."

"I don't remember that part. I remember speaking to you on the phone."

"This happened right after we talked?"

She closed her eyes and tried to remember. "I think so. I stood up. I was going to call Melinda . . . and that's all I really remember."

"Well, just rest. The doctor will be here in a little while."

"Okay." She took a couple of long, deep breaths. Closed her eyes. But she didn't sleep. She tried to will strength back into her body. After a couple of minutes, she opened her eyes once again. Hosea was still standing by her bedside.

She licked her lips, blew out a breath, and asked, "How did you know . . . that I was here?"

"Apparently, you have me as your person to contact. . . ."

". . . in case of emergency," she finished. "I forgot. I hope it was okay."

Before he could answer, the door swung open. "I hear there's someone who's awake in here," the doctor said as he stepped inside the room. "Ms. Redding?"

She was glad to see the young Robert Redford again. She nodded.

He glanced down at the digital tablet in his hand. "How're you feeling?"

She was laid up in a hospital bed; what did he think? But then, she wiggled her toes, shook her hands just a bit. And she really did feel fine. So, that's what she told him.

"Well, I'm going to have the nurse come in and check your vitals, then I'll be right back."

As if on cue, the door opened again, and a woman in a pink flowered smock and pink pants entered.

"I'll be back in five minutes," the doctor told her.

When Hosea told her the same thing, Natasia said, "No, you don't have to leave."

"I'll be right outside," he assured her.

Natasia nodded, then lay still as the nurse checked her pulse, her heart rate. She took her temperature, then checked her blood pressure.

And the whole time, Natasia tried to remember. She'd been feeling so good, thinking about Hosea, thinking that no matter how much time she had left, she knew for sure that he would be there for her — in every way that she hoped.

Those thoughts were the last ones she'd had.

"Why did I faint?" she asked the nurse.

"I'm just about finished, then the doctor will talk to you about all of that."

A couple of minutes later, the doctor strolled in, followed by Hosea. As soon as they stood by her bedside, one on each side, she asked again, "Why did I faint?"

The doctor glanced at Hosea.

Natasia said, "You can tell me anything. You can talk in front of Hosea."

The doctor took in a deep breath, then released it. "Well, we don't know why you fainted. It could be a couple of things, from your medication to your blood pressure. Your blood pressure is high, it was high last night and it's still a bit high. And we're going to look at all your medication." He paused. "But we did find out something . . ."

"My kidneys," she whispered.

He nodded. "We're going to do a test to measure your creatinine levels —"

"What does that mean?" Hosea asked before the doctor could finish.

And before the doctor could respond, Natasia said, "It means that I may need dialysis."

They both looked at the doctor and he nodded. "You've done your research."

She swallowed. "I have."

"So, she's going to need dialysis?" Hosea asked as if he was shocked.

"We still have another test to do, but it appears that her kidney function has dropped to below fifteen percent. And if that's the case, yes. Definitely. Dialysis will save your life."

"How often will she need this, doctor?" Hosea asked softly.

"There are many things we have to figure out, but it will probably be a couple of times a week."

"Wow!"

"I'm going to get some of the tests ordered," Dr. Ginsberg said. "I'll be back."

When they were alone, Hosea looked down at her and shook his head.

"Don't do that," she said. "I knew this was coming."

"But so soon . . ."

"It's not that soon; I've known for a year and because I didn't have any symptoms, my kidneys were getting weaker for years before then."

"So, what are you going to do? I know you can't work now."

"Who says?" She frowned. "Being on dialysis doesn't mean that I'm going to be laid up in a hospital bed. Plenty of people have regular . . . well, maybe not so regular, but you know what I mean. Plenty of people have regular lives."

"But if you don't have to work, then why do it?"

"Because I *have* to work for my sanity. I don't want to sit around, Hosea, and wait for this to happen."

He nodded.

"Plus, I have to work for money, unless you're going to take care of me."

She'd said that only to make him smile. And he did. But then Hosea said, "If it comes down to that, I'll take care of you."

"Yeah, right." Now, she laughed out loud, though she was so weak, it sounded like a giggle. "I'm sure your wife will be right there taking care of me, too."

"You underestimate my wife."

"No, just like a man, you do. But this is a non-discussion because I'm going to keep working."

He nodded. "Okay, but what about living by yourself?"

"Well, unless you're going to move in with me . . ."

Again, she was trying to make him smile, but this time, he didn't. He just stared at her.

"What?" she said after a few uncomfortable moments.

He sat on the edge of her bed. "I want you to hear me out."

"Uh-oh. I don't think I'm gonna like this."

"Natasia, you mean the world to me . . .

as a friend. And I'm really concerned about you. Dialysis . . . this sounds serious."

"It is."

He nodded. "I don't want you to go through this by yourself and I need you to really think about what's going to happen now."

She paused for a moment, closed her eyes, then after a few seconds, opened them. "Okay, I've thought about it. But what can I do, Hosea? I'm sick. All I can do is fight it."

"You can let me do more." He took her hands in his. "I may have a solution. We have a big house, and . . ." He stopped. "Let me think about this a little and pray about it a lot. We'll talk later, okay?"

She nodded because she didn't want to speak. If she opened her mouth, she would ask him what he was thinking, just like she'd wanted to do the other day.

But in her heart she knew it was best not to talk about his thoughts . . . not yet.

We have a big house.

Was he seriously considering moving her into his house? And if he did ask her, would she consider it?

"I have to get going," he said, interrupting her thoughts. "I'll come back in a few hours."

She nodded, and then closed her eyes when he kissed her forehead. She inhaled, wanting to savor the moment, then watched him as he stepped from the room.

Her eyes stayed on the door as she snuggled back into the bed, trying to get as comfortable as she could against the rough sheets.

There was so much that should be on her mind right now. Her kidneys were failing, her lupus was progressing . . . but all she wanted to think about was Hosea. If she had a chance of surviving, she would only survive because of him.

But truly, did he want her to live with him and his wife? Did she want to do that? No, not really. She wanted more of him, and that would never happen under his roof . . . would it?

She shook her head. None of this mattered because Jasmine would never agree. There was no need to even think about it.

But then . . . she couldn't let the thoughts go. If she did live with Hosea, she would have him for more hours than if she were not in his house. And Jasmine couldn't watch her all the time. Maria Shriver was proof of that.

"Yeah," Natasia whispered to herself. "Yeah."

She lowered the bed until she was flat on her back again and she closed her eyes. There was so much going through her mind, and if Hosea had not been there, it would've all been so scary. But he was there, and now she could handle it.

She could handle it because of Hosea. The question now, though, was WWJD — what would Jasmine do?

CHAPTER THIRTY-TWO: MARY

She was hiding out in the bathroom. That seemed to be the place of refuge from the cameras, no matter where they were taping. (Well, except for that time Chauncey snuck in and secretly taped them.) But today, the bathroom here at the W Hotel was giving her little solace.

Mary wasn't looking forward to today, and had even hoped taping would be canceled again, like Monday's show had been. Mary had heard Natasia was in the hospital, so as far as Mary was concerned, they could cancel the taping all week. But they were moving forward, taping one of the final episodes — a dedication to Jacqueline's Hope–Atlanta. Apparently, Jasmine had some national missing children's foundation and she claimed that since they'd opened a church in Atlanta, it seemed only feasible that they open a chapter of Jacqueline's Hope here as well. It was all probably a publicity stunt but Mary had been happy to take part nonetheless. Or at least, she *had* been happy.

Part of today's dedication involved having all of their children present. Jasmine's daughter and son, Jacqueline and Zaya, were already here. Alvin had come with her and Nathan, and Mary had been bracing herself for Rachel's children. For *her* son.

It would be her first time actually laying eyes on her baby, and Mary didn't know how she would react. Frankly, she'd been surprised that Rachel would even allow it. But then she'd overheard Sonny telling someone that it would only be Rachel's two older children taking part.

After hearing that, Mary had to duck into the bathroom to compose herself. All the excitement she'd felt was gone and she would've given anything to be able to leave. Even though it had been almost a week since that disastrous Women's Day event, Mary still didn't want to face Rachel. She'd only garnered the strength because of the chance to see her son. But now . . .

Mary pushed aside dreams of her son. She'd see him soon enough. Nathan had made her that promise as early as this morning — right after he kissed her and apologized for slapping her again last night.

Mary leaned toward the mirror and dabbed some more foundation on the bruise on her face. He usually was careful not to leave a bruise. This time, it was as if he didn't care. The swelling had gone down and even though a purple mark had taken its place, Mary had covered it up pretty good. She'd even covered up the bruise on her side from where Nathan had kicked her earlier in the week. What she'd never be able to cover up was the bruise on her heart.

Mary stared at her reflection and fought back the tears. Who was this woman staring back at her in the mirror? Had prison made her into this? A self-loathing, low-self-esteem-having . . . victim? Where had her fight gone? Had she lost it in prison? Had she lost it when she lost her son?

Her son. The reason she was doing all of this. The reason she was enduring Nathan's abuse.

When she left the Huntsville Women's prison, Mary had been perfectly content to come to Atlanta and be Mrs. Nathan Frazier. It wasn't until he'd started talking about her son that she began to envision a different life. It wasn't until he'd painted a picture of their happy family that she'd wanted more.

Now, Mary knew what her grandmother

meant when she said, "Sometimes you need to leave well enough alone."

She inhaled, then exhaled. She needed to pull it together. Nathan was waiting outside and she knew it would be a matter of time before he came poking his head in the doorway. Mary found herself wondering if Rachel had told Jasmine about Nathan's abuse. She was banking on the fact that the two of them didn't like each other. But Mary had no doubt it was something she'd shared with Lester. And with the courts.

She shivered as she thought of that information coming out in court. That's why she hadn't told Nathan that Rachel had seen them. He would just find some way to make that her fault.

With a new determination to get through this day, Mary dropped the compact back in her purse. But then the bathroom door swung open, and she wanted to disappear into thin air when she came face-to-face with Rachel.

"Excuse me," Mary said, trying to step around Rachel.

Rachel took a step to the right, blocking her path.

"I said, excuse me," Mary said as Rachel continued to glare at her. "What, you gonna hit me again?" Mary said. She was showing bravado that she didn't really feel.

"Nah. Seems like you get enough of that at home," Rachel casually replied.

That stung. Mainly because it was true.

"So, you're okay with that?" Rachel asked.

Mary didn't want to cause a scene because she knew Nathan was just outside the door and she didn't want Alvin to see her and Rachel fighting.

"What are you talking about, Rachel?"

"So, we're just going to pretend that I didn't see what we both know I saw?"

Mary shifted nervously. There was no sense in trying to act like what Rachel saw didn't really happen. "It's not like it seemed at all."

Rachel raised an eyebrow. "Really? Because it seemed like he was beating the crap out of you and you just laid there and took it."

"We just had a little argument that got out of hand."

"So, that's how you're going to play it? Out of hand?" Rachel looked at her like she was crazy.

"I don't owe you an explanation," Mary said, taking a step around Rachel.

Rachel grabbed Mary's arm and spun her around. "He kicked you in your side like a stray dog. And you're okay with that?"

Mary swallowed the lump in her throat. "Of course I'm not okay with that. We talked about it, he apologized, and it'll never happen again."

"That's what all abusers say."

Mary snatched her arm away. "Don't judge me."

"I'm not judging you," Rachel replied. She ran her eyes up and down Mary's body, the disgust evident. "If you don't love yourself enough to demand that your husband *not* lay his hands on you, that's on you. If you're okay with getting your behind beat, that's on you. But what's on me is making sure that my son never lives in an environment like that."

Those words cut to Mary's core. Deep down inside, she knew Rachel was right. Still, she said, "Nathan would never do that in front of *my* son." She could tell that got under Rachel's skin because her whole body tensed.

"You signed away your rights. He's *my* son."

"I wasn't in my right mind," Mary replied. "I gave him life."

"And I helped him *live.*"

They stood facing each other until Mary said, "The bottom line is, I've gotten my life together and I want my son back."

"So, your life is together, huh?" Rachel looked her up and down again. "Did you know that seventy-three percent of abusers grew up in homes where their fathers were abusers?"

Mary wondered how Rachel even knew that statistic, but she knew it was one Rachel wouldn't hesitate to use against her.

Rachel continued, "My son, yes, *my* son — because were it not for me, he'd be in the system — *my* son will not have that life. Nor will he have a life where he sees his egg donor, because that's all you are, getting her behind beat and thinking it's okay."

"He won't be raised like that," Mary said. Even as the words came out of her mouth, she didn't know that she believed them.

Mary knew one thing, though, if Nathan did ever put his hands on her in front of her son, that's when she would stand up and fight back.

"What's the holdup?" Nathan said as he stuck his head in the bathroom.

"Um, excuse me, this is a ladies room," Rachel snapped.

"So, what you doing in here?" He laughed like he really said something funny. His smile faded when he noticed he was the only one laughing. He turned to Mary. "Come on."

Mary lowered her eyes and stepped around Rachel.

"Scurry along like the good reverend said," Rachel called out after her. "Because we both know what he'll do if you don't obey him," she added as the bathroom door slammed on the sound of her voice.

Nathan froze, then glared at Mary. She immediately felt knots in her stomach. Mary knew she was going to pay dearly for Rachel's comment as soon as she and Nathan got home.

CHAPTER THIRTY-THREE: RACHEL

Rachel couldn't believe it, but she was actually ready for this reality show to wrap up. She didn't know how much more tension she could stomach. She'd almost bowed out of today's taping because it involved the children, specifically Lewis. As much as she wanted to support Jacqueline's Hope, having all of her children on was a deal breaker. Rachel had told Melinda she would walk away from everything (and face whatever lawsuits came as a result) if they wouldn't let her tape without putting Lewis on. Melinda had reluctantly agreed to tape without Brooklyn and Lewis since they were so young, so Rachel had her stepmother, Brenda, bring the other children in from Houston. They'd gotten in late last night, and since Rachel had a hair appointment before coming to tape, Brenda was just going to meet her here with Nia and Jordan.

After taking a moment to freshen up, Rachel inhaled, said a silent prayer for a drama-free day, then made her way back outside.

She had just opened the bathroom door when she heard, "Mommmyyyy!" Brooklyn and Nia came racing toward her and threw their arms around her.

Rachel scooped Brooklyn up, while looking at her stepmother strangely. "Hello, my sweeties."

Brenda shrugged. "Your sitter didn't show, so I brought Brooklyn and Lewis with me. I'll just keep them out of the way."

Rachel wanted to wring her stepmother's neck. Although she hadn't given Brenda all the details about Mary and Lewis, she'd been adamant that only Nia and Jordan were to come.

"Hey, Ma," Jordan said, hugging Rachel before she could go off on Brenda.

She hugged him as well, then looked around, "Where's your bro—" Before Rachel could finish her sentence she saw him. Her son, sitting comfortably in that sleazy preacher's arms.

Rachel almost knocked Jordan down as she bolted over to Nathan. "What are you doing with my son?" she screamed.

"I was just getting to know him," Nathan said with a slimy grin as Rachel snatched

Lewis from his arms.

Thankfully, Jasmine moved in from God only knows where and stepped in front of Rachel before her claws could make contact with Nathan's face.

"Rachel," Jasmine said.

"Move, Jasmine," Rachel growled, her chest heaving.

"Don't do this."

Rachel was shivering she was so angry. Although neither Sonny nor Chauncey were around, Rachel didn't care who saw her. She didn't care about anything anymore except making Mary Frazier a widow.

"I was just holding him," Nathan said, feigning shock at Rachel's anger. "He's such a big boy." He reached over to toussle Lewis's hair.

"You don't touch my son," Rachel hissed as she moved Lewis out of reach.

Nathan turned up his lips, and in a cocky tone said, "He needs to get to know me since he'll be living with me soon."

It was Jasmine who turned this time and looked like she was ready to clock Nathan in the eye. Mary stepped up next to her husband. "Come on, Nathan. This isn't the time." Her eyes motioned toward a curly-haired boy standing next to them.

"Daddy, why is that little boy coming to

live with us?" the boy, who appeared to be about ten or eleven, asked.

"He's not!" Rachel screamed. She didn't mean to yell at the boy, but at that moment, no one was exempt from her anger.

"Hey, what's the problem?" Sonny said, rushing over.

"Mommy, what's wrong?" Lewis asked, touching Rachel's face. Rachel hadn't even realized that she was crying until she felt him wiping away her tears.

"Hi, sweetie," Jasmine said soothingly as she stroked the little boy's hair. "Your mommy is just so happy to see you that she's crying tears of joy."

Rachel squeezed Lewis tighter as she continued glaring at Nathan and Mary. She was envisioning 101 ways she could murder them both and get away with it.

"Mom, who is that man and why is he talking about Lewis coming to live with him?" Nia asked, stepping next to her mother.

Jasmine quickly turned to the little girl. "Nia, guess who's in the back waiting to see you? My daughter, Jacqueline! You remember her?"

Nia's eyes lit up. When the two little girls first met, they didn't hit it off too well, but they'd quickly become friends. "Yes! She's here?" Nia exclaimed.

"She sure is. Why don't you go see her?" Jasmine glanced over at Rachel's stepmother. "Miss Brenda, right?"

Brenda nodded, confusion all over her face.

"Can you take all the kids in the back? We'll let you know when we're ready to get started."

"Of course." Brenda scurried over and tried to take Lewis from Rachel's arms, but Rachel squeezed him even tighter. She still hadn't said a word. She just kept glaring at Nathan and Mary as she tightened her arms around her son.

"Owww," Lewis cried, squirming.

Jasmine eased up to Rachel. "It's okay, Rachel," she whispered. "Let him go with your stepmom."

Rachel finally relaxed her grip enough for Brenda to slip the child out of her arms.

"Come on, children." Brenda glanced at Jasmine, who nodded to let her know that everything was going to be all right.

Rachel didn't know how Jasmine could be so calm. Maybe because it wasn't her kid. All Rachel knew was she was a volcano on the verge of eruption and this stunt by Nathan was about to cause her to explode.

"Again, does someone want to tell me

what's going on?" Sonny repeated.

"It's nothing," Mary finally said.

"Yeah, I was just holding my wife's son." Nathan shrugged nonchalantly.

"You bastard!" Rachel leaped toward him, but this time it was Sonny who stopped her.

"Hey!" Sonny said, grabbing Rachel and pulling her back.

"Rachel, don't let him take you there. You know he's just trying to provoke you," Jasmine said, trying to calm Rachel down once again.

"You have a son?"

Everyone stopped and turned to the little boy who was now facing Mary, a stunned expression on his face.

Shock filled Mary's eyes and she knelt down next to the little boy. "Oh, Alvin, it's a long story. We'll tell you about it when we get home." Mary's eyes darted around nervously, like she didn't want to get into this here.

"Is he gonna come live with you guys? Is that why you don't want me to live there?" Alvin said, his voice quavering.

Mary cupped his face. "Don't say that. We love you. What makes you think we don't want you with us?"

"Because I live with Grandma and Paw-Paw and I want to live with you!" he cried.

"I heard Daddy say you guys were building up your church and you didn't have time for me, that's why I have to stay with Paw-Paw."

"Oh, Alvin. You misunderstood your father." Mary cut her eyes at Nathan, and the look actually gave Rachel pause. If she didn't know better, she'd swear that was hate festering in Mary's eyes.

"No, I didn't misunderstand anything! I'm not stupid." Alvin looked at his father. "Why you trying to get her son," he pointed at Rachel, "and you don't even want me?"

"Boy, shut up all that whining!" Nathan barked, causing the little boy to flinch. "I will knock . . ."

Mary instinctively jumped in front of Alvin and put her arms up to shield him. The whole scene caused everyone to stop and stare. Nathan must've noticed because he immediately relaxed, then smiled and said, "Yeah, son, you misunderstood. But like your mother said, we'll discuss it when we get home." Then, he took in all the eyes on him and chuckled. "These kids today, I'll tell ya."

Alvin didn't say another word. He just clung to Mary for dear life.

The scene had also given Rachel time to calm down. Oh, she was still furious, but she had a new resolve. She'd die, or kill, before she let the Fraziers have her son. It was as simple as that. But there was no need to act a fool and give them ammunition against her. They would dig their own graves.

Out of the corner of her eye, Rachel noticed Chauncey off to the side — camera rolling as usual. For once, though, she didn't care. She wanted him to get it all on tape because that video would be just the ammunition she needed in court.

CHAPTER THIRTY-FOUR:
JASMINE

Jasmine released a long sigh as she tossed back the duvet, then climbed into bed. "Well, the kids are finally settled," she said as she snuggled close to Hosea. "I'm not sure if I'll do that again. I didn't think Jacquie was ever going to fall asleep."

Hosea rested his head back against the headboard, laid his iPad in his lap, and chuckled. "She was pretty excited. Her TV debut."

"It went well, though it didn't start out that way with all of that drama with Mary and Nathan."

"I know. I've been talking to Lester almost every day. He's really upset about all of this craziness." He paused. "I'm glad the only drama we have in our lives is whether or not to let Jacquie and Zaya be on the show."

Jasmine sat up and kissed Hosea's cheek. "Thanks for going along with that. I really wanted people to see that Jacqueline's Hope is all about the children."

"That's why I agreed to it. Plus, I knew you would never let them make our children look crazy."

"Not at all. Not that our adorable kids could ever look crazy, though I wasn't sure since Rachel's brats were there."

Hosea shook his head slightly. "Is it always going to be this way between you and Rachel?"

Jasmine shrugged. "I don't know. It is a weird kind of dynamic. I can say anything I want to about her, but when other people start messing with her . . ."

He laughed. "Y'all act like sisters."

"No. Serena and I love each other and you never hear me talking about her that way. Rachel is just . . . special. You know what I mean?"

"I'm not sure you meant that as a compliment, but I'm glad today went well."

"Yeah, it was cool. And the crew was great with the kids. Everyone . . ." She let her voice trail off as the questions came to her mind once again.

Natasia hadn't been on the set all week; all they'd been told was that she was recovering from a cold, or the flu, or something. Every time someone told that lie, she and Rachel exchanged glances.

But Jasmine and Rachel hadn't said a word. There was no need to, since all of their attention was now focused on Mary and Nathan and the plan that Mae Frances was putting together.

But while Natasia was no longer in the bull's eye, Jasmine did wonder what Hosea knew and when did he know it? And did he know what was going on now?

She and Hosea had kept their agreement — she wouldn't ask any questions; she would just trust him. But she couldn't keep silent any longer; she just had to know what was going on. So, she said, "Natasia hasn't been at work. . . ." She didn't put a period nor a question mark at the end of that sentence. It was open ended for Hosea. She wanted him to fill in all the blanks.

Hosea moved his iPad to the nightstand, then stared straight ahead.

She watched him for a moment before she asked, "What's wrong?"

He shook his head, but still said nothing for a while. Then, "There's something I need to talk to you about."

The pounding in her chest was immediate. Natasia had died and no one had told them! Jasmine couldn't believe it. She couldn't believe that it was over. That woman would never cause her anymore problems. She was glad about that, but still, this was so sad. Natasia was young and she had died pretty much alone.

"Jasmine?" Hosea called out to her.

She blinked back the images in her head.

He said, "Did you hear what I said?"

"Yeah, what do you want to tell me?"

"Well, not exactly tell you, but . . ." He twisted his body so that he faced her. "I need to ask you something. Now, before you say anything," he held up his hands, "let me finish everything that I have to say."

"O . . . kay," she said slowly. Before Hosea could speak, though, Jasmine had it already figured out in her mind. Hosea wanted them to plan the funeral. Even though Jasmine hadn't liked Natasia in life, she could be much more compassionate in her death. Planning a funeral wasn't something she wanted to do. She'd already been through it two times too many with her mother and father.

But she would set aside her discomfort. If this was what Hosea really wanted, she would help him. Definitely! She wasn't going to give him any grief at all.

So, her mouth was ready to say yes when Hosea said, "I want Natasia to come and live with us."

"Of course, I'll do it," she said. But then

Hosea's question caught up with her, Jasmine jumped out of the bed as if a snake had just attacked her.

"Wait. What? You want her to come live with us? I thought you wanted me to plan her funeral."

"Her funeral? Natasia's not dead."

"She's not?" Jasmine held up her hands to stop him. "Wait, can you just start all over?"

He nodded. "I wouldn't even come to you with this if I had any other solution. But I've gone over a million scenarios and I think this is best." He inhaled. "When Natasia showed up at the church that Sunday, she told me she was dying. She has lupus."

"I know," Jasmine said, and then she told Hosea all that Rachel had told her. "So, when you said that you wanted to talk, I put two and two together and with Natasia not being at work, I was thinking she'd died and you wanted me to plan her funeral."

"Wow! You put two and two together and came up with one hundred and thirteen."

"And whatever you put together, you came up with something that will never happen." She paused. "Really, Hosea, you really asked me if she could move in with us?"

He nodded. "Her kidneys have failed and she's going to be on dialysis. Plus, with her fainting, it's not good for her to live alone."

"And that's my problem . . . how?"

"Jasmine . . ."

She crossed her arms. "You know you lost your mind, right?"

"I knew that this would be a heavy lift, but she is really sick and has nowhere else to go."

"I can think of a couple of places where I can tell Natasia to go."

"Jasmine . . ."

"Look, Hosea, I'm sorry she's so sick. I really am. But that doesn't have anything to do with me. And how could you even ask me to do this after everything she's done to me and what she tried to do to us?"

"This is asking a lot, I know that. But what I also know is that no one is as bad as the worst thing they've ever done. We can't judge Natasia and her whole life from what happened before."

"That's all I have to go on," Jasmine said.

"Well, I forgave her a long time ago, and now I believe it's our calling to help her."

Jasmine shook her head as she tried to find the words. "You have been helping her, Hosea. All this time, you've been helping her, keeping her secret, going to see her, and the whole time, I've had to suck it up because you told me to trust you."

"And you did. And I thank you for that."

"And that's enough. I played my part. Not many wives would have gone along with that much, but I trusted you, I let you be with her, and now it's over."

"She's not dead," Hosea repeated.

"Well, it will be over soon. And between now and then, you can go and keep doing what you've been doing. But her coming to live here . . ." She paused. "Is. Out. Of. The. Question. It won't happen, Hosea." Before he could say another word, she whipped around and stomped out of their bedroom. "Ugh!" she groaned as she marched straight to Mae Frances's room.

She knocked on the door, but opened it before Mae Frances could invite her in.

"Jasmine Larson!" Mae Frances peered at her from her bed. She put down the Bible she held and crossed her arms. "You better stop barging in my room like I'm one of your children. I need my privacy, you know."

"What? You're not asleep."

"Well, I may not always be sleeping. You might come in here one night and your vision will be ruined for life! You better recognize."

As images went through Jasmine's mind, she scrunched up her face. "Ewww . . . and you say that with the Bible in your lap."

"So? God created every single body part,

every single thing on me. He must've put it all there for a reason."

"Mae Frances, I don't want to go into this with you," Jasmine said, pacing from one end of the bedroom to the other. "I have a real problem."

She sighed. "What did Preacher Man do?"

Jasmine stopped moving for a moment. "He wants Natasia to come and live with us."

Jasmine had known Mae Frances for a long time and her friend had helped Jasmine through just about every impossible situation imaginable. But never before had Jasmine seen Mae Frances like this . . . with her eyes open as wide as her mouth, and not a word or a laugh coming out of her.

"Did you hear what I said?" Jasmine asked because that was the only explanation she had for the silence.

It still took a moment for her to speak. "I . . . what . . . really?" was all Mae Frances could come up with.

Jasmine dropped onto her bed. "He said she's really sick, needs dialysis, and now she needs someplace to live."

"What's wrong with where she's living?"

"They don't want her to live alone, I guess because of the dialysis, plus, she fainted. But that's not my problem," Jasmine ranted.

"You got that right."

Jasmine stood and started pacing again. "I cannot believe he would ask me that."

"I know what you mean."

"I mean, who does that? Who would ask their wife to let their mistress come and live with them?"

"Technically, Jasmine Larson, she never was his mistress. She was his first love. That's different. That's special."

Jasmine glared at Mae Frances. "You're not helping."

"Well, I'm waiting."

"For what?"

"For you to ask me the question."

Jasmine frowned and Mae Frances explained, "I'm waiting for you to ask me what you always ask. I'm waiting for you to ask for my help."

Jasmine waved her hand. "Even you can't help with this, Mae Frances. Unless one of your connections can give my husband a brain transplant, there's nothing you can do."

Mae Frances shook her head. "After everything I've done for you, I can't believe you, Jasmine Larson."

Jasmine slowed her steps. "Are you saying . . ."

"I'm saying that I know how to fix this.

Just like with everything else, Mae Frances has the answer."

Jasmine pressed her hands together like she was praying. "Thank you, Mae Frances! Thank you! So, what are we gonna do?"

CHAPTER THIRTY-FIVE: MARY

Mary Frazier was seeing her husband through new eyes and she didn't like what she saw.

The man who came into her life, pulled her out of her depression, convinced her to fight for her freedom, and even introduced her to God, had actually turned out to be the devil himself. Reverend Nathan Frazier was no better than her ex, Craig, a bona fide con man. Only Nathan's cons were done under the pretense of religion.

As he paraded back and forth across the pulpit, Mary felt sick to her stomach at his hypocrisy. She couldn't understand for the life of her how, on Saturday night, he beat the crap out of her, then on Sunday morning, he could stand in the pulpit and profess his love of God. Yet, that's exactly what he was doing.

But last night had been the final straw. They'd had a huge fight after the taping on

Wednesday because of course, he blamed her. She was the reason he looked a fool. She was the reason he looked bad on camera. He was especially angry at her "coddling Alvin" as he'd said. According to him, the whole plan was falling apart thanks to her. Poor Alvin had never been so glad to go to his grandparents. Nathan wouldn't talk to him the entire ride home. He wouldn't acknowledge him. He wouldn't even tell him goodbye.

Then, last night, when Nathan's parents had dropped Alvin off because they were going out of town, Nathan's anger flared up again. Mary shivered as her mind replayed that scene. Nathan had stormed into the living room where Mary and Alvin were watching TV.

"What's wrong with you?" Mary asked. The fury on his face immediately made her want to send Alvin racing for cover.

"I just talked to Rod, one of the editors from the show," Nathan barked. "He told me that the edited version of that last taping painted a jacked-up picture of me."

Mary wanted to ask him what he'd expected, because he was jacked up. But she remained silent.

"Oh, so now you don't have anything to say?" He kicked the TV stand. "You sitting up here watching reruns on TV. You need to be watching some reality shows and taking notes because obviously you don't know how to be a successful reality star."

"Nathan, that's your dream, not mine." The words left her mouth before she knew it.

"What?" He walked over closer to her. "Now you getting smart?"

"Dad, I don't —" Alvin began.

Nathan spun on him. "Was anybody talking to you?"

Again, Mary instinctively put her arm up in front of Alvin. "Nathan . . ."

Just mentioning his name sent Nathan into a tailspin and he snatched her up by her hair. Alvin screamed as he jumped up and ran into a corner, cowering as Nathan dragged Mary off the sofa and across the living room floor.

"I am so sick and tired of you! I wish I had left you in prison." He slammed her head against the floor. "Trifling wench! You're probably working with those tramps on that show to make me look bad!"

"Nathan, stop. Please," Mary cried, tugging at her hair to ease the pain. He had her hair wrapped around his hand as he dragged her around. She felt like her hair was being ripped from her scalp.

"I have everything riding on this and you're just blowing it!" He released her hair, then kicked her in the side again. She let out a piercing scream.

"Shut up!" Nathan yelled. He raised his foot to kick her again, but before his foot could connect with her side, Alvin jumped on his father's back.

"Stop it! You're hurting her!" Alvin's fists pummeled his father. The move caught Nathan off guard momentarily before he reached up and flung Alvin off him like a rag doll.

Alvin hit the wall and slid to the floor next to Mary, who scrambled over to cover him before Nathan could hurt him anymore. She covered her stepson with her body and braced herself for more beatings. But after a few seconds, she saw Nathan take a deep breath, then retreat from the room without saying a word.

"Why do you and Grandma let them hit you?" Alvin had asked her later as he helped her put ice on her side. That question caused Rachel's words to resonate in her head. So, Nathan's dad was abusive? She resolved that she would not play a role in continuing that cycle. She would not become a statistic. Alvin wasn't seriously hurt. This time.

Mary didn't have an exit plan yet, but as her mind replayed that horrible memory, she closed her eyes and mumbled a prayer. "Lord, help me find a way out."

"The word of God is indisputable . . ." Nathan said from the pulpit. Mary opened her eyes, but still tuned him out. He might as well have been speaking in Portuguese because she would never listen to anything he said again.

It seemed like it took forever, but service finally wrapped up. Mary sent Alvin with one of his classmates and she made her way back to Nathan's office. She had just rounded the corner when she saw him leaning in toward a young female member and flirtatiously whispering in her ear. The girl saw Mary and tensed. Nathan looked up and his eyes met his wife's. Still, he didn't move.

"Okay, Rev. Thank you," the girl said, ducking from under his arm and scurrying off.

"What was that about?" Mary asked as she followed Nathan into his office. Truthfully, she didn't care. Cheating was the least of her concerns when it came to her husband.

"You know I can't share things the members tell me." He slowly removed his robe, then glared at her. "But maybe I'm looking to replace you."

"You know, I'm not trying to fight with you," Mary said, closing his office door. "I know you have the service at three. Alvin went with the Robinsons, but I was trying to see what you want to do about dinner." That wasn't the real reason she'd come back here, but she hadn't yet gotten up the nerve to say what she really wanted to say.

"Nah, I'm good," he replied. "I'm just going to hang around here until the next service. Since you and Alvin seem to be such a team, why don't you go on?"

"Why are you doing this to your son?" Mary asked. "He's just a child. He doesn't deserve your wrath."

Nathan released a small chuckle. "Oh, so now you of all people are going to tell me how to raise a son?"

At that moment, Mary hated her husband with everything inside her. "Why are you so mean?" she found herself saying.

Nathan slammed his palm on his desk. "Because my wife, who is supposed to have my back, doesn't. I'm doing this for us. For you. I'm trying to get your son."

The words that had been swirling in her head for the last few days finally found their way out of her mouth. "Maybe Lewis is better off where he is," Mary softly said. She'd waited specifically to do this at church, where he was less likely to hit her. They had court in the morning. Once again, Nathan had pulled strings and gotten their case expedited. But Mary no longer wanted to go through with it.

The look on his face showed his contempt. "You are so weak." She fought back tears as he came from behind the desk and stepped closer to her. "I handpick you from prison to try and give you a better life. You don't appreciate it. You don't appreciate me."

"I just . . . I can't take the abuse. I can't take you putting your hands on me."

"Stop pushing me, then," he replied. "As long as you're my wife, you're my property and I'll do what I want."

Mary took a deep breath and held her head up high. "I'm nobody's property," she said, finding strength for the first time since she'd stepped off the prison grounds. "As a matter of fact, I want a divorce." There. She'd said it. And no words had ever felt so liberating.

Nathan seemed shocked, but then he stepped closer. Mary's first instinct was to flinch, but she'd already told herself, if he touched her, they would be fighting right there in the church office.

Nathan was so close now, she could feel the heat of his breath. "Don't get it twisted. I bought you," he said slowly. The veins in his neck tightened as a sinister smile crept onto his face. "I own you. You don't divorce me. This is like prison, baby. This is a life sentence unless, and until, I say otherwise."

A heavy silence hung in the air, interrupted only by a knock on the door.

"Mr. Nathan Frazier?" a voice called out from the other side.

Nathan glared at her again, then composed himself and walked over to the door.

"Yes? I'm Rev. Frazier. May I help you?"

Mary couldn't see who was at the door, but she heard a man say, "I'm Detective Paul Davis. This is my partner, Lola Mc-Shan. We have a warrant to search your office and your computer."

"What? Search for what?" he exclaimed. His attitude had completely shifted.

Detective Davis handed Nathan a piece of paper as he and his partner, followed by two uniformed policemen, entered the office.

No one spoke to Mary as they immediately began going through Nathan's stuff.

"What in the world is going on?" Nathan said.

Detective Davis stopped and turned to

face Nathan. "We have cause to believe that you have child pornography in your office."

His mouth fell open in shock. "What? Are you crazy? I don't do child pornography."

Detective McShan smiled as she patted him on the back. "Well, if that's the case, we'll be in and out."

"This is ridiculous and a huge mistake!"

"We won't be long," Detective Davis said, as one of the policemen opened the cabinets over Nathan's bookcase.

"Fine," Nathan said, stepping to the side. "Check wherever you need to. I don't have anything to hide. And when this is all over, I'll demand a written apology from your department."

"Thank you, we'll only be a minute," Detective Davis said, sitting down at Nathan's desk. He began tapping away on the computer.

"This is some BS," Nathan said, pacing back and forth as the other officers went through drawers and mounds of paperwork. I'm a man of God and y'all just trying . . ." His voice trailed off as Detective Davis turned the screen around to face him. On the screen was the image of a little girl, no more than eight or nine years old. That picture disappeared and another one popped up. Then, another and another. The slideshow was filled with little boys and girls of all races, all naked as the day they were born.

"That's not mine!" Nathan yelled.

Detective Davis motioned toward a uniformed officer, who took a pair of handcuffs off his belt and stepped toward Nathan.

"Nathan Frazier, you have the right to remain silent . . ."

"That's not mine!" Nathan repeated.

". . . Anything you say can and will be held against you."

"I've been set up!"

"You have the right to an attorney."

"Mary, do something," Nathan shouted as they slapped the handcuffs on his wrists.

Mary was frozen in place. *Nathan was into child pornography?* What kind of man had she married?

"You know I didn't do this," he cried as they shuttled him toward the door. "Tell them I wouldn't do this!"

The associate pastor, Reverend Mills, rushed in. "Pastor, what's going on?"

"I'm being set up!" he continued screaming as they dragged him out. "Somebody get my lawyer on the phone. Mary, you'd better get this taken care of tonight!" His voice trailed off as they carted him out. Mary knew she probably should've followed him out. She probably should've tried to get more answers. Nathan didn't seem like the type who dabbled in child pornography. But then, he hadn't seemed like an abuser, either.

"Sister Frazier, what in the world happened?" Reverend Mills asked.

Mary shook herself out of her daze, then slowly turned toward the deacon. "God answers prayers," she said, before grabbing her purse and walking out of the office.

Chapter Thirty-Six:
Natasia

God answers prayers!

That was the mantra going through Natasia's mind as she stuffed the last of her toiletries into the overnight bag. She'd arrived at the hospital with nothing but the clothes on her back, but the way she was packing now to leave, she felt like she'd been away on a mini-vacation.

All because of Hosea. For the last five days, he'd taken care of every one of her needs so that she was more than comfortable. Being surrounded by a few of her own books and her own toiletries, wearing her own night clothes, and even having a picture of her parents by her bedside made the stay bearable. All of that was Hosea's idea.

Then, there was seeing him every day — that made this whole hospital stay worthwhile. During those days, they'd spent time together, prayed together, became closer. So close that she hoped Hosea would never want to be far from her again.

And based on the conversation they'd had last night, everything she hoped for was coming to pass.

"I'm really sorry, darlin', but I won't be able to be there in the morning."

Darlin'. Natasia pressed the phone to her ear as if that would help her hold on to that word. She wondered if Hosea even noticed that he'd started using that term of endearment with her. It was the fifth time; she'd been keeping count.

"So, I won't be able to pick you up," he continued. "I was called back to New York for an emergency meeting. I'm at the airport now."

"That's okay, boo. I mean, Hosea." Natasia had cringed when she'd made that slipup and she prayed that he hadn't heard her. He could slip, she could not.

He said, "I want you to know though, that I did talk to Jasmine."

Natasia held her breath. For days, Hosea had talked to her about living with him and Jasmine so that she would have someone to look after her. She had protested as if living with him was the very last thing on earth that she would dream of doing. She'd told him that she wasn't an invalid, she'd told him that she could live alone, she'd told him that his wife would never accept this and she didn't want to cause any trouble.

But every time, he'd waved her words away, letting her know that she was just as important to him as his wife.

Hosea broke into her thoughts. "It took a little bit of convincing, but Jasmine has agreed that we should help you."

"Oh, my God," Natasia breathed. "Are you serious? It's okay with her if I move in?"

There was the crackle of static and then, "Natasia, Natasia, can you hear me?" More static. "I don't know if you can hear me." Static. "Natasia!"

Then, nothing. She called right back, but her call went straight to voicemail. She sighed but wore a smile on her face. She'd won. She was going to live with Hosea.

Now, as she packed, she rolled it all around in her head. Every dream she'd had for the last few years was coming true. Of course, Hosea's wife living in the same house hadn't been how she'd imagined it, but it was still going to work out.

A knock on the door made her turn around, still with a smile on her face. Maybe Hosea had come back for her. Then, her smile turned right upside down.

"Natasia," Jasmine said, curtly, as if she

had a major attitude.

The creases in Natasia's forehead deepened when Rachel strutted in right behind Jasmine.

"What are you doing here?" Natasia folded her arms, but she backed up a little. Had Jasmine come here to beat her down? Is that why she had Ms. Floyd Mayweather with her?

"Didn't Hosea call you? We're here to take you home," Jasmine said as she glanced at Rachel.

"Yup," Rachel said. "You went after her man and it seems like you got what you wanted."

"She hasn't gotten anything," Jasmine snapped.

Rachel plopped onto the bed next to Natasia's bag. "Let me ask you this, Jasmine. You came to pick her up, right?" she said as if Natasia wasn't standing right there.

"Yeah."

Rachel continued, "And you're taking her home, right?"

"The only reason I'm here is because my husband asked me to do it."

Rachel raised her hands as if she'd just scored a touchdown. "Like I said, she won."

Jasmine rolled her eyes and turned to Natasia. "Are you ready to go?" she asked, her tone letting Natasia know Jasmine would leave her in the hospital if she'd said no.

"Yes, but I still have to wait for the discharging nurse," she said, just as an attendant walked in with a wheelchair.

"Are you ready to go, Ms. Redding?" the young man, dressed in all white, asked.

Natasia looked first at Jasmine, then at Rachel. Clearly, they weren't here for a fight. Hosea had sent them, so it had to be all right. "Yeah," she said finally. "I am ready." Pointing to the wheelchair, she added, "But I don't need that."

The young man's shoulder-length locks swayed as he shook his head. "Hospital policy. You wouldn't want me to lose my job, would you?"

"All right." Natasia grabbed her bag from the bed, hesitated for a moment, then handed it to Jasmine.

Jasmine looked her up, then down, before she snatched the bag from Natasia's hand.

Wearing a super-size smile, Natasia sat in the chair and leaned back. "I'm ready" — she glanced over her shoulder at Jasmine — "to go home."

Jasmine glared at her, and that just made Natasia feel like the winner she was.

"Let me push," Rachel shouted with an enthusiasm that wiped Natasia's smile away.

If the attendant had agreed, Natasia would've stood up and walked out on her own. That young man would just have to be fired.

But the young man said, "I'd lose my job if I turned her over to you."

So, Natasia sat back, relaxed, and tried to imagine the way the conversation had gone down between Jasmine and Hosea. Natasia hoped that there had been a lot of heated words exchanged, enough to create a huge chasm between them. And definitely tears. She hoped that Jasmine had cried until she could hardly breathe. She hoped that enough animosity was built up between Jasmine and Hosea so that wall would never come down. And she would be right there to comfort Hosea.

Jasmine had been a fool, really. No matter what Hosea said, Jasmine never should've agreed to this. Hadn't she ever heard the rule of never letting another woman stay in your home? Her mother and grandmother used to say that all the time when she was growing up. Natasia hadn't really understood that sentiment then, but as a grown woman, she understood it now. And if everything went according to her plan, Jasmine would understand it, too. Soon enough.

Only the attendant spoke as he rolled Natasia to the elevator. He chatted about the cool summer temperatures, and how he was sure Natasia was glad to be leaving.

But Natasia wasn't listening to any of his words. Her ears were perked to hear the whispers between Jasmine and Rachel.

She couldn't be sure, but she thought she heard Rachel call Jasmine stupid. And then Jasmine asked what was she supposed to do?

With every bit of the conversation, Natasia's smile widened. By the time the attendant got her down to Jasmine's waiting car, Natasia's grin was so wide, her cheeks hurt.

"Do you want to get in the back?" the attendant asked Natasia.

But Rachel answered for her. "No, put her right up there in the seat of honor," Rachel said, pointing to the front passenger seat. "Since she's about to be the queen of the castle."

"Would you shut up!" Jasmine growled.

Natasia wanted to stand up and applaud Rachel. Now, she wished that she'd been nicer to her. Rachel seemed to be enjoying this as much as she was. If they'd been working together, they could've destroyed Jasmine.

Maybe she would talk to Rachel again. Maybe there was still some way for Rachel to help her. And if she did, maybe she would reconsider showing the sermon scene.

Maybe.

Natasia slid from the wheelchair into the car and settled in, waiting to be driven.

This is classic, she thought. All those years ago when she'd been fired from Hosea's show, Natasia bet that Jasmine believed that she'd won. She probably believed that the two of them would never cross paths again.

How wrong she'd been, though Natasia had to admit those had been her thoughts, too. But this was just an example of how true love could wait. It could endure anything — time and space. This was an example of how God truly, truly answered the prayers of the righteous.

"So, Natasia," Rachel said from the backseat the moment Jasmine took off from the parking lot. "How are you feeling?"

Natasia froze. Had Hosea told them what was wrong with her? If he had, this was a disaster — Jasmine and Rachel would tell the world.

But then she released a long exhale. Hosea would never betray her confidence. Never.

So, she said, "I'm fine. Just had a touch of the flu," she said, repeating the story that she'd told Melinda and everyone else from OWN.

"The flu kept you in the hospital for five days?" Rachel asked.

"They were concerned that it could've turned into pneumonia. And what is this? Some kind of inquisition?"

"I was just asking to be friendly," Rachel snapped. "Which is more than you've ever been to me." She leaned forward from the backseat. "I needed to talk to you about a couple of those scenes where you set me up."

Ahhh! Now, she understood. This was why Rachel had come along. To harass her about the show.

"I didn't set you up, Rachel. This is a reality show. We tape real scenes. All of that stuff that you got into, none of that was scripted. It was all real and all you."

"Having me do a sermon at the last minute wasn't all real. Having me served with custody papers wasn't all real."

Natasia sighed. "I'm really tired. If you want, we can talk about this tomorrow on set," she said.

"You're going back to work?" Jasmine and Rachel said together.

If she hadn't been sure before, Natasia was sure now. Hosea hadn't told them anything if they didn't know that she was still going to be working.

"Yes, I'm going to work. It was just the flu, I'm over it, and we're just about ready to wrap."

Then, Natasia looked up and frowned. "Why are we here?" she said, pointing to Buckhead Tower.

"Isn't this where you were living?" Jasmine asked. Before Natasia could respond, she said, "I thought you'd want to pick up a few of your things. Hosea said he would move you out of your apartment as soon as he got back from New York. But I figured you would want at least one change of clothes."

"Yeah, you don't want to wear the same clothes every day, do you?" Rachel asked. "I mean, how you gonna get Jasmine's man wearing the same funky clothes?"

"If you don't shut up," Jasmine sneered at Rachel through the rearview mirror.

From the backseat, Rachel chuckled, and Natasia had to hold back her own laugh. All she wanted to do was laugh out loud . . . right in Jasmine's face.

But she just opened the door and slid out silently like the lady she always was.

"You can leave the bag in the car," Natasia said as if Jasmine was her assistant. "No need for you to carry it up and then back down."

Jasmine's eyes became thin slits, and Natasia could imagine her thoughts. She probably wanted to curse her out. Well, there were plenty of times when she'd wanted to curse out Jasmine, too. So, as far as Natasia was concerned, they were even.

She didn't say a word, and didn't even crack a smile. She just pivoted and sauntered into the building, the whole time, making a mental list of what she would take with her to her new home. Because Rachel did have a point. Every move she made had to be calculated, had to add up to her getting what she wanted. And that included what she would wear . . . especially her lingerie.

Natasia nodded her hello as she passed the concierge, and then inside the elevator, she pressed 17. They stood like silent soldiers, the three pairs of eyes focused on the numbers above the door, lighting up with each floor they passed.

When the doors parted, Natasia stepped off first, moving left. But Jasmine and Rachel moved to the right. When she realized they weren't following her, Natasia turned around and frowned.

"Uh . . . where are you going?"

"Oh, didn't I mention that I have a friend who lives here?" Jasmine asked.

Natasia shook her head. "No, you didn't."

"Well, you should come down here and meet her."

Natasia narrowed her eyes. She had no idea what Jasmine was up to, but it was something. She could feel it. But even though her mind told her to just go to her apartment and let Jasmine do whatever Jasmine was going to do, curiosity pulled her the other way.

She followed Jasmine to the apartment all the way at the end of the hall. From the floor plans she'd been shown when she first moved in, she knew that this was one of the bigger suites — a three-bedroom apartment.

Jasmine rang the doorbell and two seconds later, the door swung open.

"Natasia! Welcome home!"

"What?"

Jasmine stepped inside first, and it was only her natural instinct that made Natasia follow.

"Welcome home, roomie," Mae Frances said, and wrapped her arms around Natasia as if they'd always been friends. She stepped back and said, "I'm glad to see you looking so well."

"What . . . what . . . what's going on?"

Natasia asked, looking from Jasmine to Mae Frances and then to Rachel, who was standing against the wall, buckled over with laughter.

"I'm your new roomie." Mae Frances took Natasia's hand and led her to the couch.

Now, it was just confusion that made Natasia follow.

She sat down, and Mae Frances kept talking, "Now, here's the thing, I ain't never had a roomie before. The only people I share rooms and apartments with are men. But after all that you've been through, I said, I'd try it out with you. So, I got a few rules here." She reached over to the coffee table, lifted up a piece of paper, and handed it to Natasia.

"What is going on?" Natasia said again as if those were now the only words she knew how to speak.

"This is your new apartment, boo," Rachel said through her giggles.

"Yup," Jasmine said, and for the first time, Natasia saw a smile on her face. She sat down next to Natasia. "My husband was really concerned about you and he wanted you to move in with us."

Mae Frances jumped in, "But I told them, no grown woman wants to be living in another grown woman's house. Hmph, that's why I had to get out of there. Jasmine Larson was barging into my room at all hours of the night. Suppose I'd had a man up in that bed with me."

Jasmine, Rachel, and Natasia cringed together.

Jasmine picked up the story, "So, Hosea rented this apartment for the two of you. This way, you won't be living by yourself."

Natasia was smart, some called her brilliant. So, she couldn't figure out why she didn't understand. She wasn't supposed to be living in this apartment. She was supposed to be in a house . . . with Hosea.

"But . . . but Hosea said that I was moving in with you."

Jasmine shrugged. "I don't know how he could've told you that when I told him that was never going to happen."

"Now, Jasmine Larson, don't be so mean." Mae Frances turned to Natasia. "We all wanted to make sure that you wouldn't be living alone, so we all agreed that you and I should live together. And then anytime I have to go back to New York, we'll get a nurse to stay overnight. This was all my idea. Isn't it great?"

"No, no!" Natasia said, standing up and stomping her foot. "I'm not going to live here." She turned to Jasmine. "I'm moving in with you!"

Jasmine shook her head and didn't even bother to stand. "Ain't happenin'."

"Hosea told me —" Natasia screamed.

Now, Mae Frances stood up, too. "Now, see, that's one of the rules. No loud talking in here. And while we're talking about loud noises, I don't want no loud music, no loud sexing . . . oh, wait, can you even have sex?"

Natasia looked like she was about to faint again, and that's when Jasmine said, "Uh, Mae Frances, Rachel and I are gonna go down to Natasia's apartment and get the rest of her things." Glancing at Natasia, she continued, "Hosea packed up everything for you. We'll be right back."

"Okay, Jasmine Larson." Turning to Natasia, Mae Frances said, "Now, let's go over these rules one by one. . . ."

Jasmine and Rachel scurried from the apartment. Once they closed the door behind them, they leaned against the hallway walls, laughing until tears fell from their eyes.

"Oh, my God! Did you see her face?" Rachel said.

Jasmine nodded. "She doesn't know what to do."

"Either she's going to have a miraculous healing or she'll be going downhill fast."

When their laughter settled, Jasmine said, "Mae Frances will take care of her." Her tone was serious now. "I hope Natasia realizes that this is really for the best. I hope she doesn't think about moving back to her own place."

Rachel shrugged. "If she does, that's on her." She marched toward Natasia's apartment. "So, one down, and the next one to go."

Jasmine nodded. "We'll get Natasia's bags, go back to Mae Frances, and find out her plan for Nathan."

"That's what I'm talking about," Rachel said as she high-fived Jasmine. It was time to take Nathan Frazier all the way down.

CHAPTER THIRTY-SEVEN:
RACHEL

Rachel knew if her mother was here right now, she'd say Rachel should be ashamed of herself. Natasia was so sick, after all.

But the look on Natasia's face when Mae Frances opened that door was so unbelievably priceless. Rachel had to give it to that old woman. As much as she worked Rachel's nerves, Mae Frances provided unlimited entertainment.

"Finally got her settled down," Mae Frances said, walking back into the kitchen where Jasmine and Rachel were seated at the table. She glared at Jasmine. "I'm no caretaker. I'm a sitter. I sit. I can't handle her getting all worked up."

"That was just tonight," Jasmine said. "She'll be fine once everything sets in."

Mae Frances gave Jasmine a "she'd better be" look before plopping down in the seat next to Rachel.

"I have a newfound respect for you," Rachel told Jasmine, "because I couldn't do it. I couldn't help Natasia."

Jasmine smiled. "Yeah, that's what you say, but you did take in Mary's son."

Rachel paused for a moment, letting Jasmine's words sink in. "You're right," she said. "We both should qualify for sainthood."

"Hmph, sinnerhood is more like it," Mae Frances said.

"So, are you planning to torture that woman?" Rachel asked.

"Me, torture?" Mae Frances shook her head. "I'm just here to make sure she's comfortable, especially if these are her last days . . ." She glanced at her watch. "But again, all you have to do is say the word and we can speed this process up."

"Mae Frances!" Rachel and Jasmine said at the same time.

"We're not interested in killing anyone," Jasmine said.

Mae Frances threw her hands up in exasperation. "Just soft." She turned to Rachel. "Make me some tea."

Rachel raised an eyebrow and leaned back in her chair. "Excuse me, do I look like my name is Hazel?"

Jasmine stood. "I'll get it."

"No. I want Rasbushah to get it."

Rachel turned up her lip, shifted, and got comfortable in her chair. She wasn't even going to correct Mae Frances on her name because now she knew the old woman was just trying to get her riled up.

"After all I've done for you two, y'all indebted to me, so if I say make me some tea, you make me some tea."

Oh, this woman was tripping for real. "No, it seems to me you *claimed* you could help, but you didn't make Natasia sick." She leaned in, narrowed her eyes. "Did you?"

"Of course not," Mae Frances replied.

"So, yes, you're helping with the Natasia situation, after the fact," Rachel continued. "And you dang sure didn't help me because I have court at nine in the morning, trying to keep my son."

Mae Frances just scowled at Rachel, but didn't respond.

"What? Say something," Rachel said. "It creeps me out when you just stare at me."

"And just staring at you creeps me out," Mae Frances coldly replied.

"Would you two stop?" Jasmine said. "I'll make tea." She pulled a small tea kettle off the stove and began filling it with water.

"So, I didn't help you, huh?" Mae Francis asked Rachel.

"No."

"What time is it?" Mae Francis asked.

"Four fifty-six," Jasmine said. "Why?"

"Perfect timing. Turn on the TV. Put it on Channel Two." Mae Francis pointed to the small television positioned on the corner of the kitchen cabinet.

"For what?" Jasmine asked as she set the teacup in front of Mae Frances.

"Just do what I said, Jasmine Larson. Your little hardheaded bestie wants to question my capabilities." Mae Frances seemed severely offended.

Jasmine turned on the TV. The news anchor popped up on the screen. ". . . This just in, Herman Cain announced he will seek the Republican nomination in the 2016 presidential election."

Mae Frances shook her head. "I told him not to do it. If those pictures of us get out —"

"Mae Frances!" Jasmine said, cutting her off.

Rachel was getting irritated. The whole Natasia situation had brightened her mood and gotten her mind off her pending court case tomorrow, but now, sitting here talking with Mae Frances had reminded Rachel of all that the old lady *hadn't* done when it came to helping her.

"Why do you want us to see the news?"

Rachel said. "I don't care about Herman Cain."

"Oh, just hold your horses," Mae Francis snapped.

"We'll have more on that story later in the newscast," the anchor continued. "But we begin tonight with breaking news. Police have arrested Atlanta pastor Nathan Frazier."

Both Rachel and Jasmine froze as they stared at the TV.

"Authorities raided Frazier's North Atlanta church and found child pornography," the anchor continued. "The minister has been taken into custody and police say the evidence against him is mounting."

Rachel didn't even hear the rest of the story as she turned to Mae Frances, speechless.

"What did you do?" Jasmine asked, horrified.

"Let Raquel here tell it, nothing."

Jasmine fell into a chair, stunned. "Child pornography, Mae Frances?"

Mae Frances shrugged nonchalantly as she sipped her tea. "You wanted him to not be a problem, he's not a problem."

Rachel didn't know whether to feel relieved or scared. Child pornography was serious. And Mae Frances had set that up?

"Wh-How . . . Oh, my God. Nathan is in jail?"

"That's what that anchorman said."

Rachel fell back in her seat. She didn't know what to say. Mae Frances had delivered again.

The courtroom was filled with thieves, liars, and lawbreakers. Rachel couldn't process why she was even here. If Nathan was in jail, why in the world did she still have to come to court?

Rachel couldn't believe Lester wasn't here, but his flight last night had been canceled and he was stuck in Houston trying to get on the first flight out.

Thankfully, Jasmine was here. Even Mae Frances had gotten a nurse for Natasia and showed up as well, although she claimed it was just to see "the fruits of her labor."

Rachel had tried to tell her attorney that since Nathan had been arrested, the case would be dismissed, so there was no need for them to show up. Of course, he'd nixed that idea, saying that until the judge threw it out, they'd follow the rules.

"Would you stop pacing?" Jasmine said.

"That's easy for you to say," Rachel replied. "What's taking them so long?" She motioned toward the judge's chambers where her attorney and Nathan and Mary's attorney had been for the past four hours.

They hadn't seen Mary this morning, but then again, if her husband had been accused of being a pedophile, Rachel would stay low key as well.

Finally, the side door opened and Rachel's attorney, Kirk, emerged. Beads of sweat dotted his forehead and he looked unnerved.

"What's going on?" Rachel asked, racing over to him. She didn't like the distressed look on his face.

"Well, technically, since the case is being brought forth by Mary and Nathan, it can still proceed, especially because Nathan has not been found guilty of anything. He's maintaining his innocence and wants to move forward with the suit," Kirk said.

Rachel's heart sank. So, this wasn't over? "What is Mary saying about all of this?" Rachel had hoped that without Nathan pulling her strings, Mary would give up this stupid quest to take her son.

"She just arrived, her and some other lady," Kirk replied. "And well, they asked to speak to the judge privately."

"For what?" Rachel started pacing again. "Oh Lord, she's still gonna try to take Lewis."

"Rachel, calm down," Jasmine said.

Rachel wanted to cry, scream, curse, even go off on Mae Frances. What good was it to have all these connections if she couldn't make them stick?

Rachel inhaled deeply and turned back to Kirk. "What now?"

Kirk tried to appear reassuring. "The judge wants me back in his chambers in fifteen, so why don't you go get some coffee or something and meet me back here in ten minutes?"

Rachel didn't want coffee, she didn't want to wait, she just wanted this nightmare to be over.

"I'm going to call my husband." Rachel didn't give anyone time to reply as she stepped out into the hall and dialed Lester. He answered on the first ring.

"Honey?" His voice was low, nervous, almost like he was waiting on bad news.

"Hey," she said, softly. Just hearing his voice gave her comfort. "Still waiting."

A huge sigh of relief mixed with frustration filled the phone. "Baby, the thunderstorm just let up. We're boarding right now. I'm so sorry. I tried everything short of hijacking one of these planes and flying it myself in order to get there."

"I know," Rachel said. She was quiet, then said, "I can't lose him. I can't lose Lewis."

"We won't," Lester promised. Rachel had filled him in last night on the news of Nathan's arrest and like her, Lester had hoped that meant this ordeal would be over.

"How do you know we won't?" she whimpered.

"Because the Lord told me."

In the old days, Rachel would've rolled her eyes, told him to go somewhere with that "voice of God" talk, or spouted her "faith without works" mantra. But right now, that's all Rachel had — faith.

"Sweetie, I'm gonna have to go. But first, let's pray," Lester said.

Since she had nowhere else to turn — not to Jasmine, not Mae Francis, not even her husband — Rachel turned to the only place she had left. She closed her eyes and began to pray with her husband.

That prayer didn't completely wipe away her fear, but it gave her strength.

"You okay?" Jasmine asked once she walked back into the courtroom.

"I am" was all Rachel could manage to say as she squeezed Jasmine's hand. She looked at Mae Frances. "Thank you, Mae Frances. For trying to help me."

"It ain't over," Mae Frances said matter-of-factly. "So, don't come in here sounding all defeated."

Rachel was about to say something when Kirk came out the side door. This time, he had a look of pure joy on his face.

"What?" Rachel exclaimed, racing over to him. "Please tell me you have good news."

"I have great news!" Kirk said as the door opened again and Mary and some woman walked out. The woman looked extremely familiar, but Rachel couldn't place her.

"What happened?" Rachel asked, turning back to Kirk.

He grinned widely. "This case has been dismissed."

Rachel's hands went to her mouth and Jasmine had to catch her to keep her from losing her balance.

"Seems Mary told the judge Lewis should stay with you and he agreed since the charges against the good reverend are a lot more serious than we thought," Kirk continued. "He had pictures, videos, email correspondence. Looks like he was running a regular child pornography ring. The evidence was overwhelming."

"And that was enough for the judge?" Rachel finally managed to say. "I thought you said he denied everything."

"Oh, he did. But then," Kirk glanced back at Mary and the woman as they approached, "they brought in a witness. A woman to whom Nathan tried to sell the pictures." He smiled at the woman next to Mary. "I can't thank you enough, Ms. Margaret, for coming forward." Kirk glanced down at his phone as it rang. "Excuse me, ladies, I have got to take this call." He stepped outside the courtroom as Rachel stood face-to-face with Mary and "the witness." When Kirk said her name, Rachel remembered exactly where she knew the woman from. She had the same stringy hair and pale skin. The same bags under her eyes and the same dingy clothes.

"Mary, what's going on?" Rachel asked.

Mary squeezed the woman's arm and smiled. "My mother finally decided to do something right."

Margaret returned her daughter's smile. The last time Rachel had seen this woman, the state of Texas had given her custody of Lewis because Mary had been arrested. Since all Margaret had wanted was a check, and not a child, Rachel had managed to convince the social worker to let Lewis stay with her.

"I left those drugs alone. Two years clean," Margaret said proudly. "I hadn't done right by my baby" — she looked at Mary — "in, like, ever. Been trying to get her to forgive me, but . . ." She paused like she couldn't believe the words that were coming out of her mouth. "Well, when my daughter called and asked for my help, I was all too happy to oblige, especially since I've been trying to see her since she moved to Atlanta."

Rachel was stunned as Margaret rambled on. It was actually Mae Frances who spoke up. She stepped next to Rachel, a confused look on her face. "Wait, so um, how, um, so what do you mean Nathan tried to sell you pictures?" Mae Frances asked.

Rachel knew Mae Frances was thinking the same thing she was. If Nathan had been set up, how could this woman have been working with him?

Margaret shrugged. "I just do what I'm told." She looked at Mary proudly.

Rachel turned to Mary for an explanation.

"I knew that Nathan would try to wiggle his way out of this, and he might have been able to walk. I wasn't sure if he was guilty or not, but I figured if he was in jail, he might as well stay. And I knew it would be a little harder for him to plead his innocence if there was someone else who could support what the police found," Mary confessed.

"So, you manufactured a witness?" Mae Francis asked, in awe.

Mary shrugged. "Old habits die hard, I guess."

Mae Frances cackled. "Ha. Girl, I think I like you!"

"I . . . I don't understand. Why would you do that?" was all Rachel could say.

Mary looked at Rachel and her eyes teared up. "I learned to love me."

They stood in silence for a minute. Just for clarification, Rachel felt the need to ask, "So, you don't want Lewis?"

Mary closed her eyes, took a deep breath, then opened her eyes and smiled at Rachel. "I want him. Bad. But he's yours. You and Lester are the only parents he knows. I'm not going to rip him from that. And I'm sorry for all the heartache."

Rachel didn't know what came over her, but she threw her arms around Mary's neck. "Oh, my God! Thank you!" Rachel couldn't wait for Lester to arrive so she could share the news.

"Hmph, where are the cameras when you need them?" Mae Frances asked.

At that moment, the side doors opened and a disheveled Nathan was shuttled out by two officers.

"Mary! Mary!" Nathan called out to his wife.

"Ladies, that's my cue," Mary said, ignoring him. "See you at the reunion show." Mary didn't look back as she and her mother left the courtroom.

Nathan continued yelling at her and when he saw Rachel, Jasmine, and Mae Frances staring at him, he snapped. "What are y'all looking at?"

Jasmine just shook her head pitifully.

Rachel flashed a big smile.

And Mae Frances said, "Hey, Preacher Man." She pointed to the heavy hardware on his hands and legs. "You might want to learn the words to that gospel song, 'Shackles on my Feet.' "

All three of them laughed as they walked out of the courtroom.

"We make a good team," Rachel said as they approached the elevator.

"Unh-unh. I told you, y'all too soft to be on Team Mae Frances," Mae Frances said, pulling her mink tighter around her body.

"And just what is the secret to being on your team, Mae Francis?" Rachel asked as they stepped on the elevator.

"Please, you'll never get the answer to that," Jasmine replied, pushing the Down button. "Her life is like the Bermuda Triangle, information goes in but it never comes out."

Rachel eyed Mae Frances. She had literally snapped her fingers and brought Nathan down. In the short time that Rachel had known this woman, she'd discovered more secret contacts than the CIA.

"You know I'm good at investigating stuff," Rachel said. "I'm gonna go home and spend time with my babies, but this weekend, I'm starting a book about you," she told Mae Frances. "I'm going to expose how it is you do all the things you do. I'll call it *The Unauthorized Autobiography of Mae Francis.*"

Both Rachel and Jasmine laughed. Mae Francis didn't.

"And I will sue you for everything — including that twenty-six-inch yaky you're parading around like it's yours." Mae Frances tugged at Rachel's hair.

Rachel pulled her hair away. "It is mine. I bought it. And it's Remy Bohemian, for your information."

"You from Fifth Ward in Houston, wearing Korean nails, European clothes, and Bohemian hair." Mae Francis shook her head.

"Say what you want," Rachel replied, "but I'm going to find out your story. You sure you don't want to tell me?"

"If I tell you, I'll have to kill you." Mae Francis stepped off the elevator.

"And you know she will," Jasmine said, following her.

"Not personally." Mae Frances stopped, turned back to face them. "I don't get my hands dirty. Now, take me home, Jasmine Larson. I'm sure my roommate is missing me."

"Take me home first," Rachel said, "so I can see my kids."

"I'm going home first. Get it? Got it? Good. It's my world, my rules," Mae Frances said as she walked out into the sunlight.

"Hey, she stole my catchphrase," Rachel said.

Jasmine shook her head and smiled. "Let her have it. I'll help you come up with another one because somehow I think the reality show *First Ladies* will definitely be back for season two."

READING GROUP GUIDE

FORTUNE & FAME

From competing against each other to become the First Lady of the American Baptist Coalition, to joining forces to extract themselves from a murder case, Jasmine Cox Larson Bush and Rachel Jackson Adams have been through a lot together. In *Fortune & Fame,* the women must put aside their differences as production begins for the new reality series *First Ladies,* where both Jasmine and Rachel intend to become the show's biggest star. But when Rachel's husband's former lover joins the cast and Jasmine's husband's former flame turns up as the show's executive producer for the OWN network, the ladies find themselves in for a season of drama both on- and off-screen. To survive the months of filming and maintain their sanity and their marriages, Jasmine and Rachel will have to decide whether it's best for them to become friends or foes.

FOR DISCUSSION

1. The world of reality TV provides a setting rife with drama for all of the novel's characters. What do Rachel, Jasmine, and Mary each hope to gain by appearing on *First Ladies*? Is it simply fortune and fame, or something more than that? What does each character stand to lose by starring on the show? Do you think that the benefits of appearing on a reality show outweigh the negatives?

2. Each of the three First Ladies has come to her position in a different way. What does each of them gain by being a First Lady? How do Jasmine and Rachel's positions differ from Mary's, and why? Are they right to treat Mary as they do?

3. Reality shows are supposed to be unscripted. But as the novel progresses, it becomes clear that many events and scenes

of *First Ladies* — for example, Nathan exposing the secrets of Mary's past on the altar of his church — are staged by the stars and the producers. Were you surprised by how many of the characters orchestrated events during the course of filming, and by how scripted the "unscripted" show actually was? Why do the characters feel they needed to manipulate situations, and how do their manipulations help or hurt them?

4. From phone calls to Stedman to her brilliant scheming, Jasmine has a very powerful friend in Mae Frances. How do Mae Frances's connections help Jasmine and Rachel throughout the course of the novel? Could Jasmine and Rachel have made it through filming without the assistance of Mae Frances?

5. Natasia promises Rachel, Jasmine, and Mary that *First Ladies* will be a classy show, "about serving as an example of a Godly woman who finds forgiveness in the most difficult of situations." By the end of the novel, do you think Natasia's description is an accurate representation of what audiences would take away after viewing season one of *First Ladies*? Why

or why not?

6. Rachel reveals that she thinks that God is testing her by putting her on a reality show with her husband's former lover and ex-con Mary. Discuss Rachel's relationship with Mary over the course of the novel. Has Rachel accepted Mary by the end of the book and passed God's test, or not? If you think of the reality show as a test from God for all of the main characters, who passes and who fails?

7. Jasmine constantly refers to herself as classy and sees herself as above the show's drama, while Rachel struggles to maintain her composure and refrain from physical violence and altercations. How do the women's contrasting personalities push them apart and how do their differences bring them together? Do you think Jasmine and Rachel are actually more alike than they think? Do you have friends with personalities that you consider to be completely opposite from yours?

8. When Mary is released from prison, she never dreams that her life with Nathan will turn out the way it does. How does her time in prison change Mary and her

faith in God? Why are her expectations of life with Nathan so different from the reality? Why is she so submissive to her husband? Were you surprised when didn't she speak up for herself or try to leave her marriage sooner?

9. The First Ladies get the opportunity to star on a television show because they each have a powerful husband, but the pastors all have very different feelings about the show. Describe how Hosea, Lester, and Nathan each react to their wives being a part of the television show, and how their feelings about the show impact their marriages. Why are Lester and Hosea so reluctant to be a part of the filming, and why is Nathan so eager to appear on camera?

10. Natasia's illness causes her to question everything in her life, particularly her relationship with Hosea. Does Natasia take advantage of her situation to get closer to Hosea, or is she doing what anyone in her position would do? How does her understanding of her mortality impact her actions? Do you think Hosea goes too far in his support of Natasia, or are his actions justified? Is Jasmine right

to be angry with her husband for helping Natasia, or not?

11. ReShonda Tate Billingsley and Victoria Christopher Murray wrote the book in alternating chapters. Could you tell which author wrote which chapter? Did you see examples of how each author tried to put the other in situations that would be difficult to write their way out of?

12. By the end of the novel, do you think that Jasmine and Rachel are truly friends, enemies, frenemies, or something else? What do you predict will happen on the next season of *First Ladies*?

The employees of Thorndike Press hope you have enjoyed this Large Print book. All our Thorndike, Wheeler, and Kennebec Large Print titles are designed for easy reading, and all our books are made to last. Other Thorndike Press Large Print books are available at your library, through selected bookstores, or directly from us.

For information about titles, please call:
(800) 223-1244

or visit our Web site at:
http://gale.cengage.com/thorndike

To share your comments, please write:
Publisher
Thorndike Press
10 Water St., Suite 310
Waterville, ME 04901